Praise for MASANDE N~~~~~'~ *The R~~~~~~~*

"[*The Reactive* is] a searing, gorgeou⸻ ⸻ss, and death in South Africa. With exquisi⸻ ⸻asterful command of storytelling, Ntshanga ⸻ ⸻vigated the dusk that followed the dawn of ⸻ ⸻zes the casualties of the Mbeki government's fatal policies on HIV & AIDS."
—**Naomi Jackson,** *Poets & Writers*

"Woozy, touching… a novel that delivers an unexpected love letter to Cape Town, painting it as a place of frustrated glory."
—**Marian Ryan,** *Slate*

"With *The Reactive*, [Ntshanga] has created an immersive and powerful portrait of drug use, community, and health issues by exploring what it was like to be young, black, South African, and HIV positive in the early aughts."
—*VICE*

"[*The Reactive*] is an affecting, slow-burning novel that gives a fantastic sense of a particular place and time, and of the haunted inner life of its protagonist."
—**Tobias Carroll,** *Minneapolis Star-Tribune*

"*The Reactive* is not only a beautiful novel, as fierce and formally innovative as it is lyrical and moving, but also a call to inhabit as well as to critique the symbolic structures of our world that can both empower and betray us."
—**Nathan Goldman,** *Full Stop*

"Ntshanga deftly illustrates the growing pains of a new country through three friends who seem intent on obliterating their minds, but who nevertheless cling to their dreams."
—**Dmitry Samarov,** *Vol. 1 Brooklyn*

"Gritty and revealing, Ntshanga's debut novel offers a brazen portrait of present-day South Africa. This is an eye-opening, ambitious novel."
—*Publishers Weekly*

"Ntshanga offers a devastating story yet tells it with noteworthy glow and flow that keeps pages turning until the glimmer-of-hope ending."
—*Library Journal*

"Electrifying… [Ntshanga] succeeds at exploring major themes—illness, family, and, most effectively, class—while keeping readers in suspense. Ntshanga's promising debut is both moving and satisfyingly complex."
—*Kirkus Reviews*

TRIANGULUM

A NOVEL BY

Masande Ntshanga

Two Dollar Radio
Books too loud to Ignore

Two Dollar Radio
Books too loud to Ignore

WHO WE ARE Two Dollar Radio is a family-run outfit dedicated to reaffirming the cultural and artistic spirit of the publishing industry. We aim to do this by presenting bold works of literary merit, each book, individually and collectively, providing a sonic progression that we believe to be too loud to ignore.

TwoDollarRadio.com

Proudly based in
Columbus
OHIO

 @TwoDollarRadio

 @TwoDollarRadio

 /TwoDollarRadio

SOME RECOMMENDED LOCATIONS FOR READING *TRIANGULUM*:
Pretty much anywhere because books are portable and the perfect technology!

AUTHOR PHOTO→
Giorgia Fanelli

COVER ARTWORK→
Two Dollar Radio

for my parents

TABLE OF CONTENTS

"Memory itself is an internal rumour."
—George Santayana, *The Life of Reason: Human Understanding*

"The future is forever a projection of the present."
—Kōbō Abe, *Inter Ice Age 4*

"some like to imagine
a cosmic mother watching through a spray of stars"
—Tracy K. Smith, *Life on Mars*

"To administer the laws of apartheid, the bureaucracy grew
enormously. By 1977, about 540,000 Whites were employed
in the public sector [...] and Afrikaners occupied more than
90 percent of the top positions. The vast majority of the white
bureaucrats were ardent supporters of apartheid. Most of the
black bureaucrats, numbering around 820,000, were reliable
servants of the regime on which they depended for their
livelihood."
—Leonard Thompson, *A History of South Africa*

TRIANGULUM

FOREWORD

I am a woman acting of her own will and desire. Do not attempt to contact me after this communication. In all likelihood, I am no longer here.

These lines mark the beginning of the note my colleague Dr Joseph Hessler presented me with three years ago, along with the other materials I was tasked to compile into a dossier meant to inform a State Defense Report. I didn't. Instead, they became the following manuscript, which, with the now late Dr Hessler's assistance, I have prepared for the public as TRIANGULUM.

At the time of writing, the sender of these materials remains unknown. We have at our disposal the note, as well as a cover letter, detailing further instructions. Then the materials themselves: a written record in the form of a memoir, followed by what appears to be a work of autofiction, as well as a set of digital recordings.

Under all circumstances, these testimonies are to be presented as a single communication. It is not possible to make sense of one without the others. This condition is non-negotiable. For the sake of truthfulness, as well as detail—and at personal risk—I have undergone hypnotic regression therapy in order to recall the information I wish to provide this office, but I am still human, or I was human, and to understand me one must understand the life I've lived, and I require that this be an accompaniment to the text.

Herewith, then, in preparation for its tri-continental publication, is an accurate representation of the sender's findings. It is a document announcing the end of our world in 2050.

Δ

My name is Dr Naomi Buthelezi. The date is December 2, 2043. I am of sound mind and constitution and do not compose this account under duress. In a previous life, I worked as an author and writing instructor at the creative writing department of the University of Cape Town, where my career persisted on the strength of my having once been awarded both the Hugo and Nebula. I was a once-known/now-obscure science fiction writer, in other words, and assigned to this case through the office of Dr Hessler—an admirer I didn't know I had.

The two of us met at the beginning of 2040, at a quiet soiree on campus. The astronomers in the department next to ours had installed a new 16-inch telescope in the observatory north of the grounds, and a few of us in English had been invited to celebrate with them before their doors opened.

Dr Hessler, or Joseph, as I came to know him, was the night's guest of honor. He served as the chair and director of the South African National Space Agency, and had been asked to prepare a page for the evening's opening remarks. He was well known. Having contributed to our space project for a decade and a half with committed service, he'd earned a place among the nation's leaders in the field.

The gathering was modest, owing to the closed invitation. As the night wore on, I drank champagne out of a flute fashioned from a test tube and listened to my colleagues complain about ceaseless departmental meetings. I felt the same, but that didn't make it less dull. My daughter was spending the weekend at a friend's and I had a husband who was out of town for work—our relationship now openly at an impasse.

The speech was brief. After a second round of applause, I turned from my colleagues and found him smiling over the stage lights. His photograph was projected onto the walls. Then his hand was shuffled from the Head of Department's to the Dean's.

As he dismounted the podium, I realized I hadn't heard a word the man had said—which made it all the stranger when he tapped me on the shoulder and told me he was an admirer.

"It's a remarkable oeuvre," he said, refreshing my test tube.

He asked me join him at his table. Sitting across from him, I took slow sips of champagne and tried to tell him what he wanted to know about the profession—about the novels I'd published and the ones I'd abandoned. The latter seemed to surprise him. The more we spoke, the more I understood that he viewed writers as both admirable and pitiful mammals—cubs that had been separated from the pack too soon and were now frail and prone to neurasthenia; feckless neurotics, to be blunt, ruined for a life among other people, but also, because of their wandering, gifted with more sights and smells and insights than was average.

Not that he was average. From the beginning, Hessler insisted on presenting himself as a sensitive, strong man—an adventurer, able to explore those same sights and smells and insights without the writer's requisite softness; indeed, with hard science.

He told me he had one last question. "No, this one isn't about writing," he smiled. "It's simpler. I want to know if life exists in other galaxies."

I was caught off guard by the question and told him as much.

"I suppose that's fair," he sighed. He allowed a moment to pass. Then he said, "Two months ago, at our office in Hermanus, we received an unmarked package at our front desk. It was delivered by an anonymous courier, and inside, there was a locked drive containing audio recordings and printed manuscripts."

"Manuscripts?"

Hessler nodded. "Two of them. In the beginning, we tried to dismiss it, of course. There's nothing unusual about finding an eccentric in our mail haul. But from the beginning, this felt different. For one, an enormous amount of effort had gone into the materials. That much was clear. That's why I didn't mind them making the rounds in our office. Each of us engaged with them at one point or another, swapping the pages for the recordings and vice versa. I indulged it—a harmless morale booster, I thought.

"Then a narrative began to emerge and I paid closer attention. Right from the start, I'd been fascinated with how it presented itself as fact even as it veered into the fantastic." Hessler paused to drain his test tube. "Until last week, that is, which is when it stopped being an entertainment."

The room had grown louder. I leaned in. "What happened?"

"It predicted the present," he said. "Now it might be a threat."

I asked him what it had predicted and he took a moment to answer. "Last week's bombing."

I knew what he meant. An explosion had gone off on the face of Table Mountain, above the city bowl—that wide semi-oval that spread itself between Bo-Kaap and Devil's Peak. The explosion had set off a minor two-day dust storm, powdering the streets in Tamboerskloof and Gardens below. So far, the authorities had no leads.

I decided to indulge him, and asked him to explain.

Hessler reached into his jacket pocket for his cell phone and showed me an image of the explosion site—four gouges in the cliff face. "This is a pattern. The explosions were detonated to form an insignia that's referred to in the text."

I studied the photograph. "It could be a coincidence."

"I know, but it goes one better. It describes when and where the explosives were planted."

I searched his face and he didn't falter. Which is how I got involved.

Joseph confessed to having insisted on my invitation to the telescope opening, having planned on the two of us meeting. More details followed.

I waited a week as he gathered the pages and the recordings. When he drove up to campus to deliver them to me in person, he looked older, I thought, and more stooped under the merciless sunlight on Jammie Plaza. He declined an offer to cool down in the Arts Block, citing exhaustion, which from the look of him I couldn't argue with. I took the materials and drove home.

Δ

Here, I want to be clear. Joseph was not an unstable man. He was fastidious, almost to a fault. From the beginning, he exercised an extreme amount of caution in dealing with what he knew. In fact, he was still wary, all of eight months later. Despite the mounting evidence on our side, he held off on committing to belief. In his emails to me, he insisted that we still had too much room for error. That was wise, given the implications of the text; if we were right, then the threat was far greater than terrorism—and its reach wider than our continent. We only had one chance to convince the State Security Agency; if our dossier wasn't foolproof, it would fall into a bureaucratic loop that would block all further inquiries.

My task, then, was to investigate the veracity of the materials in your hands, reader—to extricate narrative allusions that might speak to a fictional grounding in the science fiction genre. In other words, I had to be as skeptical as I could bear to be as a fiction writer—which is a significant amount, most authors will attest. I took the task on, in other words, not knowing that I was hoping against hope.

The two of us worked well together. Even as Joseph's health began to decline, we never lost our temper with each other—which is rare for me. In our email correspondence, our insights often overlapped, and when his pancreas condition worsened, two years into our work, I visited him in the hospital. After we'd greeted, he'd tell me to pull up a chair and update him on our progress.

It was becoming clear to both of us that we'd have to reconsider what to do with the material. We spent weeks in discussion, before deciding that our reach would have to stretch further than the government. It took another week before we decided to release this book, which I now dedicate to the sender of these materials, in gratitude for her service to humankind.

I also want to confess that I felt a sense of loss as I approached the end of this project. Not because I went home to a vacant house (my husband and I had separated by then; my daughter was at boarding school); not even because I'd lost a friend who was dear to me. It was a different sensation from mourning in that I no longer knew who or what I was. I told Joseph this one afternoon, two days before he died, and I still do not know. Not after what I have read in these pages. Except, perhaps, I know I was never qualified to handle an assignment of this nature and magnitude. This despite its modest beginnings at the SANSA office in Hermanus, where the materials were first dispatched, out of naïveté or shrewdness, I cannot tell.

Now I'm here, with half a decade of my life given to it, and with no regrets nor doubts.

Δ

There are three things I should mention before we begin. The first is that I have left the material intact, with most of my input restricted to formatting the testimonies as per the sender's instructions. I have indicated where the written record and the recordings diverge; the section titles are also mine.

It's also worth noting that the middle of the book operates

in a manner that is distinct from the rest. Though our research has led us to believe that this section, titled "Five Weeks in the Plague," is indeed a work of autofiction, it lacks the form's traditional transparency. It is coded more than usual, no doubt for protection. For example, while we were able to discover that an eco-terrorist group did indeed plant the four explosives on the face of Table Mountain in 2026—timed to detonate only two decades later—the connection to the arts and the artists mentioned was never unearthed. Nor did we confirm the existence of a publication titled *Obelisk*. Furthermore, while no evidence exists of the alien sightings alluded to throughout the text, the Department of Social Development's collusion with Cash Paymaster Services against their grantees has been well documented; and, the kidnapping of three teenage girls in King William's Town gained national coverage in 2002.

Perhaps our most significant discovery, then, has been identifying and locating the records of the late Dr Marianne Dixon, who appears as herself in the text. Dixon earned her doctorate in cognitive neuroscience from Vassar in 1998. Her dissertation was on the topic of Jean Piaget's theory of cognitive development as applied to the education models of apartheid South Africa. Dixon was unmarried and childless, which left us no descendants to contact for testimonies, and along with her colleagues in the field (now also deceased), she maintained a low profile. There are records, however, of her attempts to publish her findings in various journals over the years, and of her applying to secure audiences at conferences in Johannesburg, New Delhi, and New York—all of which were met with rejections. Unable to prove their claims, including the existence of extraterrestrial life, which would have required them to reveal their sources, Dixon and her colleagues were excommunicated from the field. This was on the heels of a scandal—enough to cement the damage—that alleged the researchers had misused a public grant to conduct unauthorized experiments on minors.

Dismissed by their peers, Dixon and her team continued as independent researchers. Their findings, disregarded by all established cognitive neuroscience journals, can now be found collated on their website, http://www.triangulum-earth.com, whose hosting has been paid up[1], despite it not being updated in a decade. The text also explores the origins of the zones, or Delta Labor Camps as most of us know them, which are proliferating in every province—and which remain the nation's most divisive issue, bringing me to my second point, which is the setting of the manuscript.

The reader will notice that the bulk of this narrative takes place in the Eastern Cape, once known as the Ciskei[2] homeland, an apparatus of conquest implemented here by Europeans in the second millennium. This is the sender's lineage and it is also mine.

That little has changed isn't a deterrent, but a motivation for publication in 2044: to commemorate the demise of the homelands, as well as to encourage those lobbying against the state's current plan to make the North West a zoned province—a marker of 50 years of progress, we're told, since the abolition of apartheid. Which leads me to my third and final point.

I have not contacted the government. In the past, as related

---

1   The owner of the domain is hidden, but we have reason to believe the account was passed down to the sender.

2   A note for our foreign readers: the Ciskei homeland was a nominal independent state, symptomatic of the apartheid regime, that existed from 1981 to 1994. It was located in the southeast of the republic, taking up less than 3,860 square miles, and run as a dictatorship. It excluded the port of East London as well as economic centers such as King William's Town—which would later become the sender's home—and Queenstown, which belonged to the Europeans of the republic. To give the scheme a veneer of legitimacy, the land was assigned to isiXhosa speakers in two "self-governed territories." The two homelands were divided by the Great Kei River and dissolved in 1994, at the arrival of our first democratic elections, leaving behind ethnic tensions that simmer into the present.

above, scientists and authorities have not heeded the message contained in this manuscript. It is also true that, in the end, Joseph and I concluded that the instruments of power could not be trusted with our future. Instead, our aim is to deliver it to the population, even though we do not know how events will unfold, and whether or not we will survive. The choice is ours. In the end, the sender intended this work for humankind, and it is only fitting, then, that I close here with her own words.

The message I wish to pass on is not complicated. There is indeed a force more powerful than humankind. I have assented and do not know much else.

Neither do I.

Dr Naomi Buthelezi
Stellenbosch
December 2, 2043

I
THE MACHINE

October 4, 1999

I was 14 when I first lingered in front of the mirror next to our home computer, and touched myself, coming twice, so I wouldn't think about Mama's abduction.

I'd never done that in front of a mirror before, and I'd never gone beyond that number, but I told myself to stop when Tata woke up coughing. I snuck back to my room, and listened to him as he left the house. Later I'd learn that he'd gone to the clinic.

That night, close to midnight, our front door unlocked again and Tata walked back in, bringing his illness with him.

I opened his bedroom door to let out smoke. "You're doing it again," I said.

Tata told me to go to sleep.

"I don't feel well."

I could tell he wasn't sure if it was me or Mama. "It's me," I said.

"Tell me what's wrong with you."

"I don't know what it is."

"Then go back to sleep."

I turned and went to bed.

I could still smell the cigarette smoke seeping out from his room. I sat up in bed, measuring my breathing so he wouldn't know I was awake, waiting for him to fall asleep.

Lying back, I looked up at the ceiling and thought about how, 42 years ago, the Soviet Union had launched Sputnik I, the world's first artificial satellite, into orbit. Not that Tata would've cared. Although he had a degree, it was in agriculture, from a farming college in the mid-'70s.

I closed my eyes, feeling cold as the bedsheets bunched up behind me. I remembered the time I'd felt a pain similar to his. In magnitude, at least.

I was nine years old when I fell off a creaking swing in a corner of Bhisho Park. I'd seen a column of rain clouds racing toward me, and moments later, I'd flipped over and hit the ground with the left side of my head. After a minute, I couldn't see.

It was a condition the doctor at our local hospital described as corneal sunburn. It happened when I was lying on my back in the park, unable to move, staring directly into the sun before my head rolled over and everything went dark.

That was in 1994.

Afterward, Tata often told this story to his friends, pausing to mention that I never cried—a fact the doctor attributed to shock. I still remember standing in the bathroom that morning, trembling as Mama cleaned the cut on my brow and tried to dress it with an old t-shirt from Tata's closet. Then the two of them drove me to our local hospital and walked me down a long corridor that blinked under a malfunctioning fluorescent light. I got stitched seven times, prescribed 500 milligrams of paracetamol, and given a week off school.

I wasn't concussed, but for the first few days, being home felt different. My parents tottered around the house, silhouetted against the ceiling light, their shadows providing me with care, Vick's VapoRub, minestrone soup, continental pillows. Through all their efforts and between fevers, I lay on my back, hearing their voices as if from the inside of a bunker—a booming echo that preceded each one's presence inside the bedroom or the lounge, where I either slept or sat absorbing a blur of television without sound.

Mama, a counselor at the University of Fort Hare, had been a communications officer for the homeland government, and liked to leave our TV turned to the news. That Saturday, when my vision healed, I spent the afternoon drifting in and out of sleep in front of different news reports, waking up to broadcasts of conflicts in countries whose names I couldn't pronounce. At one point, Mama joined me on the sofa, stroked my neck and felt my forehead, then settled back to watch the explosions flicker into clouds of dust and fire with me, the two of us silenced.

The following summer, she went missing, and four years later, Tata returned coughing from a different hospital in a different town. I'd often wonder what connected us that afternoon as we watched the bloodshed in Mogadishu together—if that was when I inherited the machine, as one doctor would later suggest, although he didn't seem to know much about it—but feeling her touch on the wound had soothed it.

Later, I'd try to evoke this moment with Mama again, calling her back into the living room with news reports on the disasters she'd left behind with us on Earth.

I opened my eyes and breathed out again, absorbing the new-found warmth in my sheets. I could hear Tata coughing again, our house having grown still, as if the two of us had been interred inside a capsule and sent out into deep space to freeze.

Maybe on a mission to find her, I thought; but how would he know that?

As abruptly as it had started, his coughing stopped, and I could tell he was asleep.

Soon, I drifted off, too, thinking about how Sputnik had persisted for three weeks after its batteries gave out. It floated alone in the dark for two months before falling back to Earth. I took this as evidence that things came back down in the end. Including Mama.

Regression Therapy Recording (RTR): 001
Date of Recollection: 05.28.2002
Date of Recording: 06.20.2035
Duration: 4 min
Format: Monologue

Ever since I got put on medication, I've been thought of as defective. That's what people decide about me. In the 8th grade, at my last school, I was asked to join the debate team after I saw a speech coach. My grades were good, but I needed self-confidence. I didn't speak enough, and when I did, it was hard to discern how I felt. That's what my English teacher said.

The speech coach taught me how to gesture, maintain eye contact, correct my posture, and project my voice, but I didn't join the team in the end.

I was diagnosed with reduced affect display, or emotional blunting, my doctor said, from the medication he'd prescribed to me when I was 12. It meant I couldn't express my emotional responses as well as most people. It wasn't an uncommon side-effect, he said, and lots of patients could live with it. The pills he gave me, Celexa and Paxil, were treating me well for the insomnia that had brought me to his office, and he suggested we keep to the regimen. I couldn't remember how I'd been before. I sat in his office and agreed.

It's now been five years.

Picking a dandelion seed off my school uniform today, Part says she knows a bad joke and then she tells it to us. "The thing with reality," she says, "people used to have the sense for it, but now they don't buy it." Pausing for a moment, she says she means "cents."

The three of us laugh. It's the end of May, a month before our winter break, and I've just got out of detention, my second one since I stopped being a student monitor in junior high.

Litha bends down to loosen his laces and sighs. "Maybe heaven is dead," he says.

Later, at home with my earphones on, I try to sleep, but I don't.

Instead, I find myself standing in front of our bathroom mirror at 1 a.m.

I weigh 99 pounds from having had rails on both of my jaws for an underbite, and the mirror reflects my cheekbones, my neck, my lips, my hair. It needs to be braided again, I think, although it's still neat.

In the living room, I switch on the TV and find an infomercial for a range of pans—an old man in a chef's tunic uses a non-stick casserole to caramelize sugar over a low flame; he pours it into a cereal bowl and his audience claps. I switch it off.

In my bedroom, I open a drawer and take out a makeup mirror and magnifying glass. I tilt the vanity mirror on its base until it fills up with a reflection of the moon through the parted curtains. Angling the lens over the rock's surface, I count the craters that mark its damage until I fall asleep.

October 5, 1999

The following morning, after he'd returned coughing from peering into our mailbox, Tata proposed a trip to a Pentecostal herbalist from out of town. A month before, he'd been laid off from his new job as manager of a fleet of vans that delivered amasi from a farm in Stutterheim, and he'd written a note for me to miss school so we could make it in time before the lines. My presence on the trip was for good luck, he said.

We set out at noon, Tata's retrenchment letter on the console between us. Tata's double cab crossed the rail bridge at the edge of our town and entered Ginsberg, where he parked next to a sleeping German shepherd with patches of pale skin showing through its fur. It was shivering from flea bites, and I moved away, careful not to step on its tail.

We walked through a grid of one-room houses with rusting roofs, to a house with a grassy yard and long line outside the door. Tata sighed. For an hour and a half, we shuffled in line. One woman collapsed, having reached the front of the line a moment too late. It took a while before a stooped man came over and carried her away. To pass the time, I looked around. The grass grew in sparse patches over the yard, disturbed in the middle by large angular rocks that marked a path; the porch smelt of enough ammonia to cause a headache, I thought—and then got one.

Tata got to the front of the line and disappeared into a room without windows, built onto the side of a house that was larger than the rest. When he returned, without his retrenchment letter, he was holding two clear, unlabeled bottles. One was for health and the other would assure us wealth, he said, hefting them at his sides. He was to drink three times from each bottle. When we got to the car, the dog had vanished along with its leash.

Tata and I were silent as we crossed back over the rail tracks. "Tell me what you want to do with your life," he said.

I thought about it. "I don't know. Maybe take care of you."

Tata sighed, shifting into first gear. "Just like your mother," he said. "You can't think for yourself, either?"

I thought for myself. "I want to be a scientist," I said.

He didn't respond. It was only when we got home that I realized I could never tell him what I knew.

That I wanted to look for her through the longest telescope I could find.

Later that afternoon, after we'd eaten our porridge in silence and he'd drunk from each of his bottles, Tata went back to bed. I waited for his door to lock, then went to my bedroom too. I turned over my pillow and looked at the bloodstains, now turned yellow, on his old pillowcase.

This was in the spring of 1999. I'd been cured of acne. Nelson Mandela had announced his retirement, forfeiting a shoo-in for a second term, and the world was ending because of a computer bug.

We never spoke about Mama. Tata tried to keep her memory outside our walls, minimizing her in conversation, and I'd gone along with that until I couldn't. Until I no longer had the choice.

The first time I saw the machine, for example, I thought of the word *canard*, which I'd learned from a crossword puzzle Mama completed with me when I was nine. I didn't know to call it the machine, then; nor did I tell Tata about it.

Instead, the following morning, I heated up and served us two bowls of oats. Then I sat down and thought about the word again.

Myth.

"*Rumor*," Mama had said, guiding my hand over the squares.

"Falsehood?"

"That's close."

"How close?"

She smiled.

I looked up from my porridge bowl, now, and saw Tata in his worn diplomat's bathrobe—the one with the old Ciskei insignia—poring over the classifieds section of *The Daily Dispatch*. His tea had gone cold.

Ever since the abolition of apartheid, he'd been unable to find regular work. Tata and his ex-colleagues had all dropped an economic class and retreated from the public, avoiding the glares that awaited them in schools and supermarkets. In Bhisho, he'd served as a financial officer in the Department of Agriculture, working through the Ciskeian Agricultural Bank to develop "released areas," or clusters of previously white-owned farms which had been absorbed into the homeland. Men who'd been doing their duty weren't the same as the ones who'd had their boots on our necks, he said.

I sat back in the kitchen chair and spoke without expecting an answer. "I thought you had a position lined up with those new Renewable Energy people," I said. "Last week, you told me they had a logo and everything."

Tata scoffed, folding his broadsheet in half. He pinched its spine and closed his eyes. "They're all amateurs," he said. "Lawrence is the worst of them, too. He's never worked a day in his life."

I looked at the headline obscuring his face. It was about how many children were illiterate in the province. I stirred my oats and cleared my throat. "I don't believe we have an 86 percent literacy rate in the Eastern Cape. I've been to our schools."

"Come again?"

"Especially amongst the males." I raised my spoon and pointed at the headline.

Tata looked at it too, and laughed. "No, you're right. It isn't just Lawrence. Everyone's books are cooked."

We laughed together until he broke into a cough. Changing the subject, I told him how the previous afternoon I'd asked a teacher if it was true that in the year 1500, there were only half a billion *Homo sapiens* on the planet. "I told him I knew it was over six billion now, but I wanted to know if it was possible to feed that rise in population without fossil fuels."

"Using what, instead?"

"Using biofuel. Like with the Renewable Energy people."

"Then you were looking at my papers?"

I nodded. "They were there."

"Did you get an answer from your teacher?"

"I don't know. He said he likes to keep an open mind."

"Meaning?"

"That some people believe the Earth is 2000 years old."

Tata laughed again. I watched him get up, knowing I couldn't tell him about the machine, because I didn't know how to. He put the newspaper on the table, fastened his robe, yawned, and left the kitchen.

I carried his cup to the basin and emptied it, watching the cold rooibos sluice into the drain. I ran the water for the dishes. It was warm outside. The air was placid, pierced through with the sounds of birdsong and children. In a short while, parents would expect their cars to be washed by their teenage sons. Their lawns trimmed. I ran the water over my palms. Then I began on the plates, the cold water paling the tips of my fingers until each looked like a small cylinder of powder. After drying my hands, I fell asleep for half an hour in front of a muted rerun of *Noot vir Noot*. When I woke, I took the house keys from the rack.

In the garage, although the air was humid, dust powdered all the surfaces except for the treadmill in the corner, where

I'd balanced my bike. The treadmill didn't work, but the belt moved when I rode over it, and that's what I'd been doing for the past month, ever since Tata drove me to Farrer's Sports to get me a mountain bike for scoring the top grade in my class. Tata couldn't cycle himself. I'd convinced him that I'd learn to do it on the go, but I hadn't.

The lights in the garage had malfunctioned; I had to remove a large cardboard box from the window to let in some light. I balanced my bike on the treadmill and began to pedal—it was flat and long enough to hold both tires. Every time I tipped sideways, instead of spilling off, I'd clutch one of the handles on the treadmill. It was a 16-gear bike, and I wasn't tall enough to plant my feet on the ground when I lost my balance. This way, I could practice until I got tired.

That night, the machine returned.

Like the night before, as soon as I closed my eyes, the parts came out of the opposite ends of the wall, coming together to form a hole in the middle of the ceiling. The room filled up with a mechanical hum. Then I looked around and found I couldn't see.

The following morning, I woke up on my stomach with my vision blurred.

I unlocked our garage, dragged the bike off the tread-mill and rode around the block as the morning air cooled my sweat. I could tell it had taught me how to ride, and that this was the beginning of things between us. As I rode further up Wodehouse, I couldn't keep myself from blinking, the world filled with a vividness that felt capable of blinding me.

RTR: 002 / Date of Recollection: 05.29.2002 / 17 min

Today is Mom's birthday, although I forgot to watch the morning news like we used to do.

That was our ritual for the 29th. Dad couldn't understand it,
he said, but it's what Mama and I chose to do. After we were
done, he'd call us over for slices of sponge cake, her favorite,
which he ordered at the Shoprite the night before.

For a while, after she was gone, he still went out and bought
one on her birthday; but over time, without discussing it, we
both stopped touching it.

I get to school late this morning, around 8:30, a minute before
Mrs Robinson locks the front gate. She tells me latecomers are
liable for four-week suspension. It's drizzling. I cup a palm over
my forehead, another over my braids as she shuffles me to the
chapel. I follow her instructions in irritation, but silence. This
is what passes for a truce, since the two of us will never get
along. Mrs Robinson's hair is an auburn loofah, flaking off into
freckles all over her cheeks. I used to have her in 9th grade for
choir; she'd teach our class without projecting the sheet lyrics
on the wall. This was to punish us, I used to think, for getting
the words to her hymns wrong. Not thinking, once, I made the
mistake of telling her she was bleeding through the back of her
skirt. It was true, but the class ended and she didn't return to us
for choir that week.

I unshoulder my bag and join my grade at the back. I feel
relieved chapel's close to ending; a moment later, the seniors get
up and we all leave the church again, taking the gravel path to
our first period in the admin block on Huberta Square, a brick

courtyard named after a famous dead hippo from our district. I excuse myself and walk to the bathroom.

There's a text message from Litha: *I have more hockey practice.*

I tell him we'll live. I pack the cellphone back in my bag, take out two capsules of Celexa and Paxil, swallow them over the sink, and go to class.

I walk past the results of our math test from last week, the printouts pinned up in the corridor outside Mr Costello's physics classroom. Settling down at my desk toward the back, I close my eyes and listen as the pills clatter inside my backpack, the plastic tapping against a pencil case that used to belong to Dad.

Then I breathe out, and open my eyes.

Make another go of it, I think to myself.

I don't often talk about class or how good I am at school, because I don't think there's much to talk about. I know that most people here aren't, and that's fine, too.

Three years ago, sequestered at a different school—an old diocesan prison on the outskirts of East London—on a scholarship, I was awarded the Dux Litterarum. The headmistress, Mrs Primrose, cried as she patted me on the shoulder, and then apologized for her sloppiness. It was untoward of her, she explained. I took her apology, although I didn't care enough to respond. I waited for the moment to pass, pretending I didn't know about Marissa, her daughter, who was upset at losing the cup. The check went to my aunt.

A year later, I fell sick. I'd wake up in a fever, shaking at the thought of having to walk through the school grounds again. My mouth grew parched and I suffered from migraines on the benches at break. I couldn't sleep, either. I was convinced it had to do with me being there. That's what I told the counselors. Then I got passed on to new and different counselors. I did that until the school ran out of them and Dad unenrolled me.

Now I'm here.

I drop my backpack, pull out the pencil case, and stretch.

"Let me guess. Not much sleep."

Lerato's sitting next to me, and as usual her legs are shaved and shining—slathered with enough moisturizer to give a person cataracts. Gleaming on the basin behind her, I notice a beaker I could tip over to stop her smiling; but I don't.

"Thanks," I say.

"No, seriously. Hey, have you heard? Kiran was meant to come back today, but he hasn't pitched."

I hadn't heard. Two weeks after our Easter break, Kiran took a month off school after his dad, an ENT with a practice in East London, was reported missing in the dailies. This was the week after I'd asked him to lend me his MiniDisc recorder and he'd agreed, telling me he'd do it if I let him neck me at the fields outside Hudson Park.

I'd agreed to let him think I would.

It's not that he's the worst looking guy here. He's tall, with thick curls and faint sideburns, but he also thinks leaving his school shirt untucked undermines the staff. I could do without that. Last year, he'd spent most of our prep squinting at me. That's when I'd come up with the idea to record the machine with the MD.

Hence us having to make out.

I turn back to my desk. "Maybe I'm still the new girl."

Lerato laughs and I take a moment to look at her. Her face is long and faultless.

For something else to do, I open and close the pencil case my dad gave me. At the front of the class, Mr Costello tells us to settle down. He's chewing on his lip—a habit I hate, since it keeps the skin chapped.

Not that he's awful. Mr Costello's middle-aged, soft around the middle, and more bearable than most of them, here. His shoulders are often hunched, shortening his neck, and he's always blinking behind thick, tinted glasses. Today, he's holding a stack of tests close to his chest; if our class average drops below 60, he likes to make us all do the test over. It's only fair, he explains, and I guess I've never minded him for that.

I like fairness.

Most times, Part and I meet at the intersection of Queens and Joubert Roads, then head down to the park—just the two of us, if Litha's at hockey. We're all at different schools.

This town, once a mission station, was named after a monarch whose general turned natives into settlers—offering the Mfengu British citizenship in exchange for each other's blood. It spreads under us like a green tomb, its rolling hills dipping into spaces abandoned to waste. The grass is always warm, as if a giant had curled itself around the borders of Buffalo City and lain down to die, before evaporating into the atmosphere. Part and I often take shelter in the shade of a stone alcove under an elm.

Part likes to argue with me over whose life we'd grade worse, hers or mine. It's my job to tell Part to be fairer to her mom— to remind her that her mother has a vascular disease, and she should stop picking a fight with her every day of the week. Litha tells her that too.

Not that he doesn't have ideas of his own. For example, he says even adoption isn't a merciful act; it's a lucky draw. It gets to the point where you're afraid of your parents and they don't remember your name. He's lost faith in parenting, he says; these days, he loses himself in internet fantasies where the way to kill a monster is to give it a tonic of health or a life potion. He tells me to imagine a re-routed reality where life is not only the mirror of death, but also its catalyst.

I tell him I'm not sure. Most of the time we agree, though. It's been that way for two years now. Litha and I are Xhosa, while Part's grandparents are from Madeira. The three of us met one afternoon at the Master Math office on Alexandra Road, down the road from Grey Hospital and De Vos Malan High School. We were looking for tutor jobs—a week of free lessons was being provided by the state to primary students from Ginsberg and Dimbaza—and we'd settled into the waiting room, where the air conditioning spat flakes of rust over the linoleum and potted plants. It made me shiver when it almost got in my hair. I didn't like that. I yawned. I was tired, having skipped my last three meals. Part leaned back on the bench and made it creak. Next, two red-haired women greeted us, offered us a jug of water, and told us none of us had the job. I wasn't surprised; I'd suspected there'd be a school background check.

Outside, Litha told me and Part he worked at the Mr Movie up the road. He invited us over and took us back to the storeroom, where he showed us an old tape of *Debbie Does Dallas* for an hour. It had laugh tracks dubbed over the dialogue, which Litha thought we'd find hilarious, and we did. I mean, I still do.

Mr Costello reaches our desk and drops our tests in front of us.

Lerato pulls at mine. "I knew it."

I take the test back from her. My mark's more or less what I expected.

"With grades like that, I don't understand why you stopped being a monitor," Lerato says.

"It wasn't comfortable. Mr de Silva saw the report card I came in with from East London, and thought it was a Rorschach test and not just marks." The two of us learned about the inkblot test in English last week. "Like it meant I'd naturally be good at following orders."

Lerato shifts on her seat, grinning, before closing her test. "To be honest, it isn't that bad. There's the tuck shop thing, for one." I know. Monitors like her get free apple pies.

"I don't care about King Pie," I say.

"Even apple King Pie?"

"Even apple King Pie."

Lerato smiles, shaking her head, even though it's true.

Toward the end of my last year of junior high—not long after I came here—I got my student monitor badge taken away from me. I got summoned to the principal's office, where I watched our headmaster, Mr de Silva, sweating under his collar, while through the window mounds of rain clouds massed over the field the school rented for track. He was on the phone, looking down at his blotter, and I remembered how we hadn't had any sports, that year. I looked at the mist on the windowpane behind Mr de Silva's head.

He dropped the receiver and sighed, looking at his hands. "You fraternize too much," he said. "You were trusted with leadership and discipline."

I nodded, but I didn't face him.

The world outside felt muted. Two old men pushed a wheelbarrow to a landfill across the field, thin curtains of smoke rising from a smoldering garbage fire before them, and I didn't answer him, but walked to his desk when he told me to. He removed the pin from my school uniform and turned it over in his palm.

"You can go," he told me, and I left.

Before class ends, an alarm goes off for a fire drill. We file out into Huberta Square. I'm surprised they're still following regulations, even for safety; for the longest time, we've been told the school is just hanging on, on the verge of going broke. Joining the crowd at the back, I reach into my bag and feel for Kiran's MD. I can't see him anywhere.

Lerato sidles up to me. "Here's to another waste of time."

I nod and rub my hands together, feeling the onset of winter. The mist hangs low over the grounds, raking goosebumps from our skin. We get told to arrange ourselves in straight lines, slicing the courtyard into four perfect squares.

I never used to believe enough when Mom was still around. I remember that.

The first time I told Part about the abduction, her hesitation didn't surprise me.

We were in her kitchen, the first cul-de-sac off Head Drive on the other side of town; she was straining a cup of tea for her mom and telling me she'd promised herself not to spit in it. Not that I'd asked.

I sat back on the kitchen chair and watched her leaning over the basin. Part's legs could be found in an old dentist's waiting-room magazine, I thought, preserved from the '80s, like the ones I'd seen in a box of Mom's old things. Her Smashing Pumpkins t-shirt hung past her cut-offs. Her feet were slender, and if the tiles were cold, she didn't show it.

"You mean extraterrestrials?" she asked.

"I didn't see them, but yes."

"I see." Using two fingers, Part pulled the lid off the kettle, releasing steam.

I decided to try something else, before I lost my nerve. "Do you want a girlfriend?"

"I don't know. Does that happen?"

"I learned about it in Life Orientation."

Part laughed. "There's also Litha."

I sighed. Part liked to provoke me, I knew that, but I could also tell we were both scared. I dropped my head onto my fore-arms, reminding myself of all the ways I looked better than she did. I stopped when I reached the ones I'd made up. I breathed out.

Part stood and rinsed the strainer over the basin. Then she turned around and dried her hands down her sides. "I know what you're thinking," she said.

"Do you?" I looked up from my forearms and attempted a smile. "Then say yes to me."

"Yes, I do," she said, "and yes, yes to you, too."

Then I got up.

That's how Part and I first got together, that afternoon. The second time it happened, I told Part my theory of how my mom had been abducted.

The two of us headed down to the library on Alexandra Road behind the shut-down theater. We walked around the rusting cannons that sat baking on the lawn by the dried-up water fountain, ignoring the other students. I let Part walk in in front of me, absorbing the sunlight so I could savor the gust from the air conditioning in the lobby when we went inside.

We checked our bags and passed single-file through the glass doors into the main part of the library. The air was even colder here, which I liked. Under the flicking fluorescent lights, we curved into the adult section on the right, where I pulled out a hardcover with *UFO Diaries* embossed on the front.

I handed it to her. "I first found a copy of it when I was 12. It was in Mom's things. I'd snuck into the guest room, where we kept her clothes before Dad packed them up." Since then, I'd often come back here to read about people like me and Mom.

Part squinted at the cover. "These people could be insane."

"I don't know. Look."

I opened the book and she leaned over my shoulder to look, close enough for me to inhale the aroma off her skin. Thinking of my own scent, I told her to wait; I tried not to blush as I walked to the bathroom, where I tamped my armpits with damp toilet paper. I pressed it over my eyelids and between my legs. Then I washed my hands with the sweet puke-like soap from the dispenser.

I found Part sitting cross-legged in the non-fiction aisle, the book open on her lap.

"I don't know," I said, "one night she was around and one

night she wasn't. The window in the living room was open. I mean, who vanishes like that?"

I sat down next to her and she looked up at me, the book's cover sticking to the insides of her thighs. I didn't mention the other connection I had to it. That I'd found the first copy at a time when I felt foreign inside, breasts aching for the first time, and with new underarm hair. I looked taller, too. I felt like there was an exit from being a child and alone. Feeling noticed, as well, and not having a pill prescription.

"Like, aliens?" Part smiled, and I felt more stung than I'd expected. She looked down and opened the book again, creasing her brow as she read.

"Like that, huh?" she said.

"Like that."

I only met her father, the policeman, after I met his gun—an automatic 9mm.

Part's dad was out that afternoon, somewhere in town. She had the gun between us on her mother's bed.

Looking at me, Part laughed and said, "Put it in your mouth. It still has my saliva on it. It'll be like a kiss. Or even better."

Outside, the light was golden and had stuck itself to the windows, hiding behind the synthetic curtains, and there in her mother's room, on her bed, we were two humming spirits in a movie about desolation, where life was two people and death was everything else.

"It would be even better with gingivitis," Part said.

Taking the gun back, a stream of my saliva, our saliva, our kiss, fell on the bed, and then without warning me she stood in front of the dresser and raised the gun, pointing it at the wall.

I could hear her mom's voice mumbling through the wall from the living room, talking and laughing to herself.

"Imagine how easy it would be," Part said. "She wouldn't know what happened. Her head should be here, somewhere."

Part aimed, made shooting noises with her mouth. Then her arms fell limp at her sides. "I'm done. We should listen to *In Utero*." She opened the door to her room, still holding the gun in her hand. "We should do it loud, so she can hear."

I got up.

"Now come closer."

I went closer and her hand fell on my shoulder; her mom laughed again.

The next week, when I told her a third time about Mom's abduction, Part looked up at me for a moment, then reached for my hand and told me she believed me. For the rest of the afternoon, we paged through *UFO Diaries* end to end, going through each sighting, taking special note of locations and dates. This was a day before Litha came back from an out-of-town trip. Part told me she suspected his fosters might be thinking of taking him back to the children's home.

The two of us met him after school at the alcove in the park.

"Most of it was us driving around Hogsback," he said. "My fosters and I were meant to meet my biological uncle, but he stopped calling when we got to town. It happened the same way with an aunt a few years ago. It's about money."

Part and I watched him push his fingers through his hair, his dreadlocks trimmed into a new mushroom bob.

"So what did you do?" asked Part.

"Not much, except drive to Hole in the Wall and eat ham sandwiches."

"Did anything fun happen?"

Litha shook his head. "No. I wouldn't call it that."

Part patted him on the shoulder, half-joking and half-meaning it, like she often did. I looked across the field to the red roof of the public hospital, where they kept my dad under a plastic mask for two days one October, a dish the shape of a bean catching the yellow paste from his lungs.

．　．　．

Mrs Robinson clears her throat and quiets us down. "Mr de Silva's engaged today," she says. "He's had to attend an urgent funding meeting in East London, so I'll be addressing you in his place."

There's a murmur before everyone goes quiet.

"Now, I take it most of you have seen the news. Yesterday, three local girls were abducted on their way home from netball practice. They're local students, but the police are also investigating cases from neighboring towns. There could be more."

The silence deepens over the courtyard.

"It's devastating, of course, but we don't want to encourage unnecessary panic. The school's taking the required measures. Members of staff are putting together a committee to produce a memo for students. Evidence suggests the targets are girls, but there'll be an update for everyone. For now, be discerning: avoid all strangers and don't walk home alone. There'll be information on how to use the buddy system in the memo."

Then Mrs Robinson makes us file back to class in separate grades.

I pull my blazer over my shoulders, pushing through the cold as I climb the stairs to bio. It feels like there's a threat hanging over the school; I imagine it covering us like a blanket, turning the world dim and silent.

October 7, 1999

I didn't harp on about the machine, which is what I started calling it. Most of my family was already openly suspicious of me, appalled at stories of how, when I was 12, I'd convinced Tata, a man still grieving his wife, to move me from three schools in the space of 10 months. And how I'd continued to trouble him until he took me to a doctor in town—at which point I'd been awake for four days. I was diagnosed with dysthymia, which my family didn't know about, and which Tata and I found foreign too.

The doctor wrote me a prescription for a trial of SSRIs, which would change the chemical signals in my brain, he said—this was after he'd taken me alone to a separate room next to his dispensary and asked me about my period, and whether I was having sex yet, in which case I had to be warned against whoring—and which Tata pocketed but ignored. Instead, my father opted for a host of herbal remedies from friends and associates, receiving each one with what I thought was a premature sense of gratitude.

A month later, my symptoms hadn't abated and we had to drive down to town again for a second prescription. That's when I decided to tell the doctor about the machine—a mistake, I could tell. He summoned Tata into his office and told him that, aside from the dysthymia, it was possible I was suffering from severe hypnagogic hallucinations, not uncommon in epileptic patients who'd suffered brain trauma from a head injury. Though in my case, he added, it was hard to diagnose me as epileptic without the visible seizures. He leaned back in his seat and shook his head. "The hallucinations will disappear over time," he said. "The key issue is treating the dysthymia."

Tata was quiet for most of the drive home. At last he said, "I understand your injury, but now you're also unhappy with your life. Even at your age. This is what all this is about."

He creased his brow, the way he did whenever someone mentioned Mama. I knew he wouldn't face me for the rest of the trip.

I took in the sky with its thick cumulus clouds; it seemed impossible that there was no permanence to the blue that spread itself outside the windows. That from the vantage point of the universe, where light didn't refract, the only permanence we could know was darkness—or what I'd come to think of as Mama's home. I didn't tell Tata that, though. Instead, when we drove into our neighborhood, I turned to him and explained I'd never liked my teeth.

"Teeth?"

I nodded and opened my mouth at my reflection in the sunshade. My teeth were crowded and uneven. I told him that since losing my baby teeth, I'd found it difficult to talk. I was struck, most of the time, with the fear of having an audience.

Tata shrugged, but I could sense his relief. "You want to be even more beautiful than you already are," he said. "Your grandmother was the same."

Two weeks into the next month, we drove out to a maxillofacial surgeon in East London—a booming old Indian man who stooped over me and took X-rays of my skull, before presenting Tata with a sheet of paper marked with a vast sum.

"It won't be impossible to save," he said on our drive back. "The doctor said we could do the braces in a year, so why don't you give your father some time?"

I gave it to him, and he was right. I went for surgery toward the end of that year, on his insurance. By the time I got my braces fitted, I was told that my face, always described to me as earnest and severe, had improved fivefold. The pain in my jaws changed my relationship with meat, though. It gave me a diet that trimmed my reflection to that of a stranger's.

"No more new schools."

That's what Tata would say whenever he found me observing my reflection in the bathroom mirror; he detected vanity, where I felt curiosity. Not that he was far off. I'd smile back at him, not knowing how else to respond.

When I started lifting banknotes from the wallet he kept in his bedroom, hoarding full-priced halter tops in a stack at the bottom of my closet, he pretended not to notice. Tata knew the prescription for my SSRIs had gone from trial to regimen, but he'd never come with me to the pharmacy, claiming to be engaged. Only when he'd been drinking, which happened on occasion, would he call me to his room and tell me he'd been reading about what was happening with me.

"Do you still feel anything?" he'd ask, and in those moments, I would. There were times Tata dismissed me if I couldn't tell him in terms he understood what was wrong with me, but this was different. "Can you tell me what you're feeling now?" he'd say, and I'd be ready to play my part too.

I'd tell him, "Yes."

I'd tell him, "I'm happy you're my father."

RTR: 003 / Date of Recollection: 05.29.2002 / 1.5 min

I think about the missing girls until it's almost break, knowing I'm not the only one. The world still feels dim, but I hear our teachers murmuring in the corridors.

In the bio lab, we set out petri dishes to test for photosynthesis in the leaves we were told to gather from home. It's an experiment to prove the formula on the board:

$$6CO_2 + 6H_2O \rightarrow C_6H_{12}O_6 + 6O_2.$$

At our stations, we push the leaves inside test tubes using thin glass rods, then watch them boil in ethanol. The room starts to smell like iodine. We test each tube for starch. Before I hand in my answer sheet to Mrs Matten, I look down at what I've written on the page and cross it out.

It's Mom's birth date. Followed by three question marks.

I look for Kiran during break, and what Lerato said turns out to be true. He's absent. I find her instead, sitting on the benches at the front of the school with three other girls I know from choir. They sit stretched out to absorb the meager sunlight, in knee-high socks and polished Toughees, and they're talking about them, the missing girls, I can tell.

I greet and walk past them to the library, where I browse through the few interesting books I haven't read yet. Then the bell rings and I get up to walk to class, but when I reach the threshold of the library, I feel faint and lean against the door-frame; which is when I see the machine and pass out.

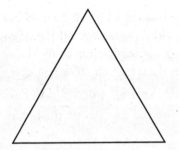

October 9, 1999

That week, Tata coughed so much I could hear him down the corridor, and he didn't stop until I'd pulled my fist back from the paneling. I was waiting for him to die. I didn't want him to.

He opened the door a crack. "Do you ever stop talking? No boy will ever kiss you," he said before I could speak. Then he got back under the covers, blowing his nose.

I drew the door closed. Whenever he was in a good mood, Tata spoke to me with this kind of impatient teasing. Ever since Mama disappeared and I'd had my braces fitted, it had been his way of cheering us up; I couldn't blame him for it. Most of the time.

I went to school, came back. I cooked for him when he felt too tired to stand for more than half an hour. Sometimes he did the same for me; often, he was the one who made sure there was something warm for us to eat, even if it meant we had to peel sardines out of a tin and spit their spines out onto a side plate.

It was difficult for him to find work. The following week, when his cough had subsided, he came home with a box of weight-loss kits to sell in our neighborhood. They contained a cream you applied to the skin before wrapping it tight with cellophane, he explained, digging through one of the boxes. "Your mother..." But he didn't finish the thought.

I went to the kitchen and served us two bowls of samp.

Mama, I thought.

I remembered how she wouldn't speak to me if I came home with less than 95 percent on a test. How she wanted to arrange me into a shape she approved of. How little I'd resisted.

Mama could intimidate me with a glance. As far back as I can remember, even when we still lived in the two-bedroom house in Bhisho, I often felt timid and slow around her. Like the rest of her, Mama's shoulders were thin but strong; from girlhood, she'd had scars on her shins. Her skin was fair; her face angular and stern, with cheekbones that would've been severe if her smile didn't feel like a window flung open.

I remember one evening when she didn't seem to care about my grades. I helped her make macaroni and cheese that night, and we both laughed when it came out lopsided from the microwave.

"Too many white things at once," she said, and we laughed until we had to sit down.

That was a part of it, too, I thought.

The two of us laughing.

I took the bowls of samp out of the oven and spooned up the beans from the bottom to see if they were heated. I almost burnt my fingers on the bars of the grill, but the bases of both bowls were still warm. Not hot.

RTR: 004 / Date of Recollection: 05.29.2002 / 7.5 min

The world is black and infinite. Footsteps thud on the floor, like something's pounding on the hull of a ship. I wake up lying under a bright ceiling light. Mrs Linden's at her desk, scratching ink into a notepad. Her clock radio crackles in front of her, dialed down to a hiss. The sick bay curtains are drawn and the door's closed.

"You were raving," she says. She turns in her chair and closes the notepad. "I don't approve, but Mr de Silva insisted on us using a sedative."

I blink back a blur, and she pulls into focus. Her hair's an auburn bob streaked with silver from the front to the back. She polishes her bifocals and perches them back on her nose.

"Raving?"

"Something about a machine."

I try to get up, but a headache pulses.

"Don't." Mrs Linden pushes her chair out. "Here, lie on your back."

She comes over to the bed, leaning in for a closer look. "You're epileptic, aren't you?"

"I don't know."

"You must be. Do you take medication?"

"For something else. Celexa and Paxil."

"I see. That could explain it. I've read about the side-effects."

"Side-effects?"

"You were seeing things. You should see your doctor. And one more thing—did you have anything to eat today?"

I shake my head.

"I thought so," she says, retrieving a small pamphlet from

her desk. "I know it isn't easy being a teen. You get saddled with more pressure than you know what to do with. I have three daughters at home."

"I'm not anorexic." I push the pamphlet aside.

"I'm not saying you are, but it's nothing to be ashamed of, either way. If anything, you should have something to eat before taking medication."

"I will."

"Trust me."

I tell her that I do trust her, since it's what she wants to hear. I thank her as she helps me up.

I get a permission slip to leave school early, although it doesn't cover scholar patrol—a punishment for talking in class last week. Mrs Linden tells me to go past reception first, because Ms Isaacs wants to see me.

There's a delivery man sweating on the couch next to the front desk. Ms Isaacs tells me to take a seat on a leather chair under the air conditioning. Her office is cramped: aside from two chairs and her desk, there's a filing cabinet and a small bookshelf behind her. There's a cut-out *The Far Side* comic stuck to the side of her monitor: a woman is telling her warrior husband to be more assertive, that she's tired of people calling him Alexander the Pretty-Good.

Ms Isaacs sees me reading it. "I know it's silly," she sighs, "but it's the only thing I could find."

"It isn't that bad."

"It is, but it doesn't matter," she says, waving her hand. "Everyone's worried sick about those girls. It's our staff agenda, this week. How are you doing?"

"I'm fine."

"That isn't convincing. Promise me you'll be safe."

"I promise."

Ms Isaacs' hair is tied in a bun above a polo neck of the same black. Most of us like her, since she's beautiful and young.

"Right, now listen," she says. "You and Kiran are on the Olympiad team together, right? I know you'll be required to prep with him."

I shift on the leather seat. "I haven't seen him around."

"Neither have we, and as far as we know, he hasn't been deregistered," she says. "The school's in a panic, of course, because of what happened with his father, but they don't want to alarm the other parents. The staff thinks there's a connection with the girls. That it might be a kidnapping syndicate."

She places the package on the table top—a white box wrapped in plastic and Sellotape.

"I looked up the return address and it's Kiran's. He sent it to himself, I suspect to keep it out of the house. He might be on those postage-stamp drugs."

"LSD?"

Ms Isaacs nods.

"Are you going to open it?" I ask.

"No. I don't know what he's involved with, but I don't want to scare him off. If he finds out it's been tampered with by a member of staff, he might not come forward."

"I still don't know what this has to do with me."

Ms Isaacs looks down at the box. "I want to give you this package. Judging from the trouble he's gone to, it must mean something to him. When he contacts you, you can tell him you have something that's his."

I nod, even though I don't understand.

"You can organize to meet with him, and then let us know how he is, and whether he's coming back. If you ask me, the school should be alerting people as we speak, but they're planning to sit on their hands until the funding meetings conclude. They don't want to scare off funders, especially with the three girls, and most of them think he moved to a different school because of his father. I don't think they're making sufficient effort, but as a member of staff, I can't act on my own. I need you to ask around about him. The administration thinks he's left the school, but I need to know he's all right."

"I don't know if he'll trust me, either."

"I've seen you with his recorder. Lord knows, I've confiscated the thing enough."

"I don't see how that's connected."

"Look, I know the two of you used to be Olympiad rivals before you enrolled here. It's clear the boy is smitten. It would be sweet, if I wasn't frightened for him. Kiran's a bright boy, but scattered." I clear my throat, but she holds up a hand. "I know I'm asking a big favor."

I look at the package. Then I tell her it's fine.

"You'll do it?"

"I'll do it."

I leave her office hefting Kiran's package. His MD recorder, which hasn't helped me, weighs down on me like something I should toss.

Kiran's a senior, and like most seniors he usually spends his lunch break skulking and sharing cigarettes behind the chapel, where the yard opens up between the tennis courts and the principal's house. That's where I'd gone looking for him a week ago, to learn how to set the recorder. There's an upended boat splintering under a gumtree at the end of the yard. A few of his friends were sitting on the hull, knocking their heels against its sides and chipping powder-blue paint onto the grass. As I walked toward them, Jonathan approached me. He had a scratched Fanta yo-yo spinning at his feet.

"You've strayed far from the flock," he said.

"I don't care."

"To what do we owe it?"

"I'm looking for Kiran."

He grinned, revealing a crowd of butter-colored teeth. "I wish I knew where he was," he shrugged, somehow managing the truth. That was a week ago.

I walk up Queens Road and head down Galloway Street. It's a different route from school to the one I'm used to. Kiran's parents own a house in Kaffrarian Heights, the wealthiest part of town, named after the word the British used to describe the natives. That's what it says at the museum in town, anyway. Now their lawns lie manicured next to their driveways, their yard walls raised high and rimmed at the top with electric fencing. The roads are vacant, except for SUVs and sprinklers that hiss out moisture even in winter.

As I get to Kiran's block, I get a text message from Part: *There's another bazaar at Central tonight. I have prefect duties as usual. Let's put Litha in the dunk tank and drown him with our sorrows.*

I close the message and stand in front of Kiran's house. I can tell the place is abandoned, with the windows and the garage doors hanging open. I'm not sure what to make of it, but I decide to keep a record. I take out the exercise book with Mom's birthdate and start sketching the façade.

I hear a car approaching and turn. The driver of the white SUV, an old woman wearing dark glasses and a rose-gold necklace, tells me to keep off the street. That it isn't safe.

October 16, 1999

My cousins, Nandi and Lihle, visited us later that October, after Tata stabilized again. Lihle and I helped Nandi unpack her suitcase in the room down the hallway, where the matron used to sleep before she died. Then the three of us spent the night eating crinkle-cut chips and watching music videos in the dark. The next day, we split our chores at 9 a.m., as soon as we got up. Around noon, I walked down to the library to page through a hardcover book on UFOs that I'd found, but it was loaned out. It hadn't been returned for a week. I bought a Coke, used the change on the Ms Pac-Man machine at Parbhoo's, and walked back home, where we warmed up leftovers and ate them in front of the TV again. Then there were more music videos.

Nandi fell asleep. When I closed my eyes to fall asleep too, laying my head on the armrest of the couch, I felt Lihle's hand on my face. His cold lips brushed against mine, and I breathed in to let his hand slip below my belt. Later, he came in my mouth.

The next morning, Lihle led me to the pool in our back yard and dared me to push my head under the water, which was green and had scummed the steps in the shallow end. He said he'd do it after me.

His father had downed two bottles of Autumn Harvest and drowned at Orient Beach the previous summer. My own had been going to the hospital twice a week, gargling his own water in his throat. I nodded.

I stood on the edge of the pool and took my shirt off, leaving my bra on. "I'll do it for something to do," I said.

One night the following week, the machine filled the entire

ceiling with the number "3"—which I interpreted as a sign from Mama. That she hadn't forgotten about us. Me and her and Tata. After that, I stopped seeing it.

RTR: 005 / Date of Recollection: 05.29.2002 / 6 min

I get home and walk past my aunt, who's fallen asleep with *The Daily Dispatch* on her lap. This has been her daily M.O. since going on leave earlier this month. I make out the photos of the three missing girls on the front page.

In my room I draw the curtains, take Celexa and Paxil, fit in my earphones and try to sleep. But when I hear Doris closing the door to her room, and then the bed springs creaking under her weight, I get up.

Out in the garage, boxes of Mom's old newspapers sit stacked in the corner. She never could toss them, even after Dad told her they were a fire hazard. I used to think the reason she kept them was because she was in them, but after she was gone, when I read through a pile of the papers, I realized there was more to it. Mom believed they'd be useful again one day, and that there was no expiration date on what was wrong with the world.

I open a box and take out a bundle. I'm looking for other cases of missing girls, but I don't find them. Instead, I read about dead bodies. Most of them are women and children from the region.

In Qumbu, a mother of four was shot, the bullet passing through her and into the forehead of her daughter, who was four and strapped to her back.

In Peddie, a mother and daughter on a fishing trip were thrown into the trunk of a car; the mother was raped and killed and the girl escaped.

I pack the papers back into the box, the world feeling dimmer.

·   ·   ·

In the living room, I switch on the VHS and push in the dub I got from Litha. In *Where Have All the People Gone?*, a middle-aged woman walks into the ocean, unable to live in a world without humans, the global population incinerated into heaps of powder. It was released in 1974 to a US TV audience, and never recouped its production costs. Litha, Part, and I have watched it together twice now.

The first time I saw it, I'd walked into Mr Movie to look for Litha after school, and found him watching it on the TV hung above the Returns Box. He looked tired, leaning against the counter with a cup of tea.

"I don't get it," I said, after a moment. "How did the vegetation survive?"

Litha dipped behind the counter and pulled up the tape's cover. "The solar flare didn't burn them," he said. "It activated a viral outbreak. A percentage of the population is immune."

Then Tom, his colleague, walked in and dropped his backpack behind the counter. "The mother of all hangovers," he announced, opening a can of Coke.

I didn't like him. Tom always stared at me like I was a coin at the bottom of a pond, a habit that made me want him covered in paper cuts, but I knew Litha admired him for his videogaming talent. In fact, I knew too much about that. Litha could never quit talking about how Tom had locked himself in his room one weekend, not leaving until he'd solved the piano puzzle in *Silent Hill*. He'd also shown Litha that the frequency for Meryl's codec in *Metal Gear Solid* was printed at the back of the jewel CD case, over the Konami logo, which the rental customers couldn't take home with them. Tom found that hilarious. He was 23 with a nursing diploma from UKZN, and had moved back in with his parents. His blond hair grew out in a mullet at the back, and his prominent Adam's apple rolled whenever he gulped one of his countless sodas.

I turned to Litha. "I have to go, but I'd like to watch more of it."

"The movie?"

"It's calming."

"I'll make a dub of it when I get home."

"Thanks."

Now my vegetable soup's gone cold and the film hasn't worked.

I let the credits roll until the end, then text Litha that I need to see him: *It's urgent.*

Later, we sit watching TV in the one-bedroom flat his new foster parents rent in Alexandra. Part's still on a field-trip to the aquarium in East London. I tell him about the articles with the murders and the rapes and he winces.

"I don't know how you read the news."

The two of us go quiet for a bit. Then I turn to him again. "The machine's back."

It takes him a while to nod. Then I tell him how the school thinks Kiran's on acid.

"He might've been ratted out by a senior he sold a cap to, I don't know," I say. "Now he's on the run and the school doesn't care. I think it's because he's not a girl."

Litha sighs. "I think so, too." Then he asks me to describe the machine.

"It's still the same."

"The same?"

"Except for one thing." I tell him about the triangle.

"You think the three are connected? Kiran, the girls, the machine?"

I pause, relieved—at least he doesn't think I'm insane.

Then he asks to see my exercise book. He turns to a sketch of the machine and one of Kiran's house. "Let's talk to Part about it at the bazaar." Then he hands me a dubbed tape of *2010* and tells me the same thing as always—that TV's not a pollutant, it's the inflation of our realities.

There's rap music on the TV now, and the way I feel is that my inflated reality is sexual ambiguity. Next, there's a sitcom and the characters get introduced one by one. Mom, dad, daughter, son, baby—a nucleus.

"The dad looks like my one father, the lawyer," Litha says. "I can't remember the year, but that foster beat me so hard I had to chew with my left molars for a week. They sent me back to Syringa Road after that, remember, next to Phakamisa Clinic, and gave me that bunk bed with Mongezi, who wanted to burn the place down?"

I nod. It happened in 1999—a year before we met. Litha's told us.

I rest my head on the couch and listen to him talk. At night, Litha says the TV illuminates the whole flat, making it hard to sleep, but now, the daylight from the windows makes it look as if it's off.

Litha says when you're a child, what you think is that you can eat anything, and when you're a parent, what you think is that you can teach anything. Leaning back on the sofa, with the light flooding in from Alexandra, he says when you're a kid, everything you see is real. There are people inside your TV and plastic fruit is edible. "That's the world you're given."

I get up and put on my scholar-patrol vest, and Litha opens the front door for me.

"The thing is," he says, "when your father has his hands clenched around your neck and your mother's screaming, trying to pull him off, what he wants everyone to think is that you've swallowed a plastic grape. He wants everyone to think you're a child, and to you, plastic is another type of fruit," he says. "That's the world we're given."

I take the stairs. Outside, the glare from the sun is blinding. I remember how my urine smelled metallic yesterday, so I stop over at Parbhoo's for tampons, but it's closed.

October 23, 1999

That summer, when Tata hadn't sold any of the weight-loss kits and his cough had worsened, my aunt arrived as his caretaker and my guardian.

I'd offered to work part-time to help him—to send out the boxes, even model the product—but Tata hadn't answered me. Instead, one day when I returned from school, I found the boxes, still full, stacked in a heap on the curb with the rubbish we'd left for collection. They'd be gone before morning. Tata went to sleep before us that night.

"You'll have to work from now on," my aunt said. "I've heard how he lets you loaf."

I turned from her and walked to my room, not bothering to hide my contempt. My aunt came from the Transkei, the poorer half of our province, and I'd never seen much of her. From the beginning, the two of us knew we wouldn't get along, and we didn't make much of it.

RTR: 006 / Date of Recollection: 05.29.2002 / 4 min

The talk with Litha calms me, and after I've said goodbye to him, I take the long way back to school. I stand on the side of the road, serving out my punishment—the lone interloper in the scholar patrol's regular afternoon troop. The rest of them are volunteers: Candice, Gareth, and Phiwe. For the time being, the four of us are shackled to the same cause—to wait for the last of the detention class to be carted out at four, facilitating the zebra crossing while we wait, monitoring the stream of traffic outside the chapel.

I heard them talking about the girls, too, when I arrived, but now it's quiet.

On opposite sides of the road, Phiwe and I raise and drop our steel beams for a maroon Corolla, followed by a white Mazda. The sunlight gets in my eyes and makes me squint, and I tell Candice, our team captain, that I need a break. I watch her smiling at me from across the road, her pale gums showing, before she blows on her whistle and walks over.

"I can only give you a minute. I'm sorry, but you'll get used to it."

"I can't. If I stand in the sun for too long my nose bleeds."

"The shift's almost done."

"It isn't. There's half an hour left."

"Fine, but please be quick."

I take a walk around the school grounds with the MD switched to record, hoping to pick up a sound from the machine. In the toilet, I kick the door closed, making sure it bangs. Folding toilet paper, I savor the shade and feel of plastic beneath my skin.

I don't bother turning the recorder off when my piss breaks the surface of the water.

I arrive home before dark, having stopped at the mall. In my room, I drop off my bag and fit a tampon. In the kitchen, I make myself a bowl of Froot Loops, eating it standing up with a teaspoon over the basin. Then I lie on my bed with the door locked.

I'm looking forward to seeing Part at the bazaar.

I remember the first time I went to her house. Her mom was in the living room, alone and giggling at a blank TV screen. Part and I were standing by the door, and I was reminded of an old tomb, or an incubator; like the light didn't enter the room, but was painted onto the windows instead.

Part started toward her room, but her mom motioned for me to sit. "How old are you?" she said. Her brow creased, but the shadows on her face didn't.

"Seventeen."

"Excuse me?"

I said it again.

I watched her edge in closer to squint at me. Then she glanced at an empty sofa, taking a moment before turning back. "Did you forget to grow?"

I told her I was born premature and that all my life, I'd been trying to catch up, but she wasn't listening. Part's mom was counting 17 with her fingers, and when she got to 10, she paused and craned her neck. Then she looked back at the sofa as if she'd left someone there, waiting to continue a conversation. I looked over, too, even though I knew Part's mom had vascular dementia—a side-effect from a mini-stroke.

"Part's turning 17, next month," she said. Then, raising her voice, she asked Part why she wasn't at school.

From her room, Part's voice carried down the corridor, saying she didn't feel like it. Then Part was at the door in her underwear, arms hanging at her sides, asking why her mom wasn't taking her medication.

Part's mom cast another glance at the sofa, then looked down at her knitted hands. "I am taking my medication," she said.

I didn't speak. The two of them fell silent, too, and the light still refused, and Part said, "Bullshit," and turned away. Then over and over again, still standing at the door and shaking her head each time: bullshit, bullshit, bullshit.

I stretch my arms out. It's a minute after 5 and the bazaar's at 7. Like most nights, I know there's a dinner plate waiting for me in the microwave—to eat from, and then wash with the rest of the dishes.

I pull out Kiran's MD, place it on the pillow next to my head and switch it on. I think about the machine—about it being a message from Mom. I wait for it to arrive, but it doesn't. I count up to 10,000. Moments before I drift off to sleep, I think of the Olympiad again, and tell myself it's 104.

Or (102) (102).

Or $\sqrt{108}$.

Or $\lim_{x \to 9} (x2 + 2x + 5)$ if it's rounded down.

October 31, 1999

Late one evening, during one of Tata's sudden bouts, I knocked on his door until two of my right knuckles went numb and almost split. I waited for a bit, then opened the door to the room that had been my grandmother's, where my aunt was lying on her back. I could tell she was awake, and that this was evidence of her being an awful person; but she was here for him, too, I thought, and here maybe for both of us.

I walked to the bathroom, where I took off my clothes and stood in front of the mirror, the tiles cold beneath my feet.

I've never been fucked, I thought, looking at the reflection in the mirror, parting my lips and taking in the gleam of my braces. I ran a finger over each wire.

My breasts were small, but showing. My hair was long and thick. My lower stomach caved in tight against the muscle, making my hip bones push out. There was a gap between my thighs and my shoulders were straight, my arms trim. My skin was bright and clear.

I drew closer to the mirror.

I'm beautiful, I thought.

RTR: 007 / Date of Recollection: 05.29.2002 / 5 min

Pulling a pair of black jeans from my wardrobe, I find a black halter top and a jacket that used to belong to Mom. Then I knock on my aunt's door.

"I'm going to a school thing," I tell her, "a bazaar. To raise funds."

I can't tell if she's sleeping or not, and I make it down the hallway before I hear her tell me it's fine. That I should make sure I'm safe.

Leaning against a streetlight two blocks up, I wait for Part's older sister, Iris, who's home on a week-long break from Rhodes, to pick me up in her black Corsa.

Part's in the passenger seat when I get in, staring at the ceiling.

"I can't believe you're dragging me to this," I tell her, climbing in.

Iris catches my eye in the rear-view mirror. "Is it that bad?"

"Think Vengaboys," Part tells her.

"Think Daddy DJ," I add.

"Think Eiffel 65."

"Think Bloodhound Gang."

"Think Planet Funk."

"Think Hit'n'Hide."

Iris slows down at the intersection on Alexandra and Maitland, indicating left. "So pretentious," she says. "You're teenage girls. You adore MTV." Then she sighs. "People at the bazaar will be talking about those girls, won't they?"

The three of us go quiet.

Then Part and I step out of the Corsa, say goodbye, and

watch Iris drive to the BP gas station. For reasons I've never asked about, Iris never stays for more than a few days when she's back from campus. I watch her sink into the dark. Then Part and I start walking up the hill.

"It's warmer here," she says.

"I know."

I pull on my jacket, undoing the zip. In the distance, in between cheers, I make out the dull bassline of an 'NSync song.

"I feel like I haven't seen you, this week," she says.

"It's everything that's happening at school."

"Lots?"

"It involves Kiran now."

Up the hill, Part bends to pick up a paper plate smeared with tomato sauce and crusted mustard, dropping it in a blue bin. "Listen, do you want to make out before we go up there and listen to Space Invaders? I meant it about it being a while."

I laugh. "I'm amenable."

I fix my hair in the bathroom mirror afterward. Then I ask Part for her lip gloss and zip up my jacket and we head back out to the grounds, holding hands until we reach the stalls. I cough at the sharp smell of smoke from the braais.

"Is Litha here?" I ask.

"He should be. He said he'd drop in after his shift."

"I take it you have prefect duties."

"I won't be long."

"I'll survive."

Part smiles and leaves for the admin block. I turn and take in the stalls and the people milling under a blanket of smoke in the congested courtyard. Most of the items on sale are pastries, baked in parental kitchens and made to be displayed. Next to them, arranged in neat, sealed rows under the gleam of flood-lights, are jars of fig jam, sugared plums, and peaches, while different species of animal, now turned to chorizo and now to biltong, hang on sharp hooks suspended above the stalls.

I weave through the crowd, walking on quiche crumbs, a crosshatch of skid marks, crunched paper cups. Placing a palm over my mouth, I wonder if what happened to me at school was a visit from the machine or if the doctors were right.

Litha waves at me from the back of the courtyard. The two of us hug next to a stall stacked with ceramic dwarfs.

"What's wrong?" he asks, pointing at my mouth.

"It's the smoke. It's also full in here."

"Do you want to go somewhere else? Hold on." He returns with two cans of Coke. "I can get cigarettes, too."

"There's enough smoke here."

Litha laughs. "I didn't know you were allergic to smoke. Or if that was possible."

I punch him on the shoulder, but let my palm linger on him as a truce.

We leave the courtyard and enter the fringes of the grounds, where the floodlights taper off, and hang our legs over a short wall behind the bleachers.

Litha sighs. "I don't have a plan."

"I'm not sure what to do, either."

"Have you opened it?"

"No."

"Maybe we can do it together."

I look up at the night sky, unable to make out the constellations through the smoke.

"Listen, do you want to lean back for a bit?" he asks.

I do. The two of us lie on our backs, taking in the pale smoke coiling against the dark.

Later, when I get home at 9:35 p.m., I see the machine again.

Its hum sounds louder than I remember.

I watch it expand to cover the ceiling, its silver parts blinking, rolling inside the darkness. From the mattress, I turn the recorder on. As I drift off, I make out the triangle again, before it sinks back into the murk.

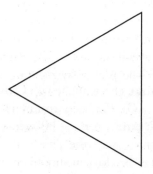

November 2, 1999

That summer, in what would be the last year of Tata's life, we drove out to see another herb specialist in East London.

At least, that's what my aunt told him as we got in the car, but when we entered the city, she turned up Oxford Road and drove us to the office of a GP she knew from university. The car went silent then. I didn't turn to look at his face when we stopped.

Inside, my aunt cut past the line in the waiting room and forewent a greeting: "Smilo, you should be able to do something for him," she told the doctor. "This is my brother."

The GP's plaque read *Dr Khathide*. He was a short man with a salt-and-pepper goatee. He sat behind his desk and listened to her. His thick glasses were tinted in the glare that came in through a picture window above his desk, and he appeared calm. He smiled at my aunt and held out his arms, dappling them in sunlight. "That's the reason I'm here," he said.

Tata was silent on our trip back to King William's Town. Each time my aunt tried to speak to him, he closed his eyes and shifted in his seat, ignoring her until she gave up. As we drove past the BP gas station in Berlin, just outside East London, he turned on the radio and dialed up the volume.

From the back seat, I watched as the two of them rode in silence. I opened a water bottle and swallowed my latest regimen, Faverin and Zoloft, and looked out of the window, thinking of Mama and what she could've done for us, if anything.

Tata's silence hung over us until we reached the driveway. Doris killed the engine and leaned back against her headrest with a sigh, taking a moment before getting out and opening the passenger door for him. She extended her hand, but as expected he waved her away, refusing to look at either of us.

My aunt stood back and watched him undo his seatbelt, taking his time. Then she went 'round to the trunk and retrieved the groceries we'd picked up on the way. "Take these inside."

I carried the bags into the kitchen and dropped them on the counter. I could hear the car door slamming—Tata's footsteps down the corridor—and then his bedroom door doing the same.

My aunt came into the kitchen and sat at the table, her palms kneading her eyes as she sighed for the umpteenth time. "Do you know how to cook?"

"I do."

"He used to like lamb stew and dumplings."

"He still does."

"That's what we'll make for him tonight then, but first go lock the front door and take his medication to him."

I didn't lock. I took the bag of pills from her and went down the hallway, where I knocked and received what I expected from him, too. His silence. When I knocked a second time, the door opened and I found him sitting at the foot of his bed. The curtains were drawn on all of the windows but one. I found the stillness of the room hard to absorb; I'd grown used to his rasping.

"I have your medication," I told him.

Raising his left palm, Tata motioned me toward his bedside table, where I put the plastic bag next to a sealed box of menthols and an empty tumbler. I filled the water glass from the faucet in his bathroom and set it back on the table.

On my way out, Tata cleared his throat and asked me to wait. He was bending down to undo his laces, taking his time to liberate each foot. "How much better do you think this is," he said, waving a hand at the table, "than the tonics I got in Ginsberg?"

"The tonics?"

"From the out-of-towner."

I knew which tonics he meant, but I'd wanted more time to think of an answer. I didn't know what to tell him. I'd never shared his belief in herbal medicine.

"I don't know, Tata," I said, and I didn't.

RTR: 008 / Date of Recollection: 05.30.2002 / 5.5 min

My aunt's engine stalls this morning just before we reach the school turn-off, which shouldn't be embarrassing, but is. Through her windshield, I watch the scholar-patrol team holding up rusting steel beams, shifting old traffic cones through the drizzle.

"This again," I say.

"Quiet." Doris sighs. "This car has its problems and that's not a new thing. You know that. Dumisani said he'd look at it, of course, but does he ever listen when a woman talks?"

"I don't know."

"He never listens when a woman talks."

I pick up a newspaper lying near my feet. The Eastern Cape Premier's office wants credit for the release of 33 political prisoners, says the front page, but the national government's refusing. Most of the inmates were attached to the ANC. I turn the page, and see a headline about how the police are still seeking help with the missing girls.

My aunt clears her throat. "Don't bother reading about the premier," she says, twisting the ignition and causing the car to cough. "Even if it was Stofile and not Mbeki who released those men, what difference does it make? He's still building the biggest house we've seen for blacks in this town."

"Is it true that 57 percent of them were convicted of murder?"

"I don't know. They would've done what they had to do."

"Tony Leon says they're criminals."

"How would he know?" My aunt laughs and shakes her head. "You know, I never understood what it was about these Model C schools that we have to send all our children to, except for the wonderful accents we hear from the learners."

I nod, since it's true. When she speaks English, my aunt's vowels are wider than mine and her r's are rough, etching out her enunciation. It was the same with Mom and Dad.

"I don't know," I tell her. "It's school."

Then the car starts and we cross the intersection, parking opposite the school entrance. Most of my grade's still milling outside, sharing homework and waiting for the bell to ring. I look for Lerato.

"I'm driving to Port Elizabeth," Doris says. "I won't be back until late."

"Today?"

"It's for a regional meeting," she sighs. "It won't be long"

"I thought you were on leave."

"I also did. Make sure to keep safe."

"I will."

"I'm serious. No strangers and keep the doors locked."

"I will."

I walk through the front gate as the bell rings, and join the others as we chart a line toward the chapel. My socks have started to fray, and I can feel the cold through the thin leather of my Toughees. Taking a seat at the back, I take out two pills from my bag and hold them in my palm, Celexa and Paxil, thinking about last night. Then I swallow them and spend the rest of chapel half-asleep.

My phone vibrates on the way back to class, and I don't have to open it to know what it is or who it's from. Last night, the three of us agreed to try and meet at the park; Part said she'd text me if she'd managed to cut class. I sit through three classes and wait until we've had our first break, before I ask to be excused from geography and walk up to the sick bay.

"What's wrong with you?" Mrs Linden asks.

I shake my head. "I don't know."

"Let me have a look." She sits me down on the cot and takes my temperature with her palm and a thermometer. "How's the head?"

"Dull and painful."

"It isn't a concussion, but you had a hard knock."

"I also feel nauseated." I look at the clock and remember to lie about eating. "I had a bowl of cereal this morning and now it wants to come up."

"I see." Mrs Linden creases her brow. "Listen. This is what we'll do. I'll write you a note to spend the rest of the afternoon at home, but only if you promise me you'll go to the doctor before coming in tomorrow. That you'll go tonight at the latest."

I promise.

I walk home, watch a rerun of *Cavegirl*, and then meet Litha and Part at the Munchies in Metlife Mall, the weather too damp for the park. Litha places three orders of hot chocolate and I take out Kiran's package.

Part leans forward. "Is that it?"

"I'll be honest. I don't know what to do with it."

Part nods. "Kiran used to be your idea of a thing, right?"

"Please kill yourself."

"I'll consider it. Did something happen?"

"I'm not sure. The teachers think he's on acid."

Part points at the box on the table. "I have to see what's inside that thing."

"I also do."

As the server lowers the tray with our hot chocolates on it, I get up for a closer look at the newspapers on the counter next to the pies and pizzas. I bring one back to our table to show Litha and Part. The front page says there's no progress on the missing girls. There's also an article about where my aunt works. I tell them about it—how 15 computers were stolen from HR at the Department of Education in Port Elizabeth, interrupting an ongoing investigation on the director. How my aunt might lose her job.

Then the place starts to fill up for the lunchtime slot and I fold the paper. "I've changed my mind. I think it's better if we look through the package at home. My aunt won't be back until late."

November 9, 1999

Tata came out of his room for breakfast the following Saturday, which surprised me and my aunt, although she was careful not to draw attention to that surprise. The three of us gathered in the kitchen, where she ladled sour porridge into his bowl and scrambled us eggs with Bisto and bell peppers. Tata seemed stronger that day, even sociable—willing to talk.

"I've been taking the medicine," he smiled, as Doris placed a mug of tea next to his plate. "Haven't you heard how quiet it's been?"

It hadn't been quiet. Tata couldn't remember his coughing anymore.

The fits now took a different course, assaulting him an hour or two into sleep. Last night he'd woken me up again, but the coughing stopped before I'd had the time to knock on his door. My aunt had slept through it.

I watched her pull on the sleeves of her bathrobe. "I'm full," I said.

"No, you're not." Her back was turned to us. "Ever since I got here, all I've seen you do is pick at whatever we eat. There's bread you've left moldering in that cupboard."

"I don't like porridge."

"Have your eggs, then." Doris dropped a plate of toast in front of me. Then she lifted my wrist and circled it with her thumb and middle finger. "Have you seen yourself? You're a stick."

"Leave her be." Tata was bent over his tea and quieter now. He didn't look up. "The child said she's not hungry. Why don't you let her eat when she wants?"

My aunt didn't release me. She drew in a breath, but didn't

concede. "You're telling me this is normal, Lumkile? This child is underfed."

Tata shrugged, seeming to lose his strength again. "Her mother was the same. The two of them, built like birds." Then he turned to me, pushing his tea aside. "Have as much as you can and then you can go out."

I pulled my arm back from my aunt and made a sandwich with the toast and eggs, biting into it without taste.

I took my SSRIs in the bathroom, using warm water from the basin, pulled on my backpack, and left.

I held back tears as I weaved through the library aisles, a heat at the base of my throat, my eyes gliding across the spines without reading them. I found a seat at the desks with the newspapers, resting my head on my arms until my eyes dried. It was close to midday when I got up again. In the aisle with the hardcover book on UFOs, I closed my eyes and felt for it, hoping I could be drawn in and lost in whatever lived inside it. The library closed at 1 p.m. on Saturday. I spent the rest of the afternoon wandering in town, wanting to be alone, waiting until I knew that Tata was in his room and Doris was visiting her friends in Club View.

I thought of going to the Musica at the mall, but the bass from the loud gospel music made me feel nauseated, and the men behind the counter were known for pushing up against our school uniforms after school. I didn't want that. I was alone and knew no one. So I went to the CNA store. The stationery shop wasn't well stocked; nothing was well stocked in our town. To make it worthwhile, I had to have a look at everything in the aisles, including the dictionaries. I'd seen most of the glossy magazines. Doris read them—she'd brought along a thick stack with her when she moved in, and each night, she fell asleep with one of them open on her lap. I went to the newspapers instead.

There was a thin one lying sideways on the top shelf, a tabloid, which reported on a murder trial which had exposed the network of a minor drug syndicate in Cape Town. There was an article on Y2K, and another on how white babies were on sale for adoption at R50,000 a head. A woman said the ghost of her dead ex-husband had forced itself on her, and there was an article on The Phoenix Strangler, who'd been sentenced to more than 500 years for rape and murder.

I was still reading about him when one of the men from Musica walked in and came to stand next to me, humming. I could smell the sourness of his sweat under his deodorant, and he was smiling, looking down at me. I dropped the tabloid and walked out down another aisle.

I took a corner table at Munchies, where I ordered a Coke and waited for a slice. I was eating pizza to spite my aunt—the way she'd held my wrist between her fingers and called me a stick. I didn't want her thinking she knew who I was, even if it made me ill.

Like this would.

I looked down at the ground beef. I pierced the lemon slice in the Coke with my straw, pushing it down to the bottom below the ice-cubes, and sucked on it hard enough to make my forehead numb. Then my vision doubled.

It was possible to forget about Tata, I thought with relief.

Then I made myself vomit in the public toilets, and walked home.

RTR: 009 / Date of Recollection: 05.30.2002 / 3 min

The garage feels like a cardboard box that's been left out in the sun. The lights don't work, so I've brought a flashlight. I let Part and Litha in, spread an old mattress on the floor, and open a window.

I drop the package between us, raising a cloud of dust, while the rain makes a soft patter against the panes. Hold on, I think. I find an old rusted cardboard cutter. Holding it close to the blade, I draw a line on the tape sealing the box, from the top to the bottom. It sighs open. There's another, smaller box inside, with a different address. I open that, too, spilling the contents across the mattress.

There's a smooth, rounded stone, and an exercise book with newspaper clippings jutting from the edges. Between Part's knees lies a locket that's snapped open, revealing a black-and-white photo of a middle-aged woman. I look at everything on the mattress.

"I don't know what to make of this."

Part reaches for the locket. "Me neither."

I flip through the exercise book. Most of the clippings are still glued to the pages, but some have started to peel, the paper yellowed with time. Then I realize what the headlines all have in common. I look at Litha and Part. "It's all missing persons."

The book slips from my hands and opens to the middle, where I see four articles about the Yugoslav Wars. In one of them, a family credits a strange, glowing presence for its survival. Next to it, there's an article on post-traumatic stress disorder.

The three of us go quiet. Litha reaches for the book. "Let me hold on to this."

I pick up the smaller box again and look at the address.

Stanfel Petrović. 10 Jameson Street, Quigney, East London.

I stop to think. It seems possible.

I turn to Litha and Part and tell them this is it: "This is the sign I've been waiting for. There's a connection between Kiran and the girls. And I know what to do. I'll wait for the machine."

"And then?" asks Part.

"If it comes back, then we should start looking for them."

"The girls?"

"The girls."

November 16, 1999

I didn't expect what followed next. Things took a different course, that summer. It started with a fire in a small garment factory downtown, a blaze that left a hundred people out of work and colored our skies black for three days.

There were the PPMs, too, as reported in *The Daily Dispatch*— small prepaid power meters that were being rolled out in our neighborhoods that year. Most people were suspicious of the devices—imagining themselves trapped in blackouts until they got paid—but we were powerless against the change. The government had decided on installing the machines as far back as 1993. Tata wasn't pleased; he spoke on it often. He liked to lament the government's wasteful expenditure, and their eagerness to trammel their own people.

My aunt and I listened.

Having watched the smoke rising over our backyard that summer, the three of us were bound to spend the following weeks discussing the fire at breakfast. Or Tata was. He commiserated with the workers, he told us, given the negligence of upper management and how the government had failed to assist them. Then he'd move on to the prepaid meters, before my aunt and I could catch a breath.

Most of the time, we would follow his argument in silence, a familiar one-sidedness. I don't doubt that Tata cared about the fire, and the power meters, and all the other things he talked about, but the complaining itself seemed to return his strength to him, I thought, and that's what encouraged him to keep on with it.

For this reason, although we never spoke about it, my aunt

and I stopped ourselves from showing impatience with his complaining. Each time Tata brought up a grievance, the two of us would begin our morning ritual, which was to absorb his unhappiness at the breakfast table.

RTR: 010 / Date of Recollection: 05.30.2002 / 3 min

I still need a sick note for Mrs Linden. I think of Rohan, who could help me with it, but whose number I've never dialed.

I remember when Litha introduced us. I'd headed to Mr Movie to find him. He was standing outside the entrance with a guy I didn't know, pinching the tip of a dead cigarette. I crossed Alexandra to join them.

"This is Rohan."

He was tall and stooped, with hair that grew down to his neck. He wore a white t-shirt with loose-fitting jeans, and thick, frameless glasses.

Litha flicked the cigarette on the road and watched it get chewed under the wheels of a flatbed. "Rohan was telling me about this new game he has. It's on Game Boy. *The Legend of Zelda: Link's Awakening.*"

"I think I've heard of it."

"I got it at a pawn shop in Maritzburg, but it's the best one." Litha placed a hand on his shoulder. "Tell her about the plot."

Rohan grinned. "It all starts with a shipwreck," he said. "There's a storm and Link, the lead character, washes onto an island called Koholint. He meets these characters, Tarin and his daughter Marin, who take him in. The daughter's fascinated by Link, having spent all her life on the island; but Link has to set out to look for his sword. Then he meets up with an owl that tells him he must wake the Wind Fish if he wants to go home."

"It sounds like most RPGs." I knew that much from Litha and Tom.

"I know, but that isn't the best part. The best part is that Koholint Island doesn't exist. It's all in Link's dream. He's still floating on a piece of driftwood in the ocean. That's after 30 damn hours of game time." He grinned, revealing his braces, and I laughed.

"Right? I sometimes think this town is Koholint Island," he said.

"I like that."

Rohan offered to lend me the game and we exchanged numbers. Later, Litha told me he was good at school, like I was, and that his dad was one of the doctors I'd been to. I nodded, but I never called.

Now I scroll through the contacts in my phone and text Rohan that I need his help. There's no response, the message pending.

There's no call from Kiran, no visit from the machine. I listen to music until I fall asleep.

When I wake up, hours later, I hear a bulletin about the missing girls on the radio, meaning my aunt's back.

November 19, 1999

My grandmother, who we all called the matron, died without her right leg when I was too young to recall most of who she'd been. It was from diabetes. She was living with us then, but we drove back to Zeleni for her burial. I was nine years old.

The village was silent during the funeral. Walking back to the homestead from the burial grounds, we formed a wide procession that waded through the autumn mist in song.

Later, I couldn't eat the meal we'd prepared to honor her; my throat closed up at each attempt at swallowing. Instead of greeting relatives who'd driven down from Gauteng, or joining the children who'd gathered from the neighboring huts, I volunteered to pass plates to the men sitting in the peaked tent. The plastic plates, worn enough to feel slicked with grease even after being washed, were stacked with samp that had been cooked over a wood fire in large three-legged pots.

But Mama first had to look for me. She found me staring at the ceiling in the matron's room. She took a seat on the bed and touched my arm, smiling down, then stroked my forehead. Her mourning regalia was beautiful; I'd never seen her cry, I thought.

"Tell me if you know the answer to this one," she said. "The year of your grandmother's birth?"

I remembered it from the service.

"That's correct. Now tell me how she got her name."

"I don't know."

And so she told me.

Three years after the matron, a teacher from the Transkei hinterland, followed her husband to settle on a plot he'd inherited from his father in Zeleni, she was promoted to the position of headmistress at the local school. That same year, two escaped convicts from St. Albans stalked into the region. They were feared. The villagers spoke of how the convicts walked with their knives on show—and how they paid shopkeepers with counterfeit money, grinning at them with lips burnt from spirits.

My grandmother, still an outsider in the village, didn't share their caution. She concocted a plan to lure the bandits to a lakeside meadow, on the pretext of celebrating the return of a rich man's son from *ulwaluko*. The two men caught wind of the news, and arrived at the meadow to exuberant singing, but no meat. Instead, they found a tall woman half-submerged in the lake, a Bible in one hand, beckoning with the other. The crowd fell silent, cleared a path.

The bandits complied and approached her, allowing her to baptize them as the village pastor gaped. It must've been her lack of fear—the men would attest to having known inmates of lesser mettle in the cages of St. Albans.

That afternoon, she enrolled them at the school, determined to teach them to read, and it was under these circumstances— in a room with two broken windows and one uneven, rocking desk—that the two convicts, in gratitude, first called her "the matron"; at which my grandmother, who was known for maintaining a stern exterior in her classes, looked up and smiled, indicating her acceptance.

RTR: 011 / Date of Recollection: 05.31.2002 / 11 min

Today drags. It's casual day, which means we're dressed in civvies, and after our first break, we get assembled in the courtyard for an apple-bobbing contest like we're 12. Then there's a presentation from a non-profit group that's visiting our school to tell us about computers. I'm surprised it isn't about condoms. It's always about condoms.

In the courtyard, Lerato asks what's happening with me. "You've had two half-days."

"Nothing's happening."

"Is everything okay?"

"I'm tired, that's all." I turn away from her toward the makeshift platform.

A thin, red-faced man in a gray suit is fiddling with the microphone, his colleagues weaving through the crowd to hand us pamphlets. The microphone screeches from the feedback, and we all watch Mr de Silva tripping over himself to fix it. Then the man's voice clears a channel through the static. The project's called Marathon for Computers, he says, and they've set up an office in town. Their mission's to make information technology accessible to areas like ours, with limited resources, poverty, and low literacy.

Lerato laughs. "He can't be talking about you."

"I'm poor."

"Far from illiterate, though. You know, Kiran still isn't back."

"I know."

"I wonder what's happened to him."

"Maybe he's at a better school."

"Maybe. It's interesting to watch you pretend you don't care, though."

"I don't.

"I think you do."

"I don't."

"I know about Hudson Park."

"That's never happening."

"That's not what his friends keep telling everyone. That thing you walk around with everywhere doesn't help, either."

"The recorder?"

"Is that what it is?"

"Kiran and I haven't fucked," I tell her.

The man on the platform tells us his organization's hosting marathons, starting from the town square, for the next two weekends.

"The proceeds go to new computers for local schools."

"I don't know if my aunt'll be hot for this," I say.

"I know my mother will. I can't wait for the humiliation."

I laugh, since it's true. Lerato's dad won a government contract a few years ago, back when our neighbors still collected inside the town hall to elbow each other for tenders. He was one of the lucky ones. He moved his family to Kaffrarian Heights— her mom couldn't move far enough—but Lerato refused to change schools. She needed one thing to be familiar, she told me. Her mom was horrified.

"Everything's about being seen, with her," Lerato sighs. "I know the apple doesn't fall that far from the tree, but there should be a limit."

I fold a pamphlet and put it in my pocket.

For the rest of the day I watch the clock, trying to keep awake at my desk while our teachers go over their marking and revise their class plans. We get shown a movie for English. Halfway through *The Dead Poet's Society*, I get called to the sick bay.

Mrs Linden's gaze is trained on her notebook. "I believe I'm owed something," she says.

I close the door.

"I'm waiting."

"I don't have a doctor's note."

"I don't recall that being what we agreed on."

"I couldn't make it to the doctor's office."

"You couldn't or wouldn't? You left school for it."

"My aunt didn't come back from work until I was asleep."

"I thought we spoke about how important it was to see a doctor." Mrs Linden closes the notebook and turns to me, motioning me closer. Then she takes my temperature again. "How are you feeling today?"

"Better."

"How's the head?"

"Fine."

"Fine?"

"I'm tired, that's all."

"Did you have breakfast this morning?"

"I had cereal."

"That's good. Now listen, because I won't repeat myself. I don't appreciate being lied to. I don't know what's happening at home, of course, but this is enough for me to call the headmaster. I'm letting you off this time, but I don't want to see you coming up here again without a sick note. You won't be having any more sick days, either."

"I understand."

"Do you?"

"I do."

The rest of the periods blur. We're released at half past 1, and I walk home through a light rain that breaks when I reach the Queens Road corner, where the clouds part and the sun beams a yellow light down over the tar.

Up ahead, I see a police van parked next to a burnt-out Toyota. There's a small crowd being kept back by the police, and I go closer, too. I hear whispers about one of the girls being inside. The car's still smoldering; its yellow paint has bubbled and blackened against the skeleton. We all wait. Eventually, one of the policemen tells us to move on. That there's no one inside.

November 21, 1999

Mama and Tata were journalists for different papers when they met, four years before I was born. In 1981, when Lennox Leslie Sebe, the chief of amaGqunukhwebe, was handed a golden pen to sign the Ciskei into an independent state, Piet Koornhof, the Minister of Constitutional Development and Cooperation, awarded him the Order of Good Hope, the apartheid republic's highest accolade. It was reported that there were over 8,000 people in attendance that night, honoring the segregation of amaXhosa from the European republic, but Mama and Tata were not among them.

It was the 4th of December and the receptionist's desk at Frere Hospital, in East London, had been vacant for an hour. A sullen cleaner slopped a wet mop over the linoleum, dragging it past the bench where they sat apart, feeling cold, their hands idling in their laps.

From another room, a radio next to a patient's bed reported on how the Ciskei had completed the process of secession. Tata walked to the counter and stood there, sighing. He went back to the bench and sucked on his teeth, which is when the woman next to him laughed. For the first time, they turned to each other.

Tata volunteered that he'd brought a neighbor's son to the hospital, a quiet child who'd fallen out of a tree and broken his shin bones. Not one, but both of them, if she could imagine.

Mama could. Her visit wasn't dissimilar. It was also a favor to a neighbor's child, she explained, a child who, on top of suffering from malnutrition, had developed an inflamed intestine. Mama, who'd worked as a teacher before, had often seen such cases: more so, she added, in the township, Mdantsane, than when she'd been in the village.

Tata nodded, unsurprised; although, he cautioned, his experience had left him with an opposing view. His people came from the other side of the river. He'd seen things worse than hunger.

Mama nodded as the receptionist returned to her post. It wasn't uncommon to use an employer's insurance on a neighbor's ill child.

Four years later, as the Ciskei began to buckle under the weight of the despot Sebe and Mama insisted on leaving before the situation grew worse, they would return to the same hospital to have their own ill child.

RTR: 012 / Date of Recollection: 06.02.2002 / 5 min

I wake up to a new stain spreading itself across our ceiling. I stare at it, passing the hours it takes my aunt to get up. The geyser might be leaking again, I think of telling her when she hauls the ironing board past my room, leaving it to stand in the kitchen while she runs water for a bath. Half an hour later, the smell of her perfume permeates down the corridor and I hear her handbag drop on the kitchen counter.

I draw my covers. "I'm up," I tell her when she knocks.

It's no different from most mornings. I have a bath, get dressed, and eat a bowl of porridge in the kitchen. Then Doris drives me to Home Affairs to get an ID made, like we arranged to do a month ago.

It's hot out, and I still haven't seen the machine. Nor heard from Kiran.

I lean my head against the window as the two of us go down Ayliff, looking out at the town center while she complains about her cousin Dumisani again.

"Isn't the car old?" I ask her.

"That's not the point."

I shrug and lean against the window again. There's a crowd gathered on the town square, in front of a man dressed in a robe woven from straw. The people before him drop banknotes at his feet. Behind them, two children dressed in matching straw loincloths race toward the memorial in the center of town, wrestling and struggling to keep their feet on the plinth.

It reminds me of how Dad used to hate seeing these monuments. From the moment we first moved here, he'd likened them to celebrating one's own prison guards. I still remember listening to him as he spoke, watching through the car window as the queen slid past us, frozen in another century, looking over a population that was kept in the dark about how much blood she'd spilt. It didn't feel like a prison, but the remains of an alien civilization which had now fled, its mission untenable; but not wanting to be forgotten, it had left behind unreadable signs, as out of place as hieroglyphs inside an igloo.

"I'd appreciate it if the cleverness was kept for school," Doris tells me.

I apologize. "I'm not feeling well."

"Have you been taking your medicine?"

"I have. I think it'll pass."

My aunt nods. We continue down the road, passing the square. "I'm surprised the pub's still open," she says.

I look up and see what she sees. For the past four years, our town's been slowly losing its old skin. Each month, an old shop closes down, to be replaced by a R99 clothing store, a cell-phone repair shop, or a café with a Coca-Cola sign.

Dad used to hate it, too, when Mom called our town quaint. The swimming baths, she meant. The bowling clubs and the horse stables. The theater facing out toward the square and the Penny Farthing store for cakes. That was back then. Now potholes and patches of broken asphalt mark the route as Doris drives us downtown, the pharmacies alone in maintaining an unshakeable trade, their turnstiles unscrewed to allow long lines to snake out from the dispensaries.

I turn back to the road.

My aunt parks in front of a white building with a brick façade and a fading government sign. We pass through the entrance under an arch, and then take the stairs. On the first floor, Doris and I join a line of old women sitting in plastic chairs, facing a partitioned counter with ringing telephones, groaning fax machines.

To my surprise, we don't have to wait—my aunt gets called

up next. She rummages through her purse for my birth certificate, and I fill out a form while she sits back down. Then I stand in another line for fingerprints, thinking about the talk we had in the car.

That's what I used to tell Dad. That I didn't feel well. I think about the machine again, and wonder if it always meant I needed to be medicated.

The line shortens and I get summoned to the front. A man takes my form and tells me to give him my hands. He dips my fingers in a vat of ink and presses my prints to the paper, and it's when he's on my second hand that I imagine seeing it.

Inside the ink.

The roiling motion of the machine.

I stare at it, but it doesn't last.

Then the man directs me to another counter, where a woman with a cropped blond wig tells me where to get the photographs I need to complete the process. When I turn around, I find Doris standing behind me with her purse. I take 40 rand from her and head downstairs, where I hand the notes to a photographer under the arch. He stands me in front of a blank wall and takes four black-and-white photos. Upstairs again, I hand the pictures to the woman, who stamps the form.

Then Doris and I head back to the car. There's a countdown on the radio, the Metro Top 40, too loud for conversation.

My aunt has to visit a friend in town. I lock the door behind her and sit in front of the TV, thinking about Kiran and the vat of ink.

In bed later, after she's come home and I'm about to fall asleep, the machine returns.

This time, I don't bother switching on Kiran's recorder.

I stare at the ceiling, watching as the it covers the new stain. The triangle appears not long after that. I turn my head to see it, but then I realize it's upside down, reminding me of the sky that day when I was nine years old in Bhisho Park, and the swing creaked behind me as I fell.

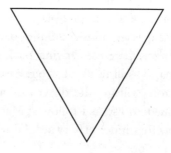

November 22, 1999

My parents built their first home without me, having moved to
Bhisho from Mdantsane to take up posts in Sebe's government.
I spent the first quarter of my childhood with the matron.
The rest was with my parents. Driving back from the super-
market with Mama, I'd still think of the gum trees and shallow
rivers in the matron's village, the dirt roads and the thatched
huts—and continue to do so as I followed Mama to the kitchen
to help set out pots for dinner. Afterward, I'd settle at our dining
table with my homework.

Before we sat down for our meal, Mama would call me to the
living room and make me recite what I'd learned from my books
that week. It wasn't hard to make my parents feel as if it was
working. I resigned myself to doing well at school because it was
an instruction that came to me without confusion.

In church, which Mama also insisted on, not wanting to set us
apart, the education was more demanding. We'd watch as scores
of adults lined up in the pews, shuffling in their high heels and
two-toned brogues, while we were given seats at the back of the
hall, next to the entrance, and banned from speaking to each
other during the sermons. The pastor stood on a stage, assisted
by a translator, but we could never see him over the congregation's shoulders or hear him over their applause.

He spoke in English, too. Even though most of his congregation needed assistance with the language, he never compromised. His sermons had intermissions, and lasted five hours in
total. We'd lean against the walls at the back, bored, prevented
from speaking by a man who wielded a switch. He used it on me

once, not to punish me for falling asleep, he said, but for having done so with my legs open.

Driving back from church, I'd often look out of the window and imagine an overlap between the world we once knew and the one we had now; as if the roads before and behind us could dissolve into brown channels, and the pavements on either side of our car—trampled under the feet of workers returning from their jobs, bearing their belongings in plastic bags—could become the banks of rivers. I'd close my eyes as we swerved into our street, making the images vanish, and then open them again to see herds of cattle throwing up dust on the horizon next to the landfills and squatter camps in Bhalasi Valley, while a flock of amasi birds divided Tata's windshield into quadrants, darkening each pane.

RTR: 013 / Date of Recollection: 06.02.2002 / 15 min

The morning after seeing the machine, I wake up with a headache, nauseated. The world is dim again. I stare up at the ceiling, waiting for it to go still.

My aunt's in the kitchen. I think about her losing her job.

When she knocks I get up and open the driveway gate for her to go to church. Then I get back into bed and watch the ceiling some more, and look through the paper my aunt was reading, the one with the missing girls on the front page.

That's when I see it. The ad. I'm not sure if it's an accident or if it's from Mom. I can no longer tell about most things.

> *Unusual paid position for top-performing local student. Must be imaginative.*

It feels a bit too convenient. Still, there's a number below and I make the call. It rings for a moment before a man's voice picks up.

"Hello?"

"I'm calling about the listing in *The Daily Dispatch*," I say. Then I raise my voice: "I'm a top-performing student."

"You don't come across as articulate."

"I'm nervous."

"Don't be."

"I can't help it."

The voice on the other end laughs. "No, of course not." Then there's more silence, the line crackling. "Tell me what your motivation for applying for this post is."

"Money."

"That's bold."

"It's the truth."

I wait through more silence. Then: "I'm sorry, we've already found a candidate. Thank you for inquiring, but we'll be taking the listing off now."

"I can do better."

"Excuse me?"

"Than the other candidate."

"Is that so?"

"It is."

The voice laughs again. "I'm intrigued."

Then he gives me directions.

Down Wodehouse Street, the air still hangs moist from the rain. I reach the cemetery next to Aloe Terrace and turn right onto the highway, then left toward town. On Alexandra, I pause for breath. Turning right again, I cross town, passing commuters, tired women, men and children, all looking to hitch rides to East London, their cardboard signs scratched with permanent marker. I walk on past the congested intersection close to Shoprite, absorbing the exhaust fumes and the screech of traffic. I'm almost in the industrial part of town.

Downing Street is narrow and congested, lined with hawkers packing up their wares for the evening. Pedestrians weave through parked cars on either side, charting paths toward the buses and the taxi rank. Past a Farrer's Sports, I catch my breath and double-check the directions. I look up at an unmarked, padlocked glass door with a steel grille, wedged between a furniture and cosmetics store.

I knock, but there's no response. I try a second time, and I'm about to phone again when the lights flick on behind the glass. Through the grille, I see a woman standing at the other end of the room, her hand hovering over a switch as the fluorescent lights flicker. Behind her, a door's been left open to the alley behind the building. I see her pull on her lab coat, close the door, and approach me, one hand reaching into her pocket to find her keys to unlock the grille.

"You're here," she says, pushing back her hair. "Please, come in. I'm Marianne."

Up close, Marianne is tall and athletic, with strong shoulders that could sit on a netball captain. I can't tell what her age is, maybe 30.

She settles herself on the other side of a small desk. "Do you have a phone? I'll need that, along with your watch and other digital devices."

I unstrap my wristwatch and reach into my backpack for Kiran's recorder. She thanks me, switches the phone off, and places all three items in a clear plastic bag that she pushes into a desk drawer. Looking up, she catches me watching. "Don't be worried. You'll get them back. This is protocol, that's all." She leans forward, creasing her brow. "Now tell me, do you have anyone waiting for you at home? It is quite late."

I think of telling her about my aunt, but I shake my head.

"That's good."

"How does this work?"

"I'll take you through it." Marianne opens another desk drawer.

To keep calm, I look around the room. "I feel like I'm the first person to answer this ad," I tell her.

"You're not."

"Then no one was chosen?"

"No, unfortunately, none of the candidates was suitable." Marianne smiles. "Despite what Devon told you over the phone. You have to understand that he's grown impatient with our progress here, but he's a good man, and a brilliant scientist. You can trust that. He was a little rattled by you, though," she adds. "That's a rare achievement."

I nod.

"Right. Now I need you to sign this before we start. It's a non-disclosure agreement."

I look at the form.

"It's not a trick. The research we're undertaking is sensitive, that's all."

"I don't know. I've heard of these things binding people."

"It's to protect the work, that's all. You're in no danger."

I take the pen from her and scan the document, before scratching my signature.

"That's great. Now I need a signature on these two as well."

One is a consent form, the other a short questionnaire on my medical history:

SYMPTON SCREEN	YES	NO
Have you ever seen a mental health provider?	X	
Have you ever been sad for over a year?	X	
Do you ever feel like you're the only person alive?		X
Have you ever had so much energy that you couldn't sleep?		X
Do you ever feel that you can't control your thoughts?	X	
Do you ever feel that all of reality is fabricated?	X	
Have you ever attempted suicide or thought about it?		X
Do you have trouble sleeping?	X	
Do you ever fantasize about moving back and forth in time?	X	
Do you have a drug prescription?	X	

I look up and tell her I'm on Celexa and Paxil.

"That's fine: when did you start?"

"Three years ago. In '99."

"You can list them below the table."

I fill out the rest of the form, until I get to a list of scientific terms I don't recognize.

"Don't worry about those," Marianne says. "They're for our benefit."

I nod and get to the end, where I scrawl my signature.

"Fantastic. I believe we're about ready to start the procedure."

"Procedure?"

She laughs. "Don't be alarmed. It's all technical talk. Protocol. You're not being operated on."

"Then what are we doing?"

"The first step is simple. You just have to answer a few questions."

"More questions?"

"More questions. They form the basis of our work, here. This time, your responses will be timed." Marianne pauses. "It means you'll have to be honest with us. That's the rule."

"I'll be honest."

"Don't worry about that, either," she smiles. "Inasmuch as we expect and value your discretion here, we extend the same toward you."

There's a knock on the door leading out to the back. Marianne turns and looks behind her. Another, louder knock. "Just a moment," she says.

She gets up and walks to the door, which she opens a crack. I don't have enough time to make out who's on the other side, before she's slipped through and closed it behind her. I wait in my chair, their voices too muffled to hear through the wood. I think of getting up and placing an ear against the door, but it opens again and Marianne returns to her seat.

"My apologies. There's been an incident," she says.

"I'm sorry?"

"Don't be. It means we'll have to reconvene, that's all. Timothy will drive you home. He's waiting for you outside. As for us, we'll be in touch. Perhaps later this week."

"I don't understand."

"There isn't much to understand. These things happen."

She reaches for the plastic bag with my phone and Kiran's recorder, and I get up and take them from her.

"Farewell," she says.

Heading back up Wodehouse, Timothy doesn't speak to me. He's even taller than Marianne, with wide forearms covered in slick hairs over pale skin. He doesn't look at me either, and when I ask about the incident, he doesn't respond.

At my house, he opens the car door for me like a chauffeur and I step out. "I do what I'm told," he sighs.

I watch him drive down our street.

The house lights are off, meaning my aunt isn't back.

Monday morning arrives and we get our memos at school. The memo has instructions on how to use the buddy system, like Mrs Robinson said it would, and which emergency numbers to call. It also tells us to watch out for people who look suspicious, whatever that means. No one talks about Kiran having gone missing, or about him selling acid.

I stop at Ms Isaacs' desk to ask if it's fine if I open the package.

"I was counting on it. I can't open it myself, as a school administrator, but a fellow student could. Let's do whatever's needed."

I look at her computer tower and notice she's removed the cartoon.

"I took my own advice," she sighs. "It was starting to bring on the opposite effect."

After school, Lerato leads me to the back of the chapel, where we sit against the hull where the seniors smoke. I ask her if she smokes now, too, and she shrugs.

"I found these at home." Pushing her braids back, she pulls out a sheet of gum and a bottle of cologne. "It's stronger," she says. "My mom's being a bore, again."

I watch her fit the menthol in her mouth and hunker down to light it. She waves the match out, digging the stick into the soil next to the hull. Rain clouds gather from the west as the two of us slide down in our blazers, leaning against the splintered wood.

I take out the newspaper my aunt was reading, and ask Lerato if she knew the girls.

"The missing ones? I think I've seen one of them around." She points to the photo on the front page. "That's her in the middle. Nolitha Ntuli. I once saw her hanging out with Lungile."

"I don't know who he is."

Lerato laughs. "That's no surprise."

"How come?"

"He's not white."

"Litha's not white."

"He might as well be," she grins. "I don't mean it mean, though."

"What's Lungile's deal?"

"Nothing. He hosts parties. His parents used to live in the Ministerial Residences, but now they own a minister's house two blocks up from me. He gets left alone a lot."

"Who gets invited?"

"Rich kids. The local ones. That's why I got confused when I saw her. Nolitha looks like she's from downtown. No offense."

I look at the article. "It says here they all go to St. Christopher's."

"Proving my point. Is there a reason I'm being questioned?"

"Pupils are to report all suspicious behavior to each other and the staff."

Lerato laughs. "You're odd. You have to know that."

"I don't."

"I can never get used to it."

"I don't know what you're talking about."

She shakes her head and gives me Lungile's address.

I meet Litha and Part at the park. The two of them have the exercise book from Kiran's package spread open in the alcove, and Litha's smoking a cigarette while Part pages through the cuttings.

"I saw it again," I tell them.

Litha looks up. "The machine?"

I nod.

"That means we'll start searching for your mom?"

"For the girls, too," I tell him. "I'm convinced there's a connection."

"You've got a lead?"

I tell them about Lungile and his parties.

"It's true," Part says. "That's unusual. The upper crust doesn't host people from downtown, or from below Alexandra."

"I know."

"I have a plan. I can go to the girls' school today," Litha says. "I have a friend there. He used to be at the Home and should be at hockey practice."

Part turns to him. "Leaving us with Lungile. Is this a plan to make us use our feminine wiles?"

Litha shrugs. "I think it might cover more ground."

"I agree." I open the sketchbook to Lungile's address. "I'll think of a cover story while we walk. It shouldn't be that hard."

Part nods and we leave the park. Litha walks up toward St. Christopher's, while Part and I walk down past the museum on Alexandra.

Its wooden doors are locked. I remember them being taller in the 6th grade, when our class used to take tours of the first two floors. The guide was Mrs Olivier, a thin, dark-haired woman who'd been assigned to teach us a class on Natural History. The first afternoon we came over, she walked us through the document collections of the first English settlers in the region, bringing them back to life through the framed remains of their journals and letters. Then she told us about a former director, Captain Guy Shortridge, who'd collected over a thousand mammal specimens from Namibia in 1927.

I'd fallen behind the others, thinking back to the settlers, among whom the captain would've ranked highly. Mrs Olivier said there'd been 4,000 of them in the beginning, and that 20 000 natives had been expelled upon their arrival, demonstrating a desire similar to the captain's, I thought, to move bodies from one corner of the land to another. The previous week, she'd told us about the bubonic plague, explaining how it had broken out in Cape Town in 1901 and spread to our town, resulting in the removal of even more bodies. In the 1930s, when the plague drifted up from the southwest coast, the settlers thought it provident, bolstering the case for segregation, which had been stalled since its proposal. Natives who lived in town would be relocated to Ginsberg, which was rural, with a population that struggled to afford the new hut tax.

November 26, 1999

I fell sick the first time Mama moved us here. The air inside our house was different to the air outside, Tata told us. He'd been reluctant about our relocation to begin with. He explained that it was the act of changing between the two that was making me ill.

Mama, who like many parents in the homeland was looking for an English-medium school for her child, made sure not to indulge him. That's how she put it. He was a man, she said, and all he wanted was to be listened to.

My illness turned out to be an allergic response to the cedar pollen in our new house, which we found could be solved through both gardening and antihistamines; the path to a suburban school, however, remained elusive. The search throughout the district deepened the lines on Mama's face, furrowing her brow each time it returned her home without reward. In the interim, she started giving me her own lessons.

Tata stopped asking her for news, resigning himself to bitter ripostes. He was satisfied, he said, with the knowledge that the large public schools had been reserved for children of different hues, whose families had been in town for longer and whose means bounded far above ours. "I told you," he said, whenever he found an opportunity to scold her from the couch. "It's discrimination." Then he'd turn and repeat the same to me, and I'd nod. But he was proven wrong a month later.

There was still His Kingdom on Earth, Mama told us one evening, a recommendation from a pregnant colleague at the university. I was in 4th grade; I'd stay enrolled until the 6th.

The school was run by the Muller clan—an extended family of eight former missionaries who'd hitchhiked their way into our town from Plettenberg Bay. Each month, the school invited a guest pastor to give a sermon. There was a man, once, with blond hair and a lapel mic, who asked us what our fears were. He stood on a raised platform at the front of our chapel—a carpeted half-circle that hid a hatch which opened to reveal a baptism pool I'd never used. I sat at the back, near the hallway leading out to the parking lot, and tried to think of Mama ascending through her bedroom window, but all I could see were the lines dividing the man's dentures.

That morning, he held up a handful of Marvel trading cards, warning us against the different disguises of the golden calf of Mount Sinai. The peace sign—which I'd seen around the necks of a number of girls in East London the previous summer, hung on loops of black string that brought out their collar bones— was a broken and inverted crucifix, he said. None of us stirred in our seats as he spoke, and none of us raised our hands for questions when he was done. That seemed to please him. He divided us into groups of four. I joined a group next to the platform at the front, in a corner awash in blue light from the stained glass above, and listened to three of my classmates—two of whom had pretended to be born again the previous term, aiming to distract their parents from their grades at the annual parent-teacher meeting—discussing whether or not a crotch was something a man could have. Then we broke for lunch. Afterward, I tried to look it up, but the modem stalled, and I walked home wondering how much we had to know about men's crotches.

RTR: 014 / Date of Recollection: 06.03.2002 / 1.5 min

Part and I find the place in less than an hour. Roman columns split the façade into three wide strips; two gardeners mow the grass. Standing in front of the wrought-iron gate, boiling in my school blazer, I press a button on the intercom and wait for a response.

"Here, let me try."

I step aside and Part kneads the button until it bleats. There's static, and then a voice arrives with a yawn. "I heard you the first time."

"Is this Lungile?" I lean over. "We want to talk. About the next party."

"I don't know who you are."

"Don't you want to?"

There's more static; I imagine him holding the receiver against his chest. Then a curtain shifts behind a window on the first floor and Lungile laughs. "Is this about getting an invite?"

"It might be."

"I see. Listen, the season's over, but leave a number and I might get around to using it."

I recite each digit.

"I like what I see," he says, hanging up.

The two gardeners push their machines up the green slope toward the back of the house, their backs hunched, sweating.

I don't feel ill, which surprises me. Then Part and I walk home.

November 27, 1999

The school was an extension of the Accelerated Christian Education (ACE) Program—an import from the United States. It was a leftover televangelist project from the 1970s, I later learned, with headquarters in Lewisville, Texas. In class, we were taught to speak Standard American English—which I still do—from an old tape recorder. The school had no teachers. Each grade was assigned a supervisor and a monitor who presided over pupils as we filled out workbooks called PACEs, all of us seated in separate cubicles. The PACEs stood for Packets of Accelerated Christian Education, and the cubicles, which were constructed from white wooden screens that rose on three sides of each desk—high enough to block out most of our peripheral view—were intended to facilitate work that took place in isolation and silence.

To seek assistance from the supervisor, we'd stick a Christian flag—white, with a red cross and navy square—into a hole drilled into the top of the partition on the right of the cubicle; to call for a monitor, her subordinate, we'd stick an old South African flag into a hole on the left. The supervisors were entrusted with intellectual and spiritual guidance, while the monitor could be called on for routine tasks.

Each time we completed an exercise, we called on a monitor to request permission to get up and walk to the scoring table in the middle of our learning center, where we retrieved dense folders packed with laminated memos. Then we proceeded to mark our own work, operating under the tenet of truthfulness, which didn't mean trust. At any moment, a supervisor could ask for a student's PACE and take it upon themselves to double-check their adherence to said tenet.

Each PACE came illustrated with a recurring comic strip meant to instill in us the values extolled by the program: among others, diligence, deference to authority, and the onus placed on Christians worldwide to deliver lesser civilizations from themselves.

RTR: 015 / Date of Recollection: 06.03.2002 / 14 min

My aunt leaves a note telling me she'll be late again. I make another bowl of noodles, spilling out half in the bin, and sit in front of the TV; but my thoughts return to Kiran's recorder. I know the machine won't return tonight, so I masturbate instead, falling asleep under the ceiling stain.

An hour later, my phone vibrates on my desk.

"He's outside."

"Excuse me?"

"Timothy's waiting to pick you up." It's Marianne. Voices murmur in the background. Then she hangs up.

I don't take a lot with me. I put on jeans and a sweater and lock the front gate. Timothy's headlights burn bright in the cul-de-sac, his van parked half on the sidewalk. Inside the van, he turns to me. "I was told to make you put this on."

He's holding a blindfold and I lean back. "I know where we're going. Downing Street."

Timothy shakes his head. "Not tonight."

I watch his silhouette in the dark. "How come this didn't happen before?"

"I don't know. I follow instructions."

I let him tie it on me.

"The trip's over if I see a finger pulling at it. Those are the instructions."

He twists the ignition and the car pulls into a U-turn.

"How do you know I won't trace the car's turns?"

"Do I have to answer that?"

"It's a small town."

He sighs.

The trip drags, but I do what he wants. I feel his gaze on me each time we stop for a red light, but I don't fidget. We come to a stop eventually, and I hear the gears of an electric garage churning. Then Timothy drives us in, parks, and kills the engine.

"I need you to wait here. Keep the blindfold on."

He leaves the van and knocks on a door. Then he climbs back in, lighting a cigarette.

The passenger door opens and a hand leads me out. "Here, let me take this off you," Marianne sighs. She undoes the blindfold. "I hope that wasn't too rough."

"It wasn't."

The garage door opens and Timothy starts the car.

"Don't worry," she smiles. "He'll be back for you when we're done."

"I'm not worried."

"Excellent."

Marianne waits for the garage door to close, then turns to me and pats her pockets. I hand her my cell phone and undo my wristwatch.

"I'll keep these safe for you," she says, "but today we have to take another precaution." She turns to a shelf and passes me two vacuum-sealed plastic bags. There's a towel in the one and what looks like a hospital gown in the other. "There's a shower through here," she says, pointing at a door in the corner of the garage. "You'll need to be as thorough as you can, and when you're done, change into this robe."

"You want me to wash? I took a bath before I got here."

"I'm sure you did, but it's protocol. I'll be here when you're done."

Marianne unlocks the door and holds it open for me. There's a short corridor beyond, lit with halogen lamps. Halfway down, I turn back, clutching the two plastic bags, but she's already locked the door.

The shower isn't much. It's narrow, the rubber flooring cracked and the vinyl curtain hanging stiff from the rail. The wall tiles are plastic, too. I turn on the faucets and scrub, using a bar of soap to clean behind my ears, my underarms, my crotch. Then I use the coarse part of a sponge to clean under my fingernails. It takes me 10 minutes. I towel off, change into the hospital gown, and fit on a pair of slippers.

When I knock, Marianne unlocks the garage door for me. "There," she says. "Now hand me your clothes and I'll keep them safe."

I hand them over and she folds them into another plastic bag. At the other end of the garage, she unlocks a second, sturdier door.

"Does this lead into a cellar?" I ask her, but she doesn't laugh. Instead, her brow furrows.

"That was a joke. I know houses don't have cellars in a town this size."

"I figured. Listen, it's not a cellar, but it's another passage. You'll have to mind your step and follow me until we get to the lab."

"The lab?"

"Another technical term. Think of it as the Living Room. That's what we call it."

The corridor's short and narrow, opening out to a bright room.

Marianne turns to face me. "Tell me, do you still remember everything we covered in our last meeting? The consent forms. The non-disclosure agreement."

"I do."

"That's good. There's no longer a need for our timed questions. I think we've established enough trust."

"Trust?"

Marianne smiles. "That's what I said. Trust."

We walk into a rectangular room, vacant except for two couches, a coffee table, and a long mirror fitted into the wall.

There's a drywall cubicle in each corner of the room, each with its door closed. Marianne walks ahead, entering a cubicle on the left. I hear her pull out a drawer. Then she comes back with a blue folder and recording equipment, settling them on the table.

"I think we should get started." She motions me over and I take a seat on the couch.

"What about the others?"

"The others?"

"The man I spoke to."

"In due time." Picking up the folder, she pulls out the questionnaire I filled out on Downing Street. "I understand you might be curious, but we'll get to that. For now, since you've told me something about yourself, I feel I should do the same. The two of us aren't that different."

She pulls out a drawer, and uses both hands to hoist a metal box onto the table. "I read your questionnaire," she says. "I was the same age when I thought the world might be fabricated."

I listen for more, thinking of Rohan and Koholint Island.

"Hold on." She opens the box, retrieving a rubber armband connected to an LCD meter. "I need to measure your heart rate."

I stretch out my arm and she fastens the cold rubber around it. When she presses a button, the meter blinks green, then steadies.

"I was also good at school," she says. "It was the combination of the two things that made me want to become a scientist."

She goes back to the box and retrieves what looks like a white Alice band with a flat, metallic disc at each end. "This is an electroencephalogram," she says, "or EEG. It measures brain waves. These two electrodes receive the electrical impulses emitted by your brain and feed them to our computer for analysis. It's common in the medical field."

Marianne fits the EEG on me, then plugs its wires into a black box and positions herself behind me. She squints at my questionnaire again, then walks around to press a button on the recorder. "Tell me, have you heard of Plato's cave?"

"No."

"It's simple. Think about being a child and making shadow puppets."

"I don't know what those are."

Marianne springs up and holds her hands below the fluorescent light, hooking them together where the thumbs meet the index fingers. It's a sudden movement, parting her lab coat. The shadow of a dove prints itself across the table top. I watch her instead of the animal.

Her arms drop and she sits back down.

"I remember making them," I tell her.

"Now imagine you'd never seen what that shadow resembles. Do you know what you'd be seeing?"

"Hands?"

Marianne laughs, then leans forward to make a mark in her notebook.

"Did I say something wrong?"

"No."

"Is this being graded?"

"No, but let me start again," she says. "Plato's cave is a fable, written as a dialogue between Plato's brother Glaucon and Socrates. Like all fables, it has a beginning, a middle, and an end. In the beginning, Socrates imagines a cave filled with prisoners chained against a wall that reaches just above their heads, while facing another, blank one, that reaches up to the ceiling."

Marianne draws an illustration of what she means, then pushes the notebook toward me.

"Now," she says. "There's a fire behind the wall that the prisoners are chained to, and once in a while, objects pass, casting shadows on the wall in front of them."

"I see."

"Do you?"

"They've never seen the objects casting the shadows."

"That's correct. The prisoners' knowledge is limited to what they see projected on the walls of the cave. They know nothing else. That's their reality."

I think of Litha, telling me this is the world we're given. "Then what happens?"

"Like the rest of us, they name the reality in front of them, not knowing it's the shadow of another more concrete reality."

"More concrete," I say, "but not the most concrete?"

Marianne stops and looks up. "Continue."

"Like with the hand. The hand would be a form of reality that the prisoners aren't aware of, since they've only seen and named its shadow."

Marianne nods for me to go on.

"That wouldn't be the most concrete, either, because the hand is in the form of the dove, representing it. The dove itself is the most concrete, and it lives outside the cave."

Marianne makes a note, flips the page. "That's correct."

"It is?"

"It is."

"Then you're saying our town is the cave?"

"Not quite. It's our perception of the world. There might be a realm outside what we know."

"That we can't see or recognize?"

"That's correct." Marianne leans back on the couch. "Listen, let's take a short break."

I inspect the room while she's gone, trying to make out if the cubicle walls have people behind them. I think of telling her about the machine, but decide against it, since it's never helped.

The door opens again. "Let's continue."

"How am I doing?"

"It's going well."

"I thought this wasn't graded."

"That's not a grading."

"That sounds like a teacher's comment."

Marianne smiles. "Time," she says. "That's what we'll talk about next. You said you think of moving back and forth in it."

I nod, and think of Mom. How thick the lines in her palms used to be, and how she'd throw her head back when she laughed. "Is that possible?" I ask.

Marianne squints at the LCD meter. Then she gets up and crouches in front of the black box connected to the EEG. "It depends," she says, "to answer your question from before." She returns to the couch and reaches for her pen, holding it between her index fingers. "Is this how you imagine time? Do you start from the end and move to the tip?"

"I do."

"How about this?" Marianne holds the pen between her palms, the angle restricting my view of the tip.

I think about it. "The first option makes it look easier to travel, but if I moved and sat somewhere else, I could say the same about this option."

"That's correct. It's the same pen, the same length, but from a different angle. Tell me, what do you see when you look at the tip?"

"The future, with the present and the past behind it."

Marianne nods, and makes another note. "There's another way to look at it. It could be a single moment, but one of three."

"I don't understand."

"It's simple." She reaches into her lab coat and pulls out two more pens, arranging them in parallel on the table top. "There's a way of thinking about time where all three of these exist together. You have to imagine that the past, present, and future are all fixed, instead of one being replaced by the other. That they all exist at once, separately but at the same time—and that each of them are a viable destination."

"The past doesn't lead to the present which leads to the future?" I ask her. "Instead, the future is in place?"

Marianne nods. "It's called 'block time.' In this conception, spacetime is a solid four-dimensional block, instead of a changing 3D one, modulated through the flow of time."

"I understand, but that still doesn't tell me how to travel from one destination to another. From each parallel."

Marianne smiles. "No, it doesn't. Unless the destinations are not separate and I'm wrong to separate the past from the present and the present from the future."

"Meaning that the block holds a single moment?"

Marianne nods. "Meaning that the block indeed does hold a single moment."

"Maybe memory is what lets us move from one pen to another, then," I tell her, feeling both disappointed and inane.

"Perhaps." Marianne takes one of the pens and places it over the other two, forming a bridge. "That's called chronesthesia… but it's not our call to solve time travel."

"Then what is your call?" I ask her, aware, again, of not knowing where I am. For the first time since I arrived, I want to ask her about being paid.

Marianne looks down at the LCD meter, then up again. "Don't be upset."

"I'm not upset. I want to know, that's all."

"It's research," she says. "To perform cognitive experiments and test cognitive development patterns. Or, to be specific, we use Jean Piaget's theory of cognitive development. Or what we call the Piaget Principle. He was a Swiss psychologist who died 20 years ago, and you could call us his disciples. He argued that the nature of intelligence was influenced by both biology and the environment. That there's a call and response with the world."

"I see, but why him and why here?"

"The two are tied. This part of our research concerns itself with the legacies of totalitarian regimes. To be specific, the homeland government and its education mandate. That's why our aim was to study the patterns in a young person—one who was born a native of this region, and is old enough to have lived through its lapsed system."

"What's it for?"

Marianne smiles. "The possibilities are endless. Peer review, policy, pedagogy—a scientific look into the past to fix the present."

"The two pens," I tell her, and she smiles.

"Not a lot to ask, either," a voice adds.

A man walks into the room; behind him are two other scientists. Marianne gets up to remove the strap and EEG from me. "This is the rest of the team," she says. "Now that you've met them, I'm curious to see if they'll hold your interest."

The man smiles. "It's good to know we've got our head researcher's confidence." He turns to me. "I'm Devon. I'm responsible for making the project a reality. These are my colleagues, Paul, Maanika—and we're all in agreement. That was impressive. I apologize for the poor bedside manner on the phone, before."

"Were you listening to us now?"

He nods, grinning. "Not eavesdropping—monitoring."

Devon looks like how I expected—a team captain, over six feet tall and clean shaven. He's lean, with square shoulders and a stare that moves between being alert and dismissive. He's clearly their leader.

"I process the data set from the EEG," Paul tells me, his face overwhelmed by wide lenses, thick ear-length hair, and a full, auburn beard.

"I help with research," Maanika adds. "I also oversee the Living Room's aseptic technique. Devon's right. That was a successful interview. To be honest, we expected our subjects to be more indisposed, finding all this too strange. I apologize for the inconvenience of the shower—we're required to do that. Because of budget cuts, we have to keep the space sterile for a pack of microbiologists."

I'm stunned at how beautiful she looks. It takes a moment for me to reconfigure her face back to a stranger's, removing it from the familiarity its symmetry invites. "It's good to meet you," I say. Then I clear my throat.

"There must be questions you want to ask," Devon sighs, frowning. "It's natural, of course, but time won't permit."

"I suppose you want to know what we specialize in," Marianne adds, and I nod, though I hadn't thought of it. "It's not that different from what we discussed," she says. "Our fields overlap—sociology, psychology and neuroscience—but in a word, we're scientists, each of us guided by the defining principles behind Piaget's work: assimilation and accommodation."

"The known and the unknown," Paul adds, thumbing his glasses.

"Take you, for example," Devon says. "You've now accommodated a new data set."

I let his words filter in.

Then Devon makes a salute, Maanika and Paul thank me at the same time, and Marianne leads me back down the corridor to the garage.

I can't tell how long it's been.

I change back into my own clothes in the bathroom, and Marianne hands me my watch and phone. Then she reaches into the pocket of her lab coat. "Timothy will be here soon," she says. "I should give you this."

I take the white envelope. Then Marianne smiles, placing a hand on my shoulder. "Look out for us in the papers," she says.

In the van, I let Timothy blindfold me without complaining. He pulls out of the garage and I hear the gears working as we set off. He opens a window and lights a cigarette. After a while, he reaches over to pull down my blindfold. I blink—we're back on Alexandra.

The town looks deserted. As far as I can see, cones of orange wash down from the streetlights and melt into each other, forming a thin, ephemeral carpet over the strip. There are no signs of life as we drive past Fort Hill, the houses all walled and gated, each as silent as a landform.

Outside the house, Timothy parks half over the curb, as usual. "Take care of yourself," he says, and I watch him drive off.

The envelope is full of banknotes. I stash the money for both of us, me and my aunt. Then I fall asleep toward dawn, not certain if my wakefulness is from fear or excitement, or both.

November 28, 1999

Our supervisor at the ACE school, Mrs Fitzgerald, was a short, round woman with long black hair who commuted from East London. She worshipped our founders and ran after their children, whom she never punished, hovering over each one with extra help for their exercises.

One week we received a new batch of PACEs with local content, an intervention from the Department of Education, which required ACEs to integrate the national curriculum. That afternoon, Mrs Fitzgerald called a meeting in the learning center, and in hushed tones told us to remember who we were. That first and foremost we were His pilgrims, sworn in under the blood of the Lamb, that we were called on to band together as soldiers in Christ, who conquered all things through faith, and to serve Him, that we may inherit His Kingdom here on Earth. Mrs Fitzgerald told us the new government wanted to hinder the work of believers. She laid out the new PACEs on her desk; a pile of photocopied pages to her left. I remember how the sunlight slanted across our learning center that afternoon; wide beams that broke over the walls of our cubicles and raised a whirlwind of motes that spun in a long cone next to the scoring table. Mrs Fitzgerald asked us to open the new PACEs to the section on The Zulu King, before telling us it would be replaced with a more accurate account—that he wasn't a general, but a man born from incest, who remained tied to witch doctors until his death, and who had ordered the deaths of countless missionaries. Then she passed around the pile of photocopies, instructing us to cut them into squares that could fit over the pages of new content in the PACEs.

None of us questioned her, I remember.
It was school.

RTR: 016 / Date of Recollection: 06.04.2002 / 5 min

I don't hold to the NDA. I break it the next afternoon when I tell Litha and Part about it. It's 4 o'clock and the three of us are hanging out in the park again.

"Two thousand rand?" Litha says. He stubs out his cigarette in the soil at the edge of our alcove. "You can't be serious? What did you have to do?"

"It was experimental. I had to do a psychological evaluation. They made me sign a non-disclosure agreement, too, and a release form."

"What for?"

"I don't know. It was about education in the province. That's all I saw." I tell them about the blindfold.

Litha's eyes widen and he shakes his head. "No way."

"It's true. There was a woman who took me through the whole thing," I explain. "Marianne, who was nice. Then there was Devon, Maanika, and Paul. Devon secured funding for the project. I spoke to him, first, over the phone, and he tried to reject me."

"Asshole," Part laughs.

"No, not really, but close. He's a team captain. Paul's a programmer, I think, and Maanika's a researcher. Maybe a lab technician, too. To be honest, all of them were nice."

"I wonder if it's illegal," Litha says.

"I don't think so."

"Then what's with all the secrecy?"

"I don't know. Maanika said something about a grant and a budget."

"Maybe they're using the money to work on an unauthorized project," Part says.

I turn to her and nod. "I think that's plausible."

"Do you think they'll test someone else from here?"

"I don't know. Marianne said they hadn't found suitable candidates."

"That's not surprising."

Despite myself, I still feel worried about the NDA.

"How did it go with the articles?" I ask Litha, changing the subject.

He shrugs. "I'm still figuring out the exercise book, but I got a lead from my friend at St. Christopher's," he says. "The missing girls were friends. They all used to attend Lungile's parties. Nolitha used to go out a lot in Ginsberg and Bhisho, before meeting up with him. That's what I heard. The other girl, Lindiwe, was about to drop out of school, pregnant. Esihle was quiet. It surprised people when she started tagging along."

"I wonder how it happened."

"It isn't clear. Lungile was seen parked outside their school a few times."

"They must've had transport, though?"

Litha nods. "The driver was young, too. His name's Loyiso, but he calls himself Luciano. He used to work in Queenstown, Cradock, and East London, which I thought was interesting."

"Interesting how?"

"Look." He opens the exercise book with the clippings. "The machine coming back is the first sign we've seen since we found *UFO Diaries*."

I nod.

"Then Kiran's package came along and I wondered what that meant." He pages through the exercise book. "Last night, I started thinking about the schools Loyiso worked in, looking for what they had in common. Then at the towns themselves. I looked at the clippings again and a pattern came out: East

London, Cradock, Queenstown. Those were the towns with the most missing persons cases, and also where Luciano had worked."

"I still don't get it."

"I didn't get the connection either, at first. Then I remembered your drawing of the machine, the triangle, and I realized Luciano might be a beacon. That he might be following a course set by the machine." Litha takes out sheets of paper from his backpack. One is a map of the province that he's printed out. He's drawn lines joining Cradock, Queenstown, and East London. "Look. They form an acute triangle that faces southeast," he says.

I look at Part and I can't tell if she's frightened or excited. I don't know which one I am, either. Litha goes on. "That's what brings me to Triangulum."

"Triangulum?"

"It's a triangle of stars, a constellation, between Andromeda and Aries. I learned about it from reading the index in *UFO Diaries*. Most recent sightings of UFOs in the southern hemisphere, when observed in the night sky, happen around those stars. The three towns, Cradock, Queenstown, and East London, form the same triangle as the Triangulum constellation. It's even facing the same direction. Here, have a look." I take another printout from him, an illustration of the Triangulum constellation, and compare it to the map. He's right.

"I think we're on a route," says Litha. "I think Luciano's guiding us. I think the machine is directing him."

"Right now?"

He nods.

I crouch down over the clippings, almost forgetting to breathe.

"Mom?" I whisper to them.

November 30, 1999

For a long time, we had no running hot water at the new house. The power bill had gone into arrears before we'd unpacked our boxes. Tata nursed puzzling ideas about scarcity, and sometimes he'd share them with us. Once, on a drive to the matron's village, we'd come across a field of mielies covered with locusts; a dark cloud eating through the summer's harvest. Tata rolled up his window and drove on, flicking on the wipers to catch a fistful of the bugs under the rubber.

When Tata laughed, Mama tensed. She could tell when he wanted to retrieve an old horror from his childhood. That afternoon, as he drove us past the field, Tata told us about 1967.

He'd wanted to be a miner when he was 17, he said, and he'd taken a bus to Alexandra, in the Transvaal, where he couldn't believe what he saw. There were families feeding on locusts and field mice, he told us. There was his uncle, who carried a plastic bucket to the abattoir to beg for blood he could boil into puree. The children looked weak even from a distance. Thin-limbed. Taut foreheads. Flaked lips.

I leaned back in the car when he went quiet again, turning up the trail that led us to the matron. Mama was silent for the rest of the trip, but I felt her anger filling up the car, imagining it as hot and bright as the sunlight beating down on the bonnet.

RTR: 017 / Date of Recollection: 06.04.2002 / 6 min

Litha calls me. He's dug up more on Lungile's parties, on Luciano.

"There might be crime involved," he says.

"Is your friend part of it?"

"I don't know. He might've been around, but I doubt it."

"Is it true?"

"That's what he thinks."

I shift on the couch and turn the volume down on *Where Have All the People Gone?* I hear Doris flushing her bathroom toilet. "What else did he tell you?"

"It gets complicated. Luciano used to be connected to parties in Queenstown, too. The upper crust, that side. He drove girls up from the townships on weekends."

"I see."

"There's more. He also used to deal at the parties. Mandrax. Roofies. He hung around schools a lot, because of the job, and picked up on the demand."

"The upper crust does buttons?"

"That's what I heard."

"The girls? Is it what I think?"

"It's worse. I heard about drugging; keeping girls in closets, running trains. Rape. Luciano delivered them."

I wince, feeling my pulse quicken. "Do you know where he lives?"

"I was hoping you wouldn't ask."

"I think we have to go."

"I know." Litha takes a long breath. "Let's meet at the park tomorrow," he says. "His place is in Schornville. He lives in a back room at his mom's house."

．　　．　　．

Litha has the address on a piece of paper in his back pocket. The place isn't hard to find. We head southeast toward the Department of Transport; then Conway Road leads us into Schornville, a small neighborhood between Ginsberg and Beacon Hill. It's known as a Colored area, meaning it has more tar roads than a township.

Luciano lives on 4th Road, down the street from a butchery and a bottle store—another rundown block with children skipping rope over potholes, Corollas rusting on cinderblocks, and yards marked with packed soil and bleached grass. The walls of number 13 are painted a peeling blue under a tin roof. Out front, there's a woman filling a concrete basin with water. When we stop in front of the gate, her shaded figure closes the faucet and turns to us, raising her palm to guard herself from the glare. I open the gate and walk in.

"Hello, ma'am, may I ask if Lungile's home?"

The woman pours a handful of detergent into the sink. The she continues sorting through her pile of soiled dishcloths. "I haven't heard what you want from him," she says eventually.

"I owe him money. He was our driver."

"How much?"

I take out a hundred from my aunt's stash and she looks at it, before turning back to the basin. "My son is dead," she says. "Like his father."

I feel stunned. "How did he pass, ma'am?" I ask after a moment.

"I'm supposed to know what he did with his time?" Luciano's mother rests her palms on the basin, hanging her head. "I never understood him," she says. "His brain was fried. He thought he was a god."

"I'm sorry, ma'am. I don't understand."

"Neither do I. He came home one day thinking he was a god. That's what he told me." She sighs. "My son was a fool. Most men are. I thought he'd be different, but who is? He died from the things he ate with the whites. There wasn't much in his head, after that."

"Drugs?"

She doesn't answer. Instead, she wrings out a pair of dish-cloths and hangs them on the sagging line behind her. Then she dries her hands against her sides. "Come, I'll show you where it happened," she says.

We follow her to the back of the house, where there's an above-ground swimming pool. It's drained, the plastic parched.

"I found him in there, drowned. I never understood what he wanted with this thing. It's for children. He had a packet of those pills on him. The doctors said it was an overdose."

I draw closer. The bottom of the pool is decorated with tri-angles, one large one scrawled with marker inside a pentagram.

"Loyiso started seeing shapes in the end," she says. "It might've been devil worship. That drawing—Thoko said she saw one like it in her girls' math book. Poor thing. Her daughter went missing a week after we found him. It's been in the papers."

"May I ask who Thoko is?"

"Nolitha's aunt. I used to work with her at Nick's Foods."

Before we leave, she pauses at the gate. "I should have said something to the police when he started bringing home school-girls," she says. "He'd have been better off in prison." Then she looks at me and holds out a hand. "I'll take the hundred. If he did honest work for it."

I hand it to her.

Nick's Foods doesn't smell like much. Dust, detergent, and cheap floor polish. It's full today, with the lines pulling back toward the aisles. The three of us look for Nolitha's aunt, walking down each row until I see a woman with her nametag at the parcel check. Her hair's in a bob that clutches her face, and she doesn't look as old as I'd imagined.

I greet her and she nods. "I'm sorry to disturb you, Sisi."

"How can I help?"

"It's about Nolitha. I'd like to interview you for our school magazine."

"An interview? What for?"

"We want to make sure the girls aren't forgotten. I can pay for your time."

Thoko watches me. "I don't understand what you're saying, but how much is it?"

"Two-hundred and fifty... but I can raise it to three."

I stand aside as she attends to a customer—an old man in a beige blazer and hat, who asks for a packet of B&B tobacco and pays her with bronze coins.

Then she turns back to me. "I'm at work."

"It doesn't have to be here. I can come over. The school allows it."

Thoko sighs. "Look, the money wouldn't hurt. The police aren't doing their job. This new government doesn't care about poor people. I weep each night, thinking of her. Ever since the news came out and her picture's been in the papers, lots of people pretend to know me, but who helps? I only had two days of leave before I had to come back to this register."

"I'm sorry."

"It's not your doing, but I'll help with your magazine. My niece is a good child. I know she hasn't run off. Since her mother passed, I couldn't afford to send her to a school with white children, but so what? Does that mean she doesn't matter? I do the best I can for her."

I ask her for an address. As she looks for a pen, I sense Part and Litha weaving past the snack aisle behind me.

"Here's one," she smiles. "I live at the edge of town. Near Sweetwaters. It's a small house, but it's not hard to find. It has a low gate, and there's no dog."

"Thank you. Do you know where the other girls live?"

"Them too? Here." Nolitha's aunt turns the page over and writes two other addresses. "Poor Esihle," she sighs, clicking the pen again. "Her mother abandoned her as a child."

Part and Litha pass a sketch of the pentagram between them. It's close to 5, and the three of us are standing on a corner equidistant from our houses.

"Why didn't you show this to the aunt?" Litha asks me.

"I'll show her later," I say. "I want to start with Esihle's house tomorrow."

"I'd come," Part says, "but I made a promise to sort out my mom's medication."

"That's fine. It's not far from me."

"I'll ask my friend more about Luciano," Litha offers.

"And I'll have a look at the exercise books," Part adds.

December 2, 1999

I grew up believing I was born indolent, a word Mama favored, and one I often heard her use to describe my grandfather, whom I'd never known. This didn't change until I was in the 5th grade, when a substitute teacher in an after-school program kept me after class. Mr Govender held up my exercise book as the others filed out, and called me to his desk.

I'd scored full marks for the test, which meant it wasn't about the grade. Maybe I'd fallen asleep in class that afternoon—I often did. But that wasn't the problem either.

I'd written a number at the top of my test. The substitute teacher pointed at it and asked me what it was. I looked. The previous month, we'd had a mascot in a red cape at our school to warn us about strangers. He was called Captain Crimestop, and he'd given us a toll-free number to call if men ever touched us. I'd been impressed by the length of the number, although I couldn't say why; and after I'd finished my sums, I'd made a table of all the answers from the test and used them to compose an equation that could lead to the long number as a solution.

"I thought I told this class not to use calculators," he said.

"I didn't."

"Let me search your bag."

I opened it for him and he reached inside.

"Then tell me how you did this."

"I did it like the other sums."

I started to point at the page, but he closed the exercise book and took out a piece of loose-leaf.

"Do you recognize the number?" I asked him.

"No."

"It's from Captain Crimestop. He was here last month."

Mr Govender grunted, shaking his head as he took out a pen and began to write out a sum, using the same numbers in my equation but changing the 48 to 52. Then he pushed the page toward me. I didn't need to do any working. I reached over and wrote down the answer. He looked at it with his head tilted, then pulled out a calculator. The number on the screen came out the same, which didn't surprise me, since the equation was familiar now.

"Is this unusual?" I asked him, but he didn't answer. He just gave me more sums and I answered them until we finished all the space on the page.

He leaned back in his chair. "It is unusual," he sighed. "How do you do it?"

"I don't know." I thought about it and told him it was like a picture.

"Picture?"

I explained that it looked like a square that was growing and that all I had to do was think of the square being large enough to hold the numbers I'd written on the page. The 48 and the 52, for example, and the ones that were smaller than that.

He shook his head. "That still doesn't explain working backward from the number."

I shrugged. "I liked the number, that's all."

"That's not what I meant."

I thought about it again, and told him it looked like a line moving through the square. That a single point leads to another until the numbers collect at the bottom.

"Like Funnels and Buckets," I said, "but with the correct numbers."

"The computer game?"

I nodded. He tilted his head back and laughed, then got up and shook my hand. I didn't understand the gesture, but I didn't stop him.

RTR: 018 / Date of Recollection: 06.05.2002 / 0.5 min

Tonight, the machine comes back with the triangle facing left, expanding between the two ceiling stains. It's late, about an hour after midnight, and I can't tell if I'm dreaming or not when I hear Doris weeping.

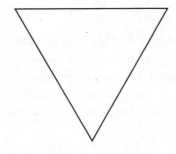

December 3, 1999

I was in the 6th grade when the school went bankrupt from a fraud case the Muller clan had imported from Plettenberg Bay. They fled town overnight, leaving our parents floundering in the dark. One day we found the buildings vacated and our school fees sunk, and we didn't know what to do except sit and wait for someone to lead us in morning prayer.

RTR: 019 / Date of Recollection: 06.06.2002 / 7 min

Esihle's house isn't far from mine—just two blocks down Alexandra toward Echovale, a pink four-room with a black gate. I find my way there after school.

There's an old woman sitting on the porch. I wave at her and when she waves back I cross the road, over the grass island.

"I apologize for disturbing you, ma'am, but is this where Esihle lives?"

The woman nods, waving me in, and I open the gate and enter the shade of the porch. She's dressed in a brown cardigan, a blue dress, and green doek. "Take a seat, child."

I sit with her on the bench, the two of us looking out onto the vacant street.

"This is where Esihle lives. Now tell me your business."

"I'm working for the school magazine. I want to write about the girls."

"I'll fix us some tea and you can tell me what you want to know."

I wait outside as she goes into the kitchen. Her stride is slow but certain. It doesn't take her long to come back: a tray with cups of Rooibos balanced on printed saucers. We each take a sip, before facing each other.

"Ma'am, may I ask about the last time you saw Esihle?"

"It was here, that morning. Later, I waited for her to come home from school in the afternoon. It wasn't like her to be late, and we had work to do. I wanted us to start baking and to take down the washing before I went to church. I had to leave the keys out for her."

I ask her if Esihle was late a lot.

"There were days when she told me there was after-school study. That was once a week. The rest of the time she was here with me at home."

"Did she talk about her weekends?

Her head moves from one side to the other. "Nothing comes to mind. My granddaughter's a quiet child; she doesn't like to use her mouth. The two of us live a peaceful life here. Her mother's in Johannesburg and couldn't be bothered. I'm an old woman, of course, and I expect her to have friends her own age."

I nod.

"Is there something you know?" she asks, and I shake my head.

"Did you know these friends?" I ask her.

"I did not. I don't meddle. It's painful enough that she has a mother like my daughter."

"I forgot to ask, ma'am, but how did Esihle get home from school?"

"I gave her enough money for transport, but she liked to walk."

"I see."

"Is that enough?" she asks, and I nod. Again. Then Esihle's grandmother sighs. "My child, I've put all my faith in the church. It's all I can do. The police sneer at us at the station, making a show of dragging their feet. I haven't been able to sleep, but my pastor told me he saw Esihle in a dream. That she's still alive. I draw my strength from that."

"This has been helpful, ma'am. I appreciate your time."

"It was nothing."

"There's a fee," I tell her, and she looks up. I hand her 300 rand, explaining that it's from the school.

"Here," she says, handing me back a hundred. "Keep that for yourself. This is more than enough for me, now that I'm alone."

I thank her. Before I leave, I take out a sketch of the penta-gram and ask her if she's ever seen it around the house. Esihle's grandmother squints down at the page and shakes her head. "No, I haven't."

Litha's at hockey practice and Part's looking after her mom, but I'm still in town. I decide to do the rest of the interviews myself. Taking out the piece of paper I got from Nolitha's aunt, I look up Lindiwe's street address. It's four blocks to the north.

There's no traffic in their neighborhood, which lies below Echovale. The grass islands grow unkempt, with dogs barking behind rusting wire-frame gates, and little girls skipping rope at the intersections.

I keep walking until I spot the house. Or until I hear it. The front yard's littered with broken dolls and building supplies, plastic cars and paint cans, and enough children to fill a crèche. Four women sit on plastic chairs on the porch, braiding hair and fitting extensions. One of them motions to a child to stop running and open the gate for me.

"I'm looking for Lindiwe's mother," I say.

"There's nothing wrong with that hair."

"Lindiwe's mother..." I repeat.

"There's no one here who can't do braids."

"Leave her be," another woman sighs, not looking up from her client. "It might be about her girl. Lindiwe's mother's inside, child."

There's no one in the living room. In the kitchen, I find a woman fiddling with a gas stove, a sleeping child bundled on her back. The room smells like fresh cement. I stop in the doorway and knock.

"I'll be with you in moment." She gives up on the stove and turns to look at me. "My girls at the front can take care of your hair."

I shake my head. "I didn't come for that."

"I see. It does look fine. Then what's this about?"

"I'm here about Lindiwe."

"Hold on." She opens a cracked window and shouts at some of the children to move off a stack of planks in the yard. "Go on," she sighs.

"It's for our school magazine. I'm writing profiles about the girls. I want them to be known as more than just the names printed in the paper." The silence grows as she watches me. "I can offer 300 rand."

She tells me to take a seat. "That's not a small amount."

I sit down as she undoes the bundle on her back and puts the child on her lap. "This is her son. Did you know that? Now she's having another."

"No."

"I'm not surprised. No one at her school knows. I told her to do that—to keep it to herself. I didn't want her thrown out. But maybe I should've let her take care of herself." She sighs.

I ask about when Lindiwe went missing.

"I was working. I'm always working. Lindiwe has her own ways, which include never listening to me. I've always tried to protect her, to keep her away from my mistakes, but we fight and she does what she wants."

I look at her seated across the table. Lindiwe's mom's skin is dark and smooth, her shoulders wide under her t-shirt. Her eyes are bright and large; the eyelids slow with each blink. "I went to the police that same night, and it was impossible to get help. Everyone pretended to be working, passing me from one officer to the next."

I imagine I can feel the table move as she talks. I look up as the stove starts hissing gas. She gets up to ignite it with a match, leaving the sleeping child on the table. I watch the flame bend the air into a blur, before she places a pot of water over it.

When I look away, it follows me. The blur. I watch it spread across the table top, reaching toward Lindiwe's mom.

I ask for the bathroom, follow her directions down the corridor, and lock the door behind me. I don't have enough time to take in the room before my body goes limp and my head falls back on the cistern. On the ceiling I see the machine, followed by the upside-down triangle, which doesn't fade this time, but intensifies, splitting into two.

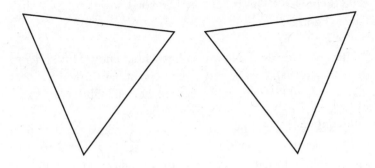

December 4, 1999

His Kingdom on Earth going bankrupt didn't mean much to me. It was all just another unsuccessful attempt by our family to integrate into the town, I thought, and even though Mama was gone, the constraints that had kept her back there remained with me and Tata. It was true that the days felt longer after we were evacuated from the ACE program, and a number of weeks passed with me idle, but Tata enrolled me at a boarding school in East London two and a half terms later. For a while I couldn't remember how things had been between us, before Mama left. Maybe that's why I didn't hassle him. I let things happen how he wanted them to.

RTR: 020 / Date of Recollection: 06.06.2002 / 6 min

I wake to a soft knock on the bathroom door, sit up, and straighten my school uniform.

"I'm putting the child to sleep," Lindiwe's mom says.

"I'm done." I run water over my hands in the basin. Then I walk out of the bathroom and sit at the kitchen table.

"I don't remember where we were," she says.

"Did Lindiwe walk from school?"

"No, my daughter's too good for that."

"Then it was transport?"

"Too good for that, too. I paid for it, of course, but she showed up here in different cars whenever she wanted to. I suspect there was a boyfriend."

I make a mark in my exercise book and watch as she pours maize meal into the water, stirring it in with a wooden ladle. "Do you know who drove the transport?"

"No, those people change all the time. I couldn't keep up. It gets busy, here, and work has me on my feet for eight hours a day."

I nod. "I have one last question." I take out a sketch of the pentagram and show it her. "Is this familiar?"

Lindiwe's mom stops stirring and looks down at the sketch. "No, what is it?"

"I'm not sure. It was in Nolitha's math book."

"I don't know a girl alive without a secret. Maybe that's the problem," she sighs, before she returns to the pot.

I take out 300-rand notes and hold them out to her.

"In the pocket," she says, cocking her hip.

I push them into her jeans.

"Now wait." She stops stirring and bends to kiss my forehead. "That's for being a sweet child."

I thank her, even though I don't agree.

Out on the street again, after I've closed the gate behind me, I see her through the kitchen window, still stirring as tears gleam on her cheeks.

The next stop's the last. Nolitha's aunt drew me a small map to her house. I walk back up to Alexandra along the edge of Echovale, weaving through the first evening traffic, past Schornville and into Beacon Hill.

The house sits on a sloping corner, next to a dirt path and a heap of gravel. It's one of the few three-rooms around. Most of the houses in the neighborhood are single units, despite having to house families. The red paint over the door is varnished but peeling. I climb the front steps and knock, taking a moment to look around. I hear footsteps approaching from the other side of the door, and Thoko opens.

"I was thinking you'd only come at the end of the week," she tells me. "How did you know I wasn't on a shift?"

"I didn't. I was in town."

"Then let's call it luck. Don't stand at the door." I follow her into a small living room, where she offers me a seat on the couch. The cement on the walls is uneven, the wall unit leaning at an angle. I unshoulder my backpack and take out the exercise book, clicking a pen.

"That looks important," Thoko says.

"It isn't. It's just for a school magazine. I won't keep you long."

"This is Beacon Hill. It wouldn't be wise to linger after dark."

I look around, taking in the silence, and ask her if she's alone now.

"No. That's all the luck I have left. I live with a man. He was gone for a long time, but now he's back."

I ask about the afternoon Nolitha went missing.

"The two of us were meant to meet at the end of my shift," she says. "That's what we usually did. If Nolitha came early, she'd wait with me at the shop. Then we'd walk to the rank and catch a taxi."

"Did she walk from school?"

"I did what I could. There were months when I could afford transport and months when things were harder. Maybe she got used to walking. Nolitha can get used to things. In that way, she takes after me more than her late mother. I was the same at school, and I came across as older, like she does. I've seen how the other girls orbit around her."

My eyes are drawn to a closed door in the corridor next to the kitchen: there's a shadow moving under it. I ask if I can use the bathroom and Thoko nods.

I get up and go to the door, but when I lean on the handle, I find it locked.

"No, the one at the end of the corridor," says Thoko.

I stand for half a minute in the bathroom, then flush and go back to the kitchen.

"Are you often home alone?" I ask.

"No, this is recent. He's back, but he needs to find work." She gets up and goes over to the wall unit, which holds a dozen framed photographs. "He's not Nolitha's father, but he's willing to do what he can. I haven't seen that man in over a decade, since my sister passed. The two of them would've been enemies."

Most of the photos are faded, taken in the '70s and '80s. "That's him," she smiles, pointing at a photo of a group of men, one of them with an afro, wearing a wide collared shirt and raising a fist. That's my man. He gave me that as a gift. Now he's out looking for work. This new government hasn't been kind to us."

I think about my dad. "What did Nolitha do on weekends?" I ask.

"I'll be honest with you. My niece likes to save money and

spend it on herself. Nolitha's a very curious child, with a hunger for the world. I told her the weekends could be her own as long as she kept up in class. That was our agreement."

I nod. "There's one last thing." I take out the sketch of the pentagram. "Do you know what this means?"

Thoko leans forward, squinting at the page. "That's the thing that was in her math book," she says. "Hold on."

I wait as she gets up to fetch something from the second bedroom, deeper inside the house. She returns with her hand held out. "I also found this."

There's a small piece of paper in her palm. I look closer and realize it's a tab of acid. It also has the pentagram on it.

"Can I hold on to this?"

Thoko shrugs.

I take out the 300 and hand it to her.

"I can't tell you how helpful this is," she says. "The whole neighborhood claims to be helping me, but no one's given me a thing I can hold on to. It's taking everything in me to wait for the police, but I know my niece needs me strong."

At the front door, she leans in to embrace me. Then she pushes a five-rand coin into my hand and tells me where to catch a taxi.

December 5, 1999

I went along on the trips Tata had to take to East London to purchase the second-hand school supplies he said were priced for a household like ours. Even though I was at boarding school on scholarship, Tata felt we could save on the supplies and use whatever we had left on ourselves.

He'd developed a taste for rich meals. He told me he'd grown up under a cloud of malnutrition that descended over their village like a fog in winter, drifting from one household to the next with the ease of smoke. He liked curried chicken, eisbein, and battered hake the most. I never felt the need to object when he sat us down at tables that were priced beyond us—unlike my school supplies—although I seldom felt like eating.

Tata and I often sat in silence as he ate. When we spoke, it was about the headlines on the different broadsheets he ferried back to our tables. The rest of the time, we were quiet until we had to go home. Often it felt like we were being powered by a malfunctioning motor, one we couldn't switch off and had long acquiesced to.

RTR: 021 / Date of Recollection: 06.07–15.2002 / 1 min

The year's 2065 and we live on an invaded planet. The world's remaining human settlements lie barricaded with dense force-fields that keep out Phantoms, an alien species that feeds off the connection humans have with the Earth. It's a two-hour battle, and it doesn't feel that implausible. Part and Litha and I walk out of the cinema.

It's been a week since I did the interviews, which gave us no leads except for the acid, which also led nowhere. Litha asked some friends who used about the pentagram, but they'd never seen one on a cap.

The news cycle has also moved on from the girls, with the memos now filling up the waste-paper baskets at school. There hasn't been a missing person's report on Kiran, but the school's de-registered him, Ms Isaacs told me.

I spend the week waiting to hear from Marianne. Or from Devon. I search for them on a laptop at school, but the internet doesn't help. The number I called them on doesn't work, either.

Doris comes home later each evening. I open the gate for her, and then the two of us retreat to our rooms again. Later, I hear her stirring in her bathroom and the kitchen. It's starting to feel like the two of us no longer share a house, which we never discuss.

I look at the tab of acid, pushing it back and forth on the table edge with my middle finger. Unable to concentrate on my homework, I go to the kitchen and heat the plate she left out. It's samp with squash and creamed spinach. I eat as much as I can, then wash both of our plates and the pots and leave them to air on the dishrack.

When I return to my room, there's a text message from Lungile.

December 7, 1999

That evening, when Mama came back from work, I told her about Mr Govender and the Captain Crimestop number. She wasn't convinced, but she also hesitated, which was unusual for her. I showed her the page with the sums and we did a few more. Then she drew me into an embrace.

"It took long enough," she said. "I apologize for being harsh. I knew you were my daughter, but this exceeds all my expectations. It took longer, that's all."

I asked her what did.

"To tune the dial."

RTR: 022 / Date of Recollection: 06.15.2002 / 7 min

The text on my phone reads: *Tomorrow. 10:30 p.m.* I show it to Part the next morning. It's a Saturday, and the three of us are hanging out at the town square in oversized t-shirts, having volunteered for the Marathon for Computers. It's peasant work, I know, but the money doesn't hurt, we decide. Litha's setting up a desk with paper cups for water, while Part and I prepare plastic bags for trash. It's still morning, but the sun's hot. Lerato and her mom haven't shown up like she said they would. I hand Part the phone.

"This is tonight?" she asks.

Litha sighs. "I'm not sure about this."

"There's no other lead."

"That's true, but it's a bad crowd."

"I know. I wanted to ask Lerato about him, but she hasn't pitched."

"Fine, but call me if anything goes wrong."

Part and I nod.

Half an hour before the party, the lip gloss I have on starts going hard. It's raspberry, close to expiring, and I decide to wash it off before I leave the house. I unlatch our gate without making it creak and walk down the block, where Litha's picking me up.

He parks in front of Part's house and I sit on the pavement and send her a text to meet us outside. The light goes off in her room and then she's standing in front of me at the gate.

"Help me over," she says.

"I don't think I'm strong enough."

"Take my hand."

In the car, Part stretches out on the back seat: she's in a tie-dye t-shirt with denim shorts. I'm in the same shorts, with a red halter top.

Litha starts up Kaffrarian Heights. "I'm not sure about this," he repeats, idling the car a block from Lungile's house. "If Lungile gives you pills, they're probably roofies," he says. "Keep them under your tongue, but not for too long. Then spit them out."

Part and I nod. Then we get out and walk the block to Lungile's house. I nod and smile at five girls standing at the intercom. The gate creaks open and we all walk inside, up a gravel driveway. The other girls walk ahead of us; Part and I follow in silence. Hearing the bass thump, I scan the lawn as we approach the Roman columns that stand past the tiered water fountain in the center.

I feel for the tab of acid in my handbag.

Then the door opens, letting out light. There's a chandelier hanging in the lobby, and beyond it a large marbled living room with people sitting and drinking on Persian rugs. A spiral staircase leads up to the left, and next to that, a large open-plan kitchen.

"Newcomers," a voice laughs.

I turn and Lungile walks down the spiral staircase. I can tell it's him from how he's grinning—arms spread out, feet in slippers, no shirt on. The girls in front of us disappear into the kitchen, while Part and I wait.

"I'm glad you came." Lungile takes a sip from his tumbler. He's heavy-set and flatfooted, but not as repulsive as I'd thought. "Everyone's in the lounge," he says. "I'll bring the drinks."

Part and I cross into the living room, where we find a group gathered smoking and drinking around a low table. Two packs of cigarettes lie on the table, filters and menthols; a joint does the rounds. Part and I let it pass. Then Lungile returns with our drinks. After nursing my tumbler for a while, I push it to the center of the table and ask if Lungile has pills.

"Pills?".

"X."

Laughter. Then one of his friends, in a trucker cap with a shadow cast over his brow, leans forward and grins. "I do." He takes out a baggie of pills and drops it next to his drink. "The high isn't free, though," he adds, and the table laughs.

I look at him, gauging his seriousness. Then I tie my braids back and walk around the table, sit on his lap, open the baggie and take out two pills. I kiss him—it takes forever, and he uses his tongue—then get up and go back to Part, handing her a pill and putting the second one in my mouth. There's a moment of silence, and then Lungile starts clapping and everyone cheers.

Part signals that she needs to piss and we go to the bathroom, where we spit the pills out in the toilet bowl. Then we walk to the kitchen and pour our own drinks. When we return to the living room, Lungile looks even more stoned.

"Can you feel the pills?" he asks.

"It's starting to have an effect," I lie, and he smiles.

"Let's go to the pool, before the place fills up. It's a house tradition."

The others laugh and get up.

I tell Part to go ahead without me. "Tell them I'm on the phone."

At the top of the spiral staircase, I go through four large bedrooms, two of them vacant, before I find Lungile's. I close the door behind me and walk to the desk at the other end. There's a window next to it, and I push my forehead against it to look down into the back yard. Everyone has their tops off, legs dipped in the water. I leave the light off and use my phone screen to look through his desk. There's nothing there. In his wardrobe, I feel through his clothes. I can hear them laughing outside. Deodorant, condoms, a tennis racket. I sit on his bed for a moment, thinking, then I hold my breath and look under it. Nothing there either.

I lift his mattress and find copies of *Hustler*, *Mayfair*, and a few other magazines without covers, and then I see an exercise book. I take it with me to the desk.

Outside, everyone's in their underwear, splashing in the pool. I hover my phone over the book and start paging. It flips to the middle, where there's a piece of cardboard stuck between the pages. I pull it out and realize it's a sheet of acid, divided into small squares with pentagrams printed on them. There's a number written on the page below it, and next to it: *Lucy Ferlain. 146 6th Avenue, Gonubie.*

I save the details on my phone. Then I go back to the window and call Part's phone, but she's in the pool, her handbag on the grass. Lungile swims up to her and strokes her hair. I send a text to Litha to pick us up.

Downstairs again, I walk through the sliding door and see two couples making out on the grass. Lungile has his head between Part's thighs. I walk up to her and kiss her neck, and then her mouth. Lungile looks up and I ask him where to get more X.

"It's all on the table. Bring it with, when you come back."

"I need to piss," Part says.

"Do it here. I don't mind."

"No."

"I'm serious," Lungile grins, but Part gets up, pulling his hand off her thigh.

I watch Part towel off and get dressed in the bathroom on the first floor. Down in the entrance hall, she finds the intercom button and presses it. Then we dash across the yard and get through the gate just as it shuts.

Litha flashes his headlights from down the block and we run toward the car.

"Are you okay?" he asks us as we climb inside.

"We're fine."

"Did you get anything?"

"I don't know."

"Nothing solid?"

"There's a number." I feel my heart slowing down again. "Also a name. Lucy Ferlain. Does that mean anything to you?"

Litha shakes his head, and then we're quiet as the car weaves through the dark, leaving Kaffrarian Heights behind.

I get to bed without Doris noticing.

Then I see the machine again: an upright triangle that splits into two.

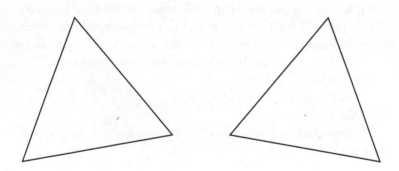

December 9, 1999

Mama never explained the dial to me. Each time I asked her about it, she acted like nothing had happened that afternoon. In the end, anticipating the precise moments at which she'd wave me away, I stopped asking.

I shelved the math exercise book.

Our closeness dissipated with it.

Mama and I retreated into ourselves again, as was our habit, padding the distance between us with small talk and different rooms. I spent most of our dinners in front of the TV with Tata.

Later, I'd recognize this as the start of what he called her Demonstrations, or protests—seeing as her life was so difficult in comparison to other people's, Tata would hiss, both of us unashamed of talking about her behind her back.

I wait for Doris to leave for church this morning. Then I get up, shower, make cereal, and take my phone to the living room couch. I slot in *Where Have All the People Gone?* and look for a text from Lungile, but I'm relieved to see there's nothing. Then Litha calls.

"I'm at work," he says, "but I've figured it out. The name's a code."

"It is?"

"Lucy Ferlain's code for Lucifer Lane."

"I've never heard of it."

"I had to do a bit of digging. Turns out Tom knows about it. He heard about it in high school. There was a kid from East London, a user named Rory. He missed class a lot and liked playing glassy-glassy. That's what he told people when they asked him how he got high. That he got loaded in Lucifer Lane. He drowned in 12th grade, high at Gonubie Beach. His school held a memorial."

"Does it check out?"

"I think so. I mean, the story holds up. Tom says Lucifer Lane's still up and running. If you ask any user or chancer with a stash where the source is, that's what always comes up. There's rumors that the drugs come from campus hippies at East London Tech, with connections to Cape Town, though no one knows where Lucifer Lane is."

"Except Lungile."

"Except Lungile. My theory's that he was fine with not knowing, too, and just buying through a middleman—until the girls, that is, and Luciano's OD. Now the information might be a bargaining tool, in case the cops get involved."

Litha considers this. "It's worth a shot, then, to call the number. I think Lungile wasn't living up to his part of the deal, either. He was burning through the caps, using them on his parties."

"I was hoping you wouldn't talk about calling."

"I have to."

"Let me do it."

"I'll be fine."

"That better be true."

I walk back to the kitchen and take my time rinsing my bowl. Then I sit back down in the living room and watch *Where Have All the People Gone?* for half an hour, before I turn the volume down and make the call, still not calm. It rings for a while before a man's voice picks up.

"How did you get this number?"

"It doesn't matter."

"It does to me."

"Not as much as what I know."

"Is that so?"

"I know about Lucifer Lane."

There's silence. Then a sigh. "I don't know what you're talking about," the voice says.

I try a different tack. "I know who's skimming off the top with the caps."

More silence. Then: "I might care if that's attached to a name. Tell me what you want."

"Not much—a few answers and I'll lose this number."

"This might be dangerous for you. Have you thought about that?"

"I don't mind."

"Then go ahead."

"The name's Kiran."

"Unfamiliar."

"That's hard to believe."

Then the voice laughs. "I might've caught a rumor or two, but who hasn't?"

"Right. Here's how this works. Three missing girls and an OD: all found with pentagrams on site. That, coupled with 146 6th Avenue, Gonubie, might be of interest to the police."

The silence stretches for longer this time. "Tell me what you want."

"Let's start with Kiran."

"Fine. I might've heard he wanted to deal in King and I might've said no."

"Is that all?"

"That's all. It wasn't serious. I didn't think he was a good fit."

On the TV screen, a bald man hijacks a family, leaving them stranded in the wilderness as he drives to LA to rescue his wife and daughter.

"This conversation never happened," I tell him.

"Tell me how you got this number."

"No." I know he wants me to give up Lungile, but the thought of helping either one of them repulses me. I hang up.

Taking my sketchbook, I sit in the living room, recording what I've seen of the machine. Then I lie on the couch, flipping through the channels. Two hours later, my aunt hoots, and I get up to press the gate button to let her in. Through the window, I see my uncle waiting for her next to our gate. I can tell he's been drinking. He follows her in.

I go back to the living room. It's not long before I hear Doris shouting. "Dumisani, don't make me throw you out of my house. If you want to kill yourself, then that's your business. You're a grown man. It has nothing to do with me."

"I'm asking for a loan, that's all."

"To do what with?"

"Things have been difficult. I need to renew my license before I can find work."

"I don't have time for this. I come back from church and find you hanging on my gate, unwashed, stinking of liquor, and you say you want me to help?"

My uncle apologizes.

"Leave, or take a seat and wait for lunch. There'll be no money, but you can eat."

Moments later, he drops his weight on the couch next to mine. My eyes are closed, but like Doris, I can smell him. His breathing is labored, pushing out a cloud of beer.

I remember learning about my uncle's scar.

The weather had been hard to predict that summer—wetter and cooler than we'd expected. Bhut' Dumisani drove us to meet my aunt at a bus station in East London. Doris was on her way back from a meeting in Pretoria. It was cold out, and my uncle was mired in a hangover, his movements as slow as the ocean current. He'd left the radio on *Umhlobo Wenene*, and as the Xhosa news droned, I could make out the Indian ocean, green and wrinkled below a blanket of rolling mist, emerging from the polluted esplanade down the block.

At the Windmill Roadhouse, we found a table by the rear window where we could wait for Doris to dock. Pulling a white lighter and a pack of Peter Stuyvesants from his coat, my uncle turned to me and smiled. His eyes were puckered, his skin giving off beer. I tried to return the gesture for him, but I couldn't convince either of us.

"How's school?"

"It's fine."

I turned back to the window while he reclined in his seat.

"Everything's different for young people these days, isn't it?"

It wasn't a question. I shifted on the bench. "That's what my dad used to say."

"He was right."

"He also used to say things hadn't changed."

"He was right there, too. That's how Lumkile was."

The waiter arrived to take our drink orders. We settled on Cokes. Then he sighed. "There was a time when none of us could imagine this," he said. "Moving to town. Everything was different, back then. It was clear we weren't welcome."

I nodded.

"We didn't listen, though, we still went out to town, but it was nothing like what people had in the cities. There were places like eGoli, where a man could get a taste of what was out there, but that wasn't for us here in the homelands—we had eDikeni, eMthatha."

I reminded him that Dad had gone to college close to Alice.

"I know. Lumkile was much too serious for all the foolishness that went on there, too. Most of the men I knew weren't half as wise or fortunate."

I hadn't noticed when the waiter brought our drinks. I stirred the ice cubes in my glass while he watched me. I didn't like it when people did that.

"How's everything else?" he said.

"Fine."

The skin on his forehead looked like it had been cleaved down the middle, a faint, light scar almost dipping between his eyebrows. I asked him about it.

"I don't think you want to hear that."

"I do."

My uncle shook his head and shifted toward his Coke. There was a curved line of sweat dotting his scar. Then he sat back again. "Do they teach you about that at school? The history of our people?"

I shook my head.

"Maybe it's for the best. I don't know if it would be the truth."

"I don't, either."

My uncle laughed. "I've always thought you were too sharp."

"Then tell me about the scar."

"Impatient, too. Is that how to talk to elders?

"I don't know."

Then he sighed and placed his lighter back on the table. "I was a thief," he said. "I didn't have the schooling your parents had, before I joined Umkhonto we Sizwe. I didn't have their options." My uncle's eyes settled on his fingers, the box of cigarettes rotating between them. "I'd heard of Mandela's soldiers, of course, most of us had, but to hear was one thing and to join another." He leaned forward and took another sip. "I hadn't felt alive, before then. It's difficult to explain, but our lives meant little to the world. I'd seen it with my parents. I had to leave school in Form 2 after my father contracted arthritis and couldn't lift hoe or hammer. It might've been his helplessness that hurried him on. Then my mother followed from her grief, and I was left with their plot."

I waited for him to go on.

"I did all right for a while. I worked the land, like we all did. I had neighbors who offered me their help, but things began to change when my father's other family came for what they felt was theirs. Each day, they had a habit of gathering around the fire and picking at whatever was left of him. His corpse hadn't even gone to soil, yet. I tried to make it work with them. I didn't know what else to do, but the bickering got worse. The woman, who'd known my father for decades, always seemed to run out of food as soon as I returned with the cattle in the evening. I'd ask for samp, taking in the scent of whatever had been hidden. There were four other children who'd arrived with them. I was told to take the eldest son with me whenever I put the animals out to pasture. The two of us got along, and when he began to smuggle half of his meals for me, the father found out and beat him."

The waiter returned and asked us if we wanted to order food. My uncle declined, then turned to me with an apology. "Have what you want," he said.

"I'm full."

"You sure?"

He waited for the waiter to leave before he went on. "He beat me, too. Not once, either. The man made a habit of it. I took to hunting with the other boys as the cattle grazed. From gardens, we took potatoes, from the fields, we took corn, and from the trees, we took sparrows and blackberries. I started spending more time outside. I'd drive the cows back in, then fasten the gate to the kraal and leave."

"To go where?"

"I didn't know, at first. I walked until I couldn't anymore. The homestead sat on a hill that dropped down in a soft slope, then met another hill, which was steeper and yielded a view of the whole village. I ran up it and down again. I did that until I dropped, the clean air scouring a path through my chest. Then, one day, as I was heading back, I saw smoke from a fire in the foothills. I'd heard of a group of guys who'd set up huts there, living on their own, free from the laws of the village. I saw one of them walk out of a low thatched doorway. I stood there and watched him stretch, and when he turned to me, I greeted him. He told me he'd seen me before, and I told him I'd seen him too. The village was small enough.

"It turned out our fathers had known each other. He held out a zol and I took it from him and smoked. Then he led me inside the hut, where the heat set to work relaxing my muscles, even though the smoke from the fire scratched me raw inside. I held in a cough. I greeted the other two who were in there, though both of them were suspicious of me. Then I sat around the fire with them and we smoked and talked until the sun came up. We shared a pot of umfino and pap. And I was getting up to leave when Luvuyo, the one who'd called me in, began to talk in a voice that made all of us turn. He was leaning against the hut wall, releasing smoke through his nose, his eyes narrowed and his gaze searching. He told us he was joining Mandela's soldiers. That he was leaving our village."

The sound of a bus coming to a stop on Moore Street broke his recollection. We both turned to look out the window, but it wasn't Doris's bus.

He went on. "It was the first time I'd heard of anyone joining MK. Most of us knew about what was happening in the country, but it never reached us. We were villagers—there were no Europeans where we lived."

I nodded.

Then he reminded me of how in 1960, protestors had been shot by Europeans at a police station in Sharpeville—and when they'd turned to flee, they'd been shot in the back.

I'd seen the documentaries. I couldn't tell if my uncle believed I didn't know about these things, or if he just wanted to hear them in his own voice.

"They wanted to be able to walk the land without restriction," he said. "That's when Mandela had also had his fill. He decided that our side needed soldiers, too."

My uncle told me that he'd followed Luvuyo and they'd joined a camp, hiding out close to the Namibian border. They were ambushed a month later, and he received his scar falling over as he fled from his friend's side. Luvuyo was killed in the fracas.

I remember Bhut' Dumisani falling quiet then, and scratching his scar.

A few minutes pass before he speaks. "Is that a history project?" he asks.

I open my eyes and find him pointing at the sketchbook. His face looks fleshier than it did last week, with a new scar next to his left ear. I follow his finger to my drawing of the machine. I shake my head. "It's not a history project."

"Look." I watch him get on his knees and pick up my pencil,

drawing a circle between all the triangles on the page. Then he makes the lines bolder, until the drawing leaps out. "How about now?"

I shake my head and he laughs. "That's as it should be. Myself, I can't forget. That's the badge of the Ciskei Police Force. The people I fought against for you and Doris."

I shrug and lie back again—then I sit up, remembering Thoko's photograph. I thank my uncle and I walk out of the living room to call Litha.

My chest feels clogged when he picks up. "It's all real," I tell him, reminding myself to breathe. "I'm coming down to the shop."

First, I make a stop at Doris's car.

Litha's standing on the pavement outside Mr Movie. "Tom knocked off five minutes ago," he tells me, stubbing out his cigarette, "and I can't leave the desk."

"It doesn't matter."

I follow him inside, take out the sketchbook and turn to my uncle's drawing. "I need the internet for this."

"No problem. The connection's slow, but it's up and running."

"My uncle says this is the emblem of the Ciskei Police. I need you to search for it for me."

"That shouldn't be hard. Here." Litha swivels the monitor to show me. I nod. "I'll print it out," he says, and disappears into the room behind the counter, where I hear the machine whirring. He returns with the printout.

"I have to go now, but I'll explain later," I say. "I think this is it."

I start running. Pulling on my hoodie, I shift from tarmac to gravel, to soil, as I cut across to Beacon Hill. I don't notice I'm out of breath until I see the house on the corner and climb the steps. I knock twice and hear shuffling behind the door. Then Thoko opens it.

"I wasn't expecting this." she says.

"I wasn't either. I won't be long."

"Hold on a moment."

The door closes again and I scan the neighborhood behind me. The street's vacant, looking leached in the afternoon light. In the distance, I see a pall of smoke rising from the new textile factory, reminding me of Dad. I turn back as the door opens.

"I'm alone again," she sighs, "and I haven't cooked. I still have some of the money left."

I follow her in. "I wish I had more for you."

"That's not a problem. I'm grateful for what I have. Let's have tea."

I take a seat on the couch. While Thoko boils water in the kitchen, I stare at the photo on the wall unit, pushing my backpack between my ankles.

"Did we forget something?" she asks, setting the tea tray down on the coffee table.

"No, it's not that." I reach for the cup. "My article's missing an important angle, that's all. There isn't enough about the parents."

Thoko crosses her legs. I take out the printout Litha gave me, and see her stiffen. "Do you know what this is?"

She squints at it. "It looks like a police badge."

I glance at the room next to the kitchen. "During apartheid, both of my parents were collaborators," I tell her. "They worked for the Homeland Government, although none of us talked about it. Then, in 1994, my mom went missing, and I've always wondered if that was the reason."

Thoko doesn't respond.

"I've never stopped thinking about it," I tell her, looking down at the emblem. Then I reach into my backpack and take out the old copy of *The Daily Dispatch* I got from my aunt's car and spread it out. "I think this is all of that coming back."

"I'm not following."

"I saw it in your photograph," I said. "My uncle was in the struggle, too, but he wasn't arrested. He talked about the badge this afternoon, and it reminded me of that picture." I point to it, standing on the shelf above the TV. "I remembered how you said the man who lives here, the one in the photo, had just come back, and that he would've been enemies with Nolitha's father. That got me thinking. Two weeks ago, I found this in my aunt's car. It's an article about the political prisoners who were released last month. I remembered it after speaking to my uncle; I wondered if the man in the photograph might have reason to do Nolitha harm, because of her father's actions."

"That still doesn't explain it."

"It was a gamble," I admit. "I thought I'd show up with the emblem and if it meant nothing to you then that would be that, but then I saw your face and kept going."

"If my man was a member of Umkhonto we Sizwe, then so what? Lots of people were."

"Then he'd be a member tied to a missing girl—and a recent inmate. Their dates overlap, too. His release and her abduction. It could mean everything or nothing." I realize that it doesn't make much sense without the machine, but I leave it at that.

"Then there was no article for the school magazine?" she asks.

I shake my head.

"Then what's all this for?"

"My mom."

"I still don't understand."

"I don't expect you to."

Thoko nods and takes my cup to the kitchen to rinse it. "Even though I don't understand this, I want it to end," she sighs. Her hands cup her face, and she closes her eyes. "That isn't all of it. Nolitha's father isn't alive. He was an awful man who deserved to die in prison."

Then Thoko walks back to the living room and settles down across from me. "It wasn't meant to be this bad," she says, and I'm about to get up and walk to her, when I see a man standing behind her—the door next to the kitchen ajar.

December 10, 1999

It wasn't that noticeable at first. Mama would arrive late from work and walk past us, going to bed without stopping to eat. We didn't think much of it; we learned to adapt.

I liked the time I spent with Tata, and even got to help him cook. He taught me recipes from his childhood, extolling the virtue of their low cost and the significance of their origins, using each meal to teach me how being modest never stole from value. But Mama left Tata's plates cold, sitting untouched on our kitchen counter. Eventually, when he broke down and asked her if she wanted to die, Mama just mumbled, "I'm full," and went to bed.

The man leans against the door frame. He doesn't look that different from the photo: mid-30s; hair trimmed but beard unkempt. He introduces himself to me as Lwanda, offering me his hand.

"I was listening from the other side of that door," he says, "but now it's my turn to speak." Letting go of my hand, Lwanda takes a seat next to Thoko and puts his arms around her. "This wasn't her doing," he sighs. "If there's someone to blame, it's me. I talked her into it."

"I don't understand."

"I never wanted to hurt Nolitha, but this is what was in front of us, unpleasant as it is."

"Is she hurt, now?"

"No."

"Then what?"

"Then nothing," he sighs. Thoko's hanging her head, and he rubs her back gently. "The plan was to keep them for a small amount of time, that's all."

"Then they're safe?"

"They were, but now I don't know. I haven't been able to sleep, knowing it was a mistake. None of us have been paid, and my comrades are getting frustrated. I fear for those girls."

"Somebody hired you?"

Lwanda nods. "The three of us. He said it would be the children of traitors, men responsible for adding a decade to our sentences. I didn't expect I'd know one of the daughters." He looks at Thoko before going on. "He promised us things, of course: social housing, cash, to be first in line for veteran benefits. Leaving prison is another sentence. We have nothing to our names."

I think again about my uncle. Then I ask him who the man was who hired him.

"He works for the Office of the Premier. His name's MC Mbusi."

"Do you know what he wants?"

"Pass me that paper." He turns to the article about the premier. "I read this when I was putting it all together," he says. "I contacted a friend in government to confirm my suspicion: Mbusi wanted to use us to embarrass the Justice Ministry for denying the premier's office credit for our release."

"The political prisoners?"

Lwanda nods. "He promised us there'd be no jail time, that we wouldn't be caught, but that it was important for us to make it clear the kidnappers were members of Umkhonto we Sizwe— and on the list of pardoned inmates."

"How would you do that?"

"With planted evidence. Manifestos and ransom notes with a political flavor. The history of collaboration in the families. It was all planned. Mbusi wanted us to wait before releasing all that, though. First he wanted to launch a search for the girls, to make him look like a hero, and ultimately boost the premier's chances of being elected deputy president in December." He glances at Thoko, who's still staring at the floor. "I know what we look like. Nolitha's my woman's niece. It hasn't been easy to see ourselves like this; but the way things are, we weren't released into a world where our ideals could hold. Like I said, we have nothing."

I lean forward. "Do you think the premier knows?"

"No. Mbusi wants him in his pocket without him realizing at first. That's my guess. He's working alone, for now, and because of that, I think I can still stop him."

"How?"

"I have to go over my comrades' heads, which isn't easy. I haven't been able to persuade them. I didn't know what to do about it, until now, when you came here, and now I see there's no other way. Even brotherhood isn't above what's right."

Lwanda releases Thoko and gets up. "I'm getting a few men to help," he says. "I also think you've done enough, now, and should go home."

I'm packing the emblem back in my backpack when Thoko speaks. "I know what you're thinking," she says. "How could I do this to my own niece and still take your money? I've known Lwanda since we were children, and we are small people who come from even smaller people. There's never been much on offer for us. Nolitha will understand."

Lwanda looks away. Thoko leads me to the door and shuts it without facing me.

I hear about it on the news, the big search for the girls Lwanda was talking about. My aunt and I are eating dinner in the living room, together for once. Doris raises the volume.

I see MC Mbusi on the screen, standing behind a podium. "It is out of great concern that we have decided to intervene in this case," he tells the crowd, before a surge of applause.

Lwanda was right, but it seems he didn't know how far along the campaign was. I feel cold. Then I get up and do the dishes, standing over the basin until Doris goes to sleep. I haven't told Litha and Part yet.

December 11, 1999

Ever since renewing a second contract at work, she'd wanted to enroll part-time for a bachelor's degree in Education. It wasn't unusual to find her poring over the application material at the kitchen table. The previous month, Mama had asked me if I thought she could teach at my school and I'd said no. The two of us had laughed, and I'd sat down and looked at the pamphlets with her. Tata walked in and planted a kiss on her forehead. He told her she was aiming low, wanting to teach high school, and that she'd be better suited to a professorship. Mama had laughed, pushing him off her shoulders. "Professorship? For a girl from Zeleni? Please don't insult me."

"The matron's done a lot for herself."

"The matron is the matron," she said.

"That's true. I can't argue with that."

My parents always got along at the end of the work week, and I could happily spend hours with them before going to find a children's book magazine or turn on the TV. But now even that changed. Mama still pored over the application booklets, but she took them out into our yard, where she sat with them on her lap for hours, coming back inside to prepare dinner only when the sun dipped low enough for the breeze to bite her skin.

RTR: 025 / Date of Recollection: 06.17.2002 / 2.5 min

On Monday, I wake up to news of the girls being found. Doris opens the door to my room at 8, and comes to sit on my bed with the newspaper.

"They found them a little malnourished, but unharmed," she says. "There were no arrests. It's strange. How they were found makes even sense less than how they went missing. According to the girls, the men who rescued them were wearing balaclavas and knew where to look. Each girl was blindfolded and then taken home."

"Really?"

Doris nods. "I'm happy for their families, though, and that those men exist. It's good to feel there's a little hope left in this place."

Then she gets up and tells me she's made porridge. I follow her into the kitchen and we eat together.

"Is it true that the machine showed you an emblem that helped you find them?" Part asks me when I meet her and Litha at the park later.

"I had to wait for my uncle to point it out, though. I think that's what the triangles were all along. I was being guided to Beacon Hill."

"Then you met one of the kidnappers?"

"He was also one of the men who rescued the girls. I think I pushed him over to the other side." Then I explain the rest of it. It takes me a while, but I cover it.

"How about Kiran and Lucifer Lane?" Litha asks.

"Lucifer Lane was a dead end. They didn't know where he was."

"I see," Litha says, leaning back into the alcove.

In the silence that follows, nobody mentions my mom.

December 12, 1999

I remember finding Mama sitting upright one afternoon, her eyes closed and her lips moving as she nursed a pamphlet between her fingers. It was a Saturday, and she sat like that for 15 minutes. The following morning, she stopped talking.

Mama responded to us with head gestures, after that, and did what she felt needed doing around the house, but she never spoke. Her movements grew more languid, too. It was then that I realized she'd become untethered from us.

Tata's aggravation shifted into panic. He just watched her, at first. Then he tried using humor, lancing her with conspiratorial smiles across the room, but Mama never responded and he tired. His face dropped. He lugged his bedding to the couch in the living room.

"It's difficult to be in the same room as a ghost," he said, staring at the TV. "It's almost as if she's upped and left us. I don't know what I'm expected to do here."

I didn't, either.

RTR: 026 / Date of Recollection: 06.17.2002 / 0.5 min

I wake up in a forest, unable to breathe, under a sky that's not clear, but white. I watch it as it blinks black, switching off; then the trees and the clouds return, and the machine appears, hovering over me. The trees continue to grow until their branches knit a half-mile above me, and I make out the faint outline of a figure swimming inside the machine. It increases in size, becoming distinct, as if approaching from a distance, until it fills the shape. I realize it's myself that I'm looking at. The swimming turns into climbing, and I feel soil packing under my fingernails. The machine flickers, then grows more vivid than I've ever seen it. Then it shatters into splinters, disappearing with a whine, and I find myself crouching on all fours on the side of a hill. A siren goes off, and I get up and run to the top of the hill, where I stand looking down at a cliff-side road as a speeding black van rounds the bend, heading toward a timber truck; just before the moment of collision, a springbok looks up at me from across the road, emitting static, and I slip backward, stumbling into an ocean current, getting caught in the undertow, waking up, again, to a blank ceiling.

December 14, 1999

In the end, Mama's Demonstrations left as abruptly as they'd arrived. Tata and I still didn't understand what had happened, but it gave me relief to watch our household recover. Tata collapsed his fort in the living room and ferried his bedding back to their room. He and I no longer ate our dinner in front of the world's unending blur of marches and murders.

Instead, we spoke.

Mama regaled us with anecdotes from work, and Tata took to acting out what he saw each week at the office, miming the actions of his superiors and subordinates alike. Listening to each word, Mama would throw her head back and laugh. For my part, I no longer parsed large numbers in exercise books, inviting the attention of substitute teachers.

"Learn to look at it from the other side," she said one evening, when Tata came back from work in low spirits—unable to mine the humor in a recent row with a superior.

"How?"

"Look at all we have," she said, smiling. "The three of us can touch it, for now, but it won't always be here."

I didn't understand, but when I turned around and looked at Tata, he was collapsed into his chair with his chin hung against his chest. The kitchen grew silent, and then his shoulders began to shake, convulsing in place, and he looked up at her in tears.

The silence deepened, and I wondered what currents were passing between my parents; thinking, as I had been since the end of her Demonstrations, that they'd been born with languages I would never speak.

• • •

That night, Mama, Tata and I linked hands around the kitchen table, and following Tata's lead, we danced around it until our dinner went cold. His eyes were still wet, but the tears had dried on his beard and fingertips, and I couldn't stop watching the two of them, our hands still linked when we sat down to spoonfuls of cold samp.

RTR: 027 / Date of Recollection: 06.18.2002 / 1 min

This morning at school, we get told in assembly that the missing girls have been found. It's Mrs Robinson who gives the announcement, and she tells us it isn't a license to forgo caution. Kiran's still missing, but no one seems to care under the noise of the girls being found. The school's covering its tracks, I figure, and most of the students don't notice.

Afterward, when I meet Litha and Part to walk home together, I explain that the machine's gone.

"It's over. I felt it leave after the dream. Maybe it was always about the girls and not my mom."

"Don't give up hope," Litha says. "There's still Stanfel in East London."

"Right." I think about it for a moment. "I still have money left, too, and the address."

"Exactly. Maybe we can explain everything and ask him about those articles. His clippings were laid out in a pattern that involved the girls, but I think it's much bigger than them. Those other disappearances, for example, including Kiran's and your mom's." Litha pauses. "I think we can still find her."

"You don't have to try and make me feel better."

He shakes his head. "No, I mean it. I think we can find her. Let's do it on the weekend."

December 16, 1999

I thought we'd never change how we were. After Mama came back to us, our habits remained the same. For instance, I once watched Mama finish a crossword puzzle when she thought no one was around to see her. She did it backward, like she always used to—starting with the last letter and filling each row and column in a single go.

Tata was out drinking at a friend's house in Phakamisa, and I'd come back home to collect coins I'd seen in a pocket of his jeans in the hamper. I stood at the kitchen door watching Mama. I wondered if she'd look up, but she didn't. She just sat at the table, staring at the crossword. Then she sighed and picked up a pen. I was close enough to see her fill in the squares. When I opened the fridge door she started and looked up, covering the page with both hands.

"What's another word for hierarchy?" she said.

"Ladder."

Mama nodded. "Not pyramid?"

"I don't know."

"Don't be indolent," she said, closing the magazine. "It's unbecoming."

"I'm not being indolent. I don't like puzzles—you do."

Her brow creased and I waited for the worst, but then Mama smiled.

"My beautiful child," she said.

I hadn't expected that.

RTR: 028 / Date of Recollection: 06.22.2002 / 3 min

On Saturday, Litha gets us bus tickets to East London. It's an early trip: we meet at the station just after 12, waiting on a steel bench as the bus docks. Forty-five minutes later, I look up from my watch as our coach enters East London and turns into Moore Street.

Litha's the last to wake up. I pull on his arm and tell him we're here, and he opens his eyes and nods. We join the line down the center aisle, waiting to get off.

"It's three blocks south of here," Litha says, closing his map.

The house in Jameson Street has a line of cars parked outside, a pillared porch half-hidden behind the garden shrubs, and a small iron gate. As we approach, we see two old women on the porch, balancing teacups on porcelain saucers, both dressed in black and seated on backless wooden chairs. The woman on the left looks up at us, tilting her head. I tell her we're here to see Mr Petrović.

"Stanfel?"

"Yes, ma'am."

"Please, inside," she says. Her accent is thick, but I can't place it.

Part, Litha and I follow her down a short corridor to the sitting room, which is crowded with more people dressed in black and holding drinks. Which is also when I see the coffin and realize we're at a wake.

That Stanfel is dead.

"I'm so sorry," I say. I turn to Part and Litha: "We should leave.'

But the old woman shakes her head. "No, please. Don't go. Stay. Have drink. Eat."

Before we can reply, she leads us to a small, sun-washed kitchen and hands us each a beer. "My brother come here to East London and think this big opportunity for better life. He leave Johannesburg with us, wanting to be fisherman," she laughs. "He is carpenter, before, in Europe, before war. He live in small town, like me. Not having a lot, like most of the family, but not missing something, either."

I take a sip from the beer, feeling it cool me as it courses down.

"You are neighbors of Stanfel?" she asks, and I nod. She smiles. "Stanfel has big heart for everybody. It is over, now, but he has peace. He work hard at factory. He get nice house. He get nice neighbors." She sets a plate of cheese pastries on the table. "I am Petra," she smiles. "I must go, now."

We thank her, and she disappears into the sitting room. Then we take turns looking at Stanfel inside his casket. We thank Petra again and leave.

The next bus sits docked at the Windhill Roadhouse. We break into a trot when we see it, catching it just as the door shuts. The trip home feels longer than it is, and we spend most of it in silence. In King, we get off and walk up Albert Road, headed to the corner equidistant from our houses. We stand in silence for a moment.

Part sighs. "I suppose this is it then."

Litha looks up. "I think it was worth having a look."

I nod. "I think so, too."

Then we hug and say goodbye.

December 17, 1999

Before she disappeared, there were times when the frequencies emitted by Mama's Demonstrations would resurface—she wouldn't ignore us, but her behavior would grow erratic again. I thought of her actions as tools older women needed in order to keep themselves afloat. I wasn't sure if they worked. A friend accompanied her home from work, once, and put her to bed, explaining that Mama had intervened in a squabble between a lecturer and the student he was involved with. Not long after that, she pushed herself into the middle of a fight between a neighbor's wife and her husband, realizing only after the fact that the man was armed. Tata couldn't recall these afternoons without impatience; whatever admiration he felt was drowned in his disapproval of her recklessness.

He often thought she was dim and said as much; to which she'd respond that he was the same, but that wasn't the sum of who they were.

Mama went back to inquiring about me and school, and asking Tata about work, but in a different manner from before; her motivation had changed. Now it went beyond the duties of a mother and a wife, I thought, and was grounded in her desire to see us—me and Tata, the two people she'd chosen to spend her life watching.

She'd page through my exercise books, quipping that the curriculum was spoon-feeding a generation that was destined to inherit a country in ruins. The two of us would laugh, and then Mama would loosen her grip on me—a gesture I first experienced as abandonment, but would later interpret as inoculation, understanding the intensity with which she experienced her feelings. Sometimes, I'd ask her about her girlhood, and she'd tell me not much had changed. Then Mama would leave me, and I'd listen to the murmurs from their bedroom, which occasionally rose to the pitch of an argument, but not all the time. More often than not, it was laughter that escaped and tumbled down our corridor, pushing against our walls with as much might.

Two weeks pass. Part, Litha, and I spend most of them apart. Part's mom's condition worsens in the wintertime, as usual, trapping her and her sister in their house. Litha didn't leave a note before our trip to East London, and that gets him grounded in the flat on Alexandra.

For my part, I don't see the machine again, even though I still put the recorder out.

Maybe in memoriam.

Doris gets cleared in the investigation at work, and wins a promotion to keep her compliant—that's how she puts it to me. The raise helps her to get on a better medical plan and I use her benefits to see a new psychiatrist, a thin man who smiles at me and shakes his head when I tell him my previous diagnosis.

"Dysthymia? That's a quaint term. I'll be treating you for persistent depressive disorder."

He changes my drug regimen, adding a third medication.

"That's a mild antipsychotic," he explains, "for if the hallucinations return." He emphasizes the word *if.*

My aunt and I fill the prescription at a pharmacist in Vincent Park and drive home in silence. Later, I lie on my side and stare at the pill bottle until I fall asleep.

Hallucinations: I've started to believe that's what it was, the machine.

They don't return.

Other things happen. The lower half of the atlas starts to slide toward the winter solstice, and to keep distracted from thinking about the machine, I find an old notebook in the sitting

room and start writing letters to Mom, my final communication
with her.

Letter No. 1

Dear Nobomi,

Lerato still pretends to smoke cigarettes, even though she's
had a surgical procedure on her throat: a tonsillectomy, to be
exact. This afternoon, as the two of us walked down the corridor from math toward Huberta Square, she told me she was
leaving. Her dad's moving them to East London, and she'll go
to Clarendon.

I asked her if she was sure. I told her I'd miss her.

Me too, she said.

Then I helped her pack her locker. I gave her Dad's pencil
case.

Letter No. 2

Dear Nobomi,

I went to the Olympiad and it felt different without Kiran.
I admit that. I walked around the fields afterward, until a group
of seniors jeered at me from the clubhouse. I ignored them.
Later, waiting for the transport to take me back to King, I made
out with a boy named Lee. I didn't take his number, but I remember he was from Graff Reinet.

Letter No. 3

Dear Nobomi,

Monday morning arrived and Ms Isaacs called me down to her office. I found her moving a bookshelf. She told me that they'd heard from Kiran—his people got in trouble, but he's all right now. He's with his sister Jivinka. Apparently he's going to call me.

Then she asked me to tell her what I thought about her shelf. It's a shelf, I said, and she laughed. Then she showed me what was on it: a slip from the post office. Ms Isaacs had asked for a scholarship form from the University of Cape Town, even though I'm only doing 12th grade next year, and I had to go collect it. She reminded me to take my ID. I thanked her.

Before I left her office, she showed me the cartoon on her computer. I didn't get it—it was the same *Far Side* comic that she had before. She smiled and told me it was better than nothing, and that she wanted me to think about that.

I said I would.

Letter No. 4

Dear Nobomi,

I ran into Iris in the line at the post office. She was getting books delivered from the internet, because the people at her Grahamstown dorm keep losing her mail. It's a shitshow, she told me.

I told her about the scholarship and she nodded, telling me UCT's a good school.

She's having friends over from Rhodes for the weekend, and there's a party in Headlands on Friday. Iris said Part could bring her friends, too. She said she needed a break from helping out with their mom. Maybe you'll learn what it's like to be a varsity student, Iris said.

I thanked her and said I'd come.

Then I realized I'd forgotten my ID book.

Letter No. 5

Dear Nobomi,

Doris drove us to Pick 'n Pay tonight, and I helped her pick what we'd need for the week, while flipping through a *Time* magazine that I left behind in the chocolate aisle. It's the second week of the month, meaning most of her debit orders have been drawn, and it didn't take us long to head to the checkout. Even with her promotion, we still count out coins.

Then I heard someone say, "It's a runt. I'll only give you a five Rupees prize for that."

I turned around and saw Rohan grinning in the next checkout line over. His hair was cut short and his glasses were narrower than I remembered. I hid my surprise at seeing him.

He told me it was a quote from a game, The Legend of Zelda: Link's Awakening. Apparently he's got a new phone number, so he never got my text about the doctor's letter.

When we said goodbye, he told me he hoped I made it off Koholint Island. I hope you do too, I said.

Then Doris came back to the checkout with *The Daily Dispatch* and the bottle of amasi she almost forgot. I started offloading our groceries with the mielie-meal and the mince— our staples, and the two things Dad used to hate the most.

Letter No. 6

Dear Nobomi,

Doris ladled bowls of porridge from the mielie-meal she bought for us last night, and then she pushed the newspaper toward me. On the second page there was an article about Central, the school in Echovale, close to the edge of town:

School Head Faces Dismissal

Principal Robert Weir is the subject of an investigation after he raised tuition and made unapproved curriculum changes at Central Primary School.

Sources reveal that new curriculum was developed by a secretive team of renegade cognitive scientists, who now work in hiding after misappropriating a government grant.

"This is all very bizarre," said an anonymous staff member, who raised concerns with the Department of Education. "It's quite clear Robert is willing to make a profit at whatever cost. That, or he's insane."

Mr Weir, who holds a diploma in Operations Management from UNISA, says he plans to resign and found his own private college.

Doris said it all made more sense to her than these Model C schools, and that it was too bad it wasn't a high school.

Letter No. 7

Dear Nobomi,

Kiran called me after school. It took a moment for me to recognize his voice. That's how long it's been.

I told him I still had his MiniDisc recorder, and he laughed. Then I told him I'd spoken to Ms Isaacs, and that I'd opened his box. He said he didn't mind. But when I told him about the exercise book, the locket, and the stone, he went quiet. His breathing just got louder. Then I got up from my desk and lay down on my bed.

At last he started talking again. Kiran told me his father was dead, like Stanfel. It turns out the two of them met 10 years ago, after the Croatian War of Independence. Stanfel was a refugee, and Kiran's dad treated him for free and gave him a job at the factory that he managed. It was Stanfel's wife in the photo. The rock was all he got to take with him from his house. He sent these items to Kiran when he heard that Kiran's dad was missing. He wanted to send a package with a lucky stone and articles about others who had lost people. Things that had comforted him. He knew he was old and would be dead soon, but he wanted to share how he'd managed to live without his wife. Kiran told him to send it to the school, in case Kiran's family had to leave town.

Kiran paused again, and breathed out. Then he told me his dad's corpse had been found in Port Elizabeth. The murder was linked to an embezzlement scheme at the East London plant. His mom was involved since she was in debt to the cartel, but his dad wasn't. His refusal is what got him killed, and that scared her. Now his mom was on the run, maybe overseas. There'd been a lot of press.

I nodded, even though he couldn't see me. Then I apologized, and once I'd started that, I couldn't stop. I did it again.

And a third time. Until the two of us were wiping our tears on either side of the line. Then Kiran ran out of minutes.

Later, Iris arrived with Part to pick me up. I was still hoarse from crying, but I got in the car and greeted them both. Then Part left the passenger seat and joined me in the back, and I let her take my hand.

Letter No. 8

Dear Nobomi,

Iris took us to a large house with a steep driveway at the edge of Headlands. The electric gate sat between date palms and ferns. Iris pressed a button and the gate pulled back behind a wall, and she pulled inside and parked. There was a sliding door above us on the first floor, and a patio overlooking a large pool. People were sitting or standing around, laughing, drinking, smoking. Iris told us to hang out, to feel free to check the place out.

Litha was walking up the hill. He waved and we waved back. We all headed to the patio, where we found beers and sat on cushioned wicker chairs. I told them about Kiran's call and we went quiet for a bit, until someone pulled us into a drinking game.

Things blurred after that, but I remember feeling lighter, too. The music was loud from the TV in the living room. Part and I danced. Litha did, too.

Then the three of us folded into a couch in the corner on the second floor. I woke up at 4 a.m. with a scorched throat. I went downstairs for water and to piss, walking over half-emptied bottles, and when I came back up, Part and Litha were awake. We cuddled and spoke until dawn, and walked home while everyone else was still asleep.

Letter No. 9

Dear Nobomi,

Part, Litha and I spent a few hours apart, and then we had sex together for the first time the following evening, at Litha's flat on Alexandra. His parents were out of town. Litha brought a PlayStation from Mr Movie on overnight rental; Part and I brought money for pizza and soda. After watching *Where Have All the People Gone?* again on his parents' set, we spilled their sofa cushions across the kitchen floor. Then we touched each other. Litha asked me to go down on him, and I did. I reached up to kiss Part, touching her with my other hand until she shook and I felt Litha's come running down my arm. We went down for a swim at the complex pool after that. Later, Litha wasn't hard enough when he pushed into me a second time. I lay back, smelling the chlorine seeping into his sheets while Part leaned over him, bending her elbows to use her mouth.

Letter No. 10

Dear Nobomi,

I'm learning how to live with schizoaffective disorder, and I'm learning how to live with persistent depressive disorder. That's what the doctor told me I have. He gave me more mild antipsychotics and I didn't fight him this time.

Letter No. 11

Dear Nobomi,

I never see the three girls around in town, and I doubt I'll see Thoko and Lwanda again either, but I feel glad about their freedom—even though I see now it's possible that you and I never communicated after '95. That the machine wasn't from above, but something cracked within.

Letter No. 12

Dear Nobomi,

I've learned something new about humankind, but it's not from the machine, or from what you called the dial, it's from a book. I've learned that from our vantage point on Earth, we can't make out our own galaxy, the Milky Way, in its entirety. Instead, interstellar dust—like human thoughts and emotions—occludes the view, limiting our appraisal of the whole to 20 percent. This is how it was between us, and how it was between you and Dad, and how it is between everyone else, too. It's called the Zone of Avoidance, and it starts down here where we all are, and it reaches up to the heights of supernovas.

II

FIVE WEEKS IN THE PLAGUE

PART A: 2025

ONE

001

D. and I weren't meant to get along. Not that well, I mean. We met in Cape Town during a rare rain-soaked evening in January, when I was still sleeping with a man I no longer wanted to be sleeping with. It was at the exhibition of a famous local artist who'd announced his retirement, in a small gallery crosstown from the hotel that Nathanial had booked us into. I'd spent years working as a science writer for a national paper, where I'd met Nathanial, an art critic. Later I resigned for a government job. We still had sex on occasion, but we'd never been exclusive, given his marriage.

I'd accepted his invitation to Cape Town because he'd told me it had something to do with him separating from his wife, and that he needed a friend to vent to. Not that I bought that. Not then, nor when I'd woken up and taken a shower that morning, nor when I met him to board the afternoon flight at OR Tambo. He looked like he hadn't slept for more than an hour. His shirt was wrinkled, his stubble pronounced.

"Is this about getting into my pants?" I asked.

We'd scanned our boarding passes and joined a line of tired human cargo in front of the security gates.

"Excuse me?"

"This trip."

Nathanial smiled. "No," he said, glancing at his phone. A message from work or home—I didn't know and he wouldn't tell me.

"Then let's act like I believe you," I said, to tease him.

"I agree. I like it a lot better that way."

． ． ．

In any case, I ran into D. at the gallery bar that night. She was dressed in a black polo neck, a stained burgundy coat, black fitted jeans, combat boots, and she'd been staring at me from across the white-walled room. She told me her name was D, and that she wouldn't force me into conversation if I wasn't keen on talking.

I didn't have time to respond; champagne flutes clinked behind us, marking the evening's speech from the gallerist.

D. leaned against the bar. "How do all these people not get tired of this?" she said.

I didn't know what to tell her except for the obvious: "You're here too."

D. smiled. "That's true. I blame it on being a curious person," she said. Then she gestured at the server with her empty eight-ball glass and I held back a laugh.

Nathanial had tangled himself into a somber conversation with a dour, ancient man in dark glasses across the room. I felt relieved to have the time to myself. I turned back to hazard another drink. D. had stayed put.

I asked her what her grievance with the art world was, but I couldn't hear her response over the sound of applause. I drew closer as the gallerist patted her microphone, holding it tight against her chest, her palm muffling the feedback.

"I'm sorry. I didn't catch that."

D. sighed. "I said I can't tell if it's the sense of importance or where the money comes from," she said. "The paper trail. But I'm glad you're indulging me."

This time, I laughed. It wasn't my first exhibition. Nor the first time I'd felt like licking the earlobes of a woman I didn't know.

"It's an interesting view," I said, and D. smiled.

"You seem nice," she told me. "I like this whole thing."

"This whole thing?"

"I think you're a nervous person. It's endearing. Honest, even."

I didn't agree, but I thanked her.

We turned to watch the artist, Oscar Molope, fumble with the microphone's tangled cord, drop the device between his feet, reach down, and drop it again.

It annoyed her. "It's all an act," she said. "Performance art. The artist is the centerpiece. His name is only thing these people care about owning."

I was quiet.

"Do you know why I'm here?" she asked.

I didn't, of course. "Are you an artist, too?" I said.

D. laughed. "If I ask you to follow me, will you do that?"

"I might."

The air was still damp from the afternoon rain. We went out back to a narrow alley between the gallery and Buitenkant Road, where D. pulled out a joint from her coat and lit it for us. "I used to be guilty of being an artist," she said, "a little bit, but now I have different interests. Like inviting you for a drink somewhere less tiring."

I took the joint when she passed it. We walked out to her car, where D. changed out of her coat with its coal-like smear, and then she led me to a bistro near Greenmarket Square. We sat in a corner with apéritifs. Losing the burgundy coat had the effect of making her seem more present, I thought, while also diminishing her frame and blurring her into the people around us. She was small.

We talked, and D. showed me her work—I'd expected her to be more reluctant. The glow from her cell phone was an electric stain that slipped up her face, lighting her chin, revealing the soft fangs in her grin, cresting on her cropped silver dreads. From genuine appreciation, I was encouraging about her painting and installations; I even listened to an audio file of her music. Out of obligation, I thought, she asked me why I'd written the book I'd written.

I took a sip of wine. "That was a long time ago."

Usually, I never spoke about my writing, but with D. it felt effortless. Not that there was a lot to talk about. My only book, a collection of short stories titled *Obelisk*, was written while I was a student at the University of Cape Town, enrolled as a double major in biology and psychology. It had begun as a distraction, but grown into a preoccupation—a collection of science fiction stories about girlhood and illness. My own, of course. I'd called it *The Machine*, before deciding, after receiving the proofs with my name under the title, that it reminded me too much of where I was from. I convinced the editorial team to change it to *Obelisk*. It did all right, I suppose, and when D. probed me about it, I didn't mind as much as I'd expected.

The conversation felt natural, familiar. When she mentioned she was looking to move up to Johannesburg, I told her I had a room I could sublet.

"I'll slash the rent," I said—a genuine offer.

We ordered a second round, and then D. told me the truth about that night.

"It's in the oils," she said. "The work itself. That's what we look into."

We stepped out to the back of the bistro, next to the bathrooms, to sneak more of the joint. I thought about what she'd said. I told her I didn't understand.

D. nodded. "It takes a while. I don't know if it's wise to tell you this, but I will—the artist is a plant, a recent recruit. I'm from The Returners. Have you heard about us?"

I hadn't. "No, I haven't."

"Molope wasn't hard to turn," she said. "The clues were in his paintings." D. took a deep breath. "Listen, you have to stay behind after I'm done with what I'm about to tell you. Then head straight back to your hotel, all right?"

I was too surprised to protest. "Okay."

D. leaned forward and spoke into my ear.

I still remember how it felt: like being dropped into the ocean, cold and weightless, floating in a dark expanse with no land in sight.

I lingered in the bistro after she left. I walked down to an Ethiopian kiosk, bought a pack of Lucky Strikes, and hailed a cab. Nathanial wasn't back from the exhibition when I carded myself into the hotel. I poured a glass of pinot noir, took his laptop to the balcony, and lit a cigarette while it booted up.

The wrought-iron chair I sat on was uncomfortable, straight-backed and hard, but I could see Table Mountain from it. The floodlights had been switched on, the municipal wattage washing a teal light across the cliff-face. I thought back to when I was a student, only 19, in 2004. They'd projected the image of a rhino across the crag that year, part of an anti-poaching campaign, calling attention to how all five species were disappearing from the continent. The previous year, poachers had slaughtered almost 700 rhinos, sawing off their horns and selling them for traditional medicine.

The light-show gesture didn't help. Afterward, the stakeholders went back to charging 5,000 rand a night, renting the lights out to corporations for annual leadership conferences.

Nathanial's password was his wife's name, a fact I didn't feel enough shame about. I connected to the wifi and pulled up a search on Oscar Molope. I opened a document of notes Nathanial had prepared for the show. Most of them were bullet points from the gallerist. I leaned in closer and clicked a link to Molope's work, looking for what D. meant when she'd said she'd found the clues in his oils. The first link contained a biographical note on the artist. It was a dutiful paragraph without a photo, mentioning that he'd been born in 1961. Molope's parents were farm workers in the Free State, but he'd been educated across

Europe. His leanings were naturalistic and figurative, delving into the pastoral and the urban with oils, mixed media and found materials. Most of the latter came from garbage dumps.

I clicked through to his paintings. The first sample was dated 2025—a brown and platinum blur brushed over a large canvas. I clicked to enlarge it.

The door opened and Nathanial walked in, taking off his blazer and draping it over the bed. He lumbered to the bar fridge to retrieve a beer, and I thumbed the power off on his computer as he stepped out on the balcony.

"I don't blame you for leaving," he said, smiling, "but I'm glad you made it back."

He took a sip of beer and leaned his weight against the door-frame, making it creak. He wasn't an awful-looking man. Not an awful man either. He loosened his collar, rolled up his cuffs, and asked me if I was smoking. "Is there one for me?"

He came up to me from behind, but I slipped out of his arms. "Let's get real drinks, first." I'd seen cognac in the cabinet.

Later, I let Nathanial go down on me for 10 minutes, before I put on his shirt and let him fuck me in it. After he came, I waited until he was asleep before I took his computer to the bathroom. Sitting on the toilet seat, I navigated back to Molope's landscape paintings, clicking through them, but nothing stood out.

In bed, later, Nathanial drew toward me and I endured his pawing until I fell asleep.

The kidnapping was reported the next morning. I was toweling myself dry in the shower, nursing a hangover and preparing for the flight back to Johannesburg, when Nathanial called out. He was sitting on the edge of the bed, holding up the TV remote control, but I didn't join him. The night before, when D. left me at the bistro, I'd felt like I was paralyzed. I looked at the screen, and felt it again—the sensation of being dropped into the ocean.

The Returners, D. had told me the night before after we'd returned to our table for another drink, were individuals whose concern for our landmass ran deep—with regard to both its past and future.

I was confused. I asked her if she meant the continent.

"In the end, the continent, the planet, yes. But for now, the tip we're sitting on."

"The past?"

"Think a billion years. Think a billion and then add another billion. That's how long ago it was when an asteroid hit our planet, forming the Vredefort Crater in the Free State. Here's what that means. The impact created a fork in the path for us."

"Us?"

"Humankind. It altered the course of human development in this region. Hominid fossils, ancient ones, were pushed closer to the Earth's surface, but then so was gold."

D. paused for a waiter to bring our bill. She went on: "It was a test—that's what we believe. The path on the left or the path on the right. The impact revealed secrets to our ancestors about our origins, through those fossils; but it also warped the basin in the north, allowing colonists to discover gold in 1886."

I watched her mouth while she spoke. "That began the purchasing of machines and petroleum en masse. That part's not a secret. The consolidation of the Union of South Africa as a manufacturing state, a slave camp, and whatever we have now. This is what we call The Left Hand. The Path of the Machine. The Returners wish to direct our course back to the fork, in search of The Right Hand." She reached for her glass and finished it. "That's the short version."

I nodded. "I'm following, but I'm not sure why you're telling me this."

D. half-turned in her seat. "It's because I read *Obelisk*," she said.

"You did?" The book was more than a decade out of print.

"I know. I couldn't believe it was you, either, but there you were. I don't have a lot of time, but I read the book and I think you can help us."

"The Returners? How?"

"By putting us in an accurate frame."

D. got up and told me to keep a distance from the exhibition. "I can't explain right now."

"Is it dangerous?"

"No, but it's important. It's the start of our work together."

She got up and left.

I didn't know it then, but The Returners were an eco-terrorist group founded in the late 1990s. They operated as a covert cell, responsible for monkeywrenching—as they called it— companies that were involved in deforestation, mining, GM crops, energy production, and later manufacturing. Their manifesto was classified as esoteric by reputable intelligence agencies. Within rural enclaves, their numbers were rumored to be growing. There were varied reports of vigils, sermons and disciples—of ascetic men and women who arranged themselves in cross-legged circles, leaning forward to hum and whisper inside crumbling buildings. They appealed to the majority, calling for opting out of data and fighting from below the grid. Technological enterprise and technocratic rule were a forgone conclusion, they said, that dead-ended at the assured destruction of our habitat. The Earth buckled under man's idea of property, both physical and intellectual. This had all been seen. In response, the Returners stood opposed to the doomed path of the Industrial Revolution. It was a direction that had taken us off course, they argued, and compromised our survival in the universe. Now this also included digitization, the Industrial

Revolution's youngest heir and our presiding ruler, or what they called The Path of the Machine. The Left Hand.

My eyes regained focus. "I can't believe this," Nathaniel said. "That's where I was standing, last night."

I walked over to him and took his hand. The TV reporter was saying that Oscar Molope had been kidnapped the previous night at his exhibition. The suspects were unidentified and still at large. Apparently, when power went off, several individuals charged into the gallery; when the generator came on, buckets of unrefined cobalt were seen scattered across the floor, and the artist was gone. Later, results from the city's chem labs revealed the mineral was fake.

I remembered the stain on D.'s coat; it must have been from handling the stones.

I told Nathanial we had to go.

It was raining again when we checked out, but the flight was on time, at least.

In Johannesburg, two hours later, there was an accident on the N12: an articulated diesel truck had jackknifed after its driver got heatstroke, passing out with his foot on the pedal. The fuel caught alight and the bridge was cordoned off. It was more than 86 degrees out, but not with clear skies. The air was arid, trapped under a pink dome of dust and smog; according to the pilot, we had to be careful of molten tar.

Nathanial caught a cab on arrival while I stopped at the CNA for a newspaper, a bottle of water, and a boxed fruit salad. There was a man standing behind me in line, rotund, dressed in a white soccer t-shirt and black slacks.

"I've given up on reading the paper," he sighed. "My money's all for medicine, now."

I smiled to be polite.

I paged through the broadsheet on the platform upstairs,

waiting for the train and thinking about D. and how I had no means of finding her. I was still parsing that thought when I saw the article.

Two gold mines had been sabotaged. The government had sanctioned both, the report revealed, even though neither had a working water license. They were among several that were responsible for raising the levels of toxins in the metropolis's water.

That's when I felt I understood. I took out my phone and pulled up the website with Molope's paintings. I opened satellite images of the two mines, and quickly found their matches on his canvasses. It took me a while to breathe again.

The train arrived and I boarded, thinking of *Obelisk*, and whether it had led me here.

I lived in Doornfontein, in the gentrified section of downtown, in a small two-room north-facing apartment. The kitchen window looked onto a vacated building with a faded mural of Nelson Mandela. He was pictured taking a break from being a solicitor and exercising as a boxer—a photo taken in Jerry Moloi's famous D.O.C.C. boxing club in the 1950s. The streets below the former statesman were often choked with traffic, the call of women selling mielies a warm intermission in the chorus of machines.

That night, I allowed myself a waking dream of her, in which I combined the parts of D. I recalled from the bistro with other parts I didn't know. Across the ceiling, headlights from the cars coursing the thoroughfare below slid from one panel to the other, keeping my thoughts of her suspended in intermittent shimmers.

I went to work the next morning, clocking in at Population Control, which was the name we gave the Grant Regulation Office in east Johannesburg—an unofficial wing of the Department of Social Development. Our offices were situated on the edge of Edenvale. To the public, we were grant officials, government hires performing a national service. On induction, that's the appearance we were told to maintain. This was part of the job, our contracts stipulated.

G.R.O. had begun as a corrective government initiative in the second half of 2017, after our national social welfare dispenser, and the US corporation that rolled out its payments, were found colluding against their grantees, coercing them into high-interest loans and cellphone packages that generated billions in profit instead of nutrition and housing. G.R.O. was put in place to research and regulate both grant and grantee fraud.

However, two years later, G.R.O. was bought by a Silicon Valley investor, who replaced the staff of clerks and social workers with scientists and programmers like myself, while continuing to roll out foreign aid to ensure the Department's silence. The prevailing assumption among us at the office was that our purpose was data mining—to monitor the rise and decline of the worker population in the metropolis and beyond, and to note their consumption patterns in the townships and the CBD, where commuters clocked in each day to stoop their backs and pack on calluses for pennies. We had our reservations, but we went to work.

I can't remember who first came up with the name Population Control, but it made us laugh. It felt apt for our office. Maybe it was a way to deal. I don't know. Our work was not unrelated, I often thought—stuck in traffic, inching home with my wheels sloshing over potholes in the rain—to the history of labor in the metropolis. I sometimes saw myself as a different woman, one from seven or eight decades earlier: a worker at the Social Welfare Department of the Non-European Section of Johannesburg, driving to Alexandra and handing out surveys to families whose children were bedridden as a matter of course, their bellies swollen taut with kwashiorkor.

I walked into the office and found Henry, one of the few colleagues I could bear, hung at an angle over his keyboard, a blue IT repairs screensaver—SICK AND WIRED? CALL US FOR ALL YOUR NETWORK REPAIRS—ricocheting over his head like the fragment of a bad dream. I patted him on the back as I made my way to the kitchen, where I found a scraped-out can of Nescafé containing just enough weak coffee for both of us. I returned and handed him the mug.

"I'm not hungover."

"I know."

"I've been working."

"I know."

I sat down and turned to the office TV. Henry raised the volume. We fell silent, like we always did when we watched the news.

There were more housing strikes in Alexandra, which wasn't surprising. Ever since the 2019 launch of the Delta Urban Renewal Project—an initiative to redevelop township space in the province, using local labor—there'd been a shortfall in both materials and wages, especially in Alexandra, which had served as the vanguard. The mayor had taken to a podium on behalf of the developers—Delta—citing similar projects across Asia. The townships were meant to serve as micro-cities, we were told: self-contained, privately owned zones with standardized populations of 200,000, and streamlined economic functions, including energy production, recycling, manufacturing, and urban farming. This meant that in 10 years, each zone would fall under corporate, rather than governmental, regulation.

Not too different to us at Population. It marked a trend: the nation was transitioning from underdeveloped state to multifaceted corporation. In order to avoid the fiscal collapse of the late 2010s, multinationals were incentivized into direct investment by being offered a citizen's rights to land. This meant that the settlements would ultimately be available for purchase.

But the flagship project was experiencing difficulties. The residents still awaited work, education, and healthcare, while the trial companies that had signed on waited for Delta to deliver their infrastructure and sourced labor.

In the TV studio, a sociologist who'd been invited to share his view—a bald man with thick glasses and a grey moustache—spoke with passion against the urban renewal project, describing the zones as a new form of apartheid. On the other side, a community organizer—a woman in a green doek and red tunic—told him that people needed to eat. The usual.

Henry flipped the channel to another news report. I closed my eyes, feeling a headache growing from how little I'd slept.

The studio guest was a man who made a show of rolling his R's to affect the enunciation of Umkhonto we Sizwe vets. He presented himself as a politician of generous and gregarious disposition, and introduced each response with a winding, self-deprecating anecdote, before piling into the opposition parties who were calling for the president's impeachment. Where were we were headed as a nation, he wanted to know, if we were eager to fit our heads back into an old noose? Henry flipped the channel again.

This time, my eyes were open and I could see the repeat screening of a live broadcast from the previous morning. There was an aerial shot of a taxi on the TV screen, driving ahead of a presidential convoy. Further on, another taxi had overturned in a ditch. The accident had been caused by a cell phone, the anchor reported, when an oncoming driver had dropped the device between her feet. As the second taxi drove past, the passengers took photos of the wreckage.

The taxi traveled on to Constitution Hill, where a congregation of men and women in red berets, hundreds of them, were forming a wall and holding up placards. They were chanting a protest song and blocking the traffic at the intersection. That morning on my way to work, headlines from the dailies plastered on streetlights reported that the Economic Freedom Fighters had revived their old call for the stock exchange to be returned to workers. The march had started in Newtown and was set to end in Sandton. The taxi driver rolled down his window and hooted, whistling his support as he rapped out a drumroll on his door. The men and women in berets laughed and began to separate, letting him through, then reassembled as an even bigger mass in front of the president's car.

It took 18 canisters of tear gas to clear them, the bulletin reported.

I turned to my computer as Henry muted the TV.

Half an hour later, our team was summoned to one of our two boardrooms on the third floor. *You are special*, a recorded voice saluted us as we walked in. *Each of you chosen with purpose.* This was an old routine, which preceded us sitting down like children to listen to Pius, our department head. It had been recorded in Northern California, and the voice belonged to Ian Carpenter, our CEO, whose face we'd seen once in a video conference call. It was rumored that he was an eccentric former stockbroker, now a recluse. His digital trail was faint, and most of us had given up on discerning his motives.

There was a carafe of water on the table, standing on a decaled silver tray bearing G.R.O.'s logo, surrounded by stacked pastrami sandwiches. This wasn't normal for our meetings. We took our seats and faced front, looking at the projected screen, even though Pius was still missing.

Then his second-in-command, Phil, walked into the boardroom. He was wearing a bright lavender tie, his frameless glasses misted despite the air conditioning. In one hand he held a manila envelope and in the other a ballpoint pen. "I know I'm not your superior," he said, clicking the pen-tip in and out of the shaft, "but I'll be standing in for Pius. There's been an accident. He was found dead in his bathtub earlier today at his house in Westcliff, bleeding out from both wrists. It's a tragedy, of course."

There was an uproar around the table. I excused myself to the bathroom and headed back to my desk, feeling nauseated. I hadn't expected this.

I logged five out-of-office hours, and pushed a work laptop into its sleeve. Then my phone rang. I sat back down, letting my bag sag down my arm.

It was Nathanial. "I need to see you," he said.

"What's this about?"

"Not over the phone… but it's about Cape Town. I was told to bring you down there."

"What?" I asked, confused. "Come again?"

But he'd hung up.

During my lunch break, I often went on long drives that weaved through the grid of the metropolis—wasting fuel, I reprimanded myself—pretending to be an aid worker, living in a blighted civilization caught in the advanced stages of a plague. In this fantasy, I was also one of the sick. As I drove further, I imagined the plague dissolving all of us together.

Nathanial had sent a text suggesting we meet at O'Grady's, and I'd told him I'd be there in half an hour. It was a sports bar the team at the paper used to frequent after hours, back when I still worked as a science writer on the same floor as Nathanial. It was dim and cavernous, adorned in the required Irish trappings, and known to fill up at noon and 5, giving us an hour to talk in private.

The bar was in a student mall, jammed between two large campuses. The building was under constant construction, aiming to build enough retail space to sink all the students into debt, I imagined. I found a parking spot close to the entrance.

Nathanial skulked behind the frosting on the pub's window. He was sitting at the rear, his back to the wall as he gazed out at the parking lot. Two drafts of beer stood foaming in front of him and he looked up as I approached. Taking a deep sip from his pint, he motioned for me to sit.

"I'm here," I said. "What's all this about?"

He sighed. "Listen, I can't tell if you're in danger or not, but I could never forgive myself if I didn't tell you. Please understand—I was threatened."

I waited. Nathaniel adjusted his beer on the coaster. "Last week, before the Molope show, there was a phone call to the paper," he said. "It was through our tip hotline, but it asked for the culture desk."

"Nadine?"

He shook his head. "Nadine still edits the insert, but the request was for my line. It was a man's voice. He asked me if I knew you. No—he *told* me that I did."

"That's a strange formulation, but it's also no secret. I used to have my name in the paper."

"Sure. Anyway, then it all came out." He leaned forward, taking another sip. "I received an email with attachments. Photos of the two of us. With a note at the bottom, saying the guy knew Doreen's email address and cell number."

I winced and reached for the beer. Doreen was his wife.

"Then the instructions. I had to take you to the Molope show and act oblivious. If I complied, that would be it. The evidence would be deleted. There was no interest in me. I asked if it was dangerous and I was reassured. I told myself I'd be alert and track your movements, but then you slipped out. It took everything in me not to collapse when I found you in the hotel room. I had to touch you to see if you were real."

I reached for his hand and thanked him for telling me. "There's something you're leaving out, though, I can tell."

Nathanial sighed again. "That's true. It's about Doreen. The timing of the email sent me into a tailspin. There's a job opening for her in a firm in New Zealand. If this came out, now, she'd be shattered. It's meant to be a second chance for us."

"New Zealand?" It was news to me.

He looked down at his knuckles. "I know I won't blend in as well as she will, but it's better than Australia. I figured I'd give us one last go." His brow creased again. "All that aside, though. This could be dangerous. Do you have any leads?"

"Leads. Is this a thriller?"

"Leads about who might have sent the pictures. Did anything happen to you in Cape Town?"

I thought about it. "Nothing happened in Cape Town," I said. "Maybe it was someone from the office."

"Now I'm moving from being frightened to irritated."

"I think it's nothing, a prank." I took a sip of beer and looked at the email on his phone. "The pictures are outdoors, with both of us in clothes. It isn't espionage. I could've left a desktop unattended, or whoever did this might just have been out at the same restaurant as us. I don't know."

"Then what's the deal with Cape Town?"

"Oh, I don't know. It's immature, Nathaniel. Nothing would surprise me."

He leaned back. "I'll be honest, I'm relieved this isn't alarming for you. It's almost enough to put me at ease, this cavalier response to blackmail."

I smiled. "Learn to trust a woman for once."

"Isn't that the problem here? That I do?"

We finished our beers, stretched the rest of the hour as much as we could, and said our farewells. It would turn out to be for good, this time.

I thought about Pius on the drive home, imagining him like the rest of us, a configuration of chemicals and flesh burdened by consciousness—which I thought of as a vague collection of ideas, both cumulative and transient, running the motor of a warm and wet machine.

I couldn't stop thinking about Pius, though I tried; he'd been a diplomatic leader, his loyalties often split between us and management. But there was nothing I could do except go back to work. All of us waded through the gloom left in the wake of the news.

Our work stations were divided by frosted-glass partitions beneath a line of fluorescent lights, 15 crammed into a room of no more than a thousand square feet. Forty hours a week, we sifted through data mined from the census records of the working class, which we tested against algorithms, each built to predict and replicate the behavioral patterns in our archives. We corrected deviations and sent the amended information back to the international developers. In simple terms, we were teaching machines how to think and consume like the poor.

This same data Ian Carpenter sold, in incomplete packages and at a mark-up, to his competitors—after he'd used it himself, that is, in service of a venture we'd been instructed not to inquire about.

There was a premium on our information, that much we knew: all the tech start-ups, responding to market saturation in both the West and the East, had focused their sights on our continent. It was public knowledge that in order to take advantage of this development, and in amendment of our constitution, the government was legislating digital access as a human right, which would open a new and untapped market of users that numbered in the millions, as well as creating new government tenders and subsidies. Regulations were loosened, no doubt to facilitate zoning—which promised companies a market economy and the freedom to experiment with products without government intervention. The official line was "to foster competition and growth."

All of it meant more work for us.

That's what I was preoccupied with when I received the email from Phil.

Mr Carpenter is bringing in a special directive, it said. *I am in charge of selecting the most gifted among you to make up an elite team. I am happy to inform you that you have been chosen as one of the new team's five members.*

I read the email over, the sound of keyboard strokes drumming against my temples.

We assembled in the first boardroom on the second floor— members of a new team, seated in front of even more elaborate sandwiches and refreshments.

Phil stood at the head of the table as the recorded voice reminded us again why we were there. This time, it was as if the man was seated among us. Phil cleared his throat, then motioned to the speaker above him—the ghost of Ian Carpenter. He beamed. "Indeed, each of you is special and has been chosen with purpose."

I turned and looked at who he meant. The new team was me, Henry, Rose, Micaela and Lindani. Those of us who stayed awake the most at work. No one moved as he spoke, not even toward the refreshments. All of us felt tethered by the same mixture of relief and trepidation. If we hadn't been picked, we suspected, we'd have risked being released back into a barren market, the details of our roles at Population redacted from our resumes as per our signed agreements.

Phil clasped his hands behind his back. "It's a special honor," he said, "to be selected for this promotion. The work involved is classified as our most confidential. Meaning there will be additional rules. For one, upon signing, no team member is permitted to discuss their work with a colleague. That goes for both inside and outside this boardroom. Is that clear?"

It wasn't a question, but we answered in the affirmative. Then Phil distributed documents for us to sign. It was archaic, this practice of using paper, but our courts didn't accept digital signatures. This was us being bound once more in accordance to the law; par for the course at G.R.O.

Phil told us Ian Carpenter would be addressing us: "It's a pre-recording, but it's still the man's time." He dropped a handful of flash drives on the table. "Take those home and watch the video. Then report back to the office tomorrow morning. There'll be a driver available."

He let us out before quitting time. Thinking about the meeting, making even less sense of it, I joined the 3 o'clock traffic on the N3. I pushed through the jam and stopped at a garage a block away from my flat to buy a Moroccan salad—my third that week. After keying myself into my flat, I observed a ritual I hadn't been able to knock off lately, despite it concerning me, which was to stand at the door and stop breathing.

I imagined myself disappearing.

The sound of traffic drifted up to the kitchen as the sun began to dip west, drawing long shadows across my living room. On its trail were the familiar sounds of screeching tires and shouts, hawkers, taxi drivers, commuters, schoolchildren, and the rest of the embattled human stream below, rising each morning to course across the contours of the crumbling metropolis.

I turned and locked the door.

I peeled off the packaging on the salad and sat in front of the computer in the lounge. The noise from the street made it feel as if I had no walls—that the room was an extension of what I'd left outside. I pushed in the flash drive and opened the video file. The screen went blank, then brightened.

A man appeared seated against a white background: Ian

Carpenter, our CEO. He didn't look as old as I'd imagined. Instead, he was fit and well fed, with blood in his cheeks, clear skin, and bright teeth. His smile might've disarmed me, if I could forget who he was.

"It's true. You've been selected to see behind the curtain," he said, "to be part of an initiative to give this nation a seat at the table in determining the future of the modern world."

I chewed on chickpeas and listened to him elaborate on what he called "our great nation," lauding the social cohesion we'd achieved since the end of apartheid. Those were his words, each indicative of a foreigner.

He knitted his fingers together. "This is a crucial moment in global history. Human enterprise has advanced far enough, at last, to allow us to create the foundations of a new civilization. This is its beginning."

I put the salad down and leaned back on the couch, watching the screen as my pulse quickened. Carpenter grinned. "These are exciting times. Indeed, exciting times. More information will follow, but for now, I want you to bask in making the cut. It won't be without its challenges, of course, but I have no doubt each of you will rise to the task."

The video ended and I looked at my reflection on the screen. After a minute, I got up and put the rest of the salad in the fridge, took off my shoes, and got into bed, trying to clear my mind of both Pius and Carpenter.

I didn't succeed.

I watched the world outside darkening, and eventually took a pill to sleep.

005

I woke up to the whir of machines. The construction seemed to be starting earlier and earlier each morning.

I sat up in bed and looked out of the window. I could make it out in the distance: the Tower reached up, cleaving the smog that hovered over the horizon. It was supported by cages of scaffolding, with cranes creaking on either side of it, the earth at its base gouged into wide, shallow pits of red dust. There'd been resistance to the construction of the Tower, I'd heard, although I hadn't paid much attention to either side of the argument. It was at odds with the history of its site, which for decades had been a nature reserve—a 40-acre island of fertile parkland, known as The Wilds, which traced its origins back to the 1920s. Before being donated to the city, the park had belonged to the private Johannesburg Consolidated Investment Company, a mine investor. But now it was private again, belonging to a different set of men who were gutting the earth for profit. History in the metropolis often felt like a circle.

I got up and ran a shower, brushed my teeth, got dressed. I unplugged the flash drive and dropped it in my handbag. At the kitchen counter, I drank coffee I'd cooled down with water from the tap. I didn't hesitate over what to wear. I didn't know what to expect, so I left it at that.

I beat the traffic on the N3 headed into Edenvale, making me the first to arrive at the G.R.O. offices. As I walked toward the entrance, Phil rounded the corner.

"Impressive!" he said. "The first to arrive. Is this dedication I'm seeing?"

I nodded to be polite. "I couldn't sleep," I told him.

"Nerves?"

"It's the construction. I don't live that far from the Tower."

There was a flat smile on his face. "Now, that's interesting," he said.

The others arrived. In age, Henry and I were in the middle. We were both in our late 30s, although Henry looked older than me: red-headed and freckled, with stooped shoulders and a gaze as tired as it was suspicious. Rose and Micaela, who'd been inseparable since they'd joined our office, were coding prodigies in their 20s. I often felt for them—out of all of us, their generation had inherited the least in the metropolis. It was said that seven in ten would never find work. Then there was Lindani, who stood against the entrance, smoking. He was in his 50s, with dark skin and a smooth pate that gleamed in the morning light. He had one hand in his pocket, the crook of his arm cradling his enormous stomach. He asked Phil if we were heading up.

"Not today. The car will arrive to take us to the facility."

Then, as promised, the car arrived.

006

Ten minutes into our trip, I understood the blankness behind Phil's smile. The reason he'd behaved like a marionette. It was unexpected, but understandable. He was driving us to the Tower. I'd mentioned the structure without knowing.

I stared ahead as Rose and Micaela chatted in lowered voices, their hands fixed to their laps. There was plenty of room in the van, but it didn't feel like it. It was impossible to find comfort, and easier to remain silent. The closer we got, the louder the whirring noise of the construction grew, until I could feel it in my skull and at the back of my throat.

Phil flashed a clearance card at the gate and the driver parked in a designated space close to the entrance. There was a substantial number of guards. I didn't have to wonder why.

The scale of it.

I'd seen the Tower countless times from my apartment, but this close, I had to take a step back and gape. Even under construction, it was an imposing machine—a high-rise commissioned from a famous architecture firm in New York and built in collaboration with the provincial government. Revolution Tower, as it was known, was meant to be the tallest building on the continent; when complete, it would boast 65 floors and a spire that stood 820 feet above our heads. It was a gift from Delta, meant to draw attention to the city of Johannesburg, to attract investors and signal an economic shift toward information trading. No civilians were permitted onto the construction site.

Lindani lit a cigarette and pulled. "I've never seen anything like it," he said.

I turned to Phil. "Is that where we're going?"

"Not quite, but close." He held up his hands. "Here, follow me. I'll demonstrate."

He led us past the barrier, toward a small windowless building to the north of the Tower. His clearance card made the censor on the wall beep, and the reinforced-steel doors drew apart to let us in. It was dark inside.

Phil took the lead without waiting on us. He went up a small ramp and was swallowed into the gloom. Lindani followed, and we went after him. Up ahead, there was an elevator built into the far wall. Phil went to it and raised his clearance card again; the censor on the wall beeped and glowed blue.

"It's underground," he said.

The elevator doors parted and a red light washed into the room. Then the doors drew shut behind us.

"Each of you will receive your own clearance credentials. From now on, this will be your second place of work."

We mumbled back understanding. As we began to descend, I noticed that the whirring from the machines outside still registered as a faint tremor on my skin. I wondered if Pius had been here, and what it was, exactly, that Phil had been entrusted with. The lift doors opened onto a narrow corridor.

"Today will be an orientation," he said, "to get you acquainted with the facility. We have a number of offices down here. The wing you'll be using will be kept exclusive to you. I have to warn you, though. The whole facility is kept under surveillance."

"I thought we were special and chosen."

"That hasn't changed, Rose."

"It sounds like we're not trusted, either."

"None of us are. It's the nature of the work. It demands it."

"Phil," I asked, "How were we chosen?"

"Performance."

It's what I would've expected to hear from him. I didn't bother asking anything else.

. . .

The last door we walked through opened onto our new offices. Six in total, each a perfect square with glass walls and doors. Inside, the furnishings were sparse: a desk, a work station, a swivel chair, and a filing cabinet. There were two other doors in the far wall, made of steel—lavatories, Phil explained—and what he called the Observation Room. Each desk had a small stack of paper on it.

"Feel free to choose a station."

I walked to the nearest one. As the five of us took our seats, we heard the door at the end of the corridor draw shut. I didn't have to look up to know that Phil had left us. He was gone for half an hour.

We all went through the files on our desks, then rolled our swivel chairs into the corridor to deliberate.

"Is it a test?" Rose said to no one in particular. I could see her panic, how much she wanted to do well.

Henry sighed and massaged his eyelids. "I have no idea."

"None of us do," Lindani said.

He got up and tested the door, but it was locked. He took out his cigarettes and fondled the box, creasing his brow as Micaela paged through her stack of paper and frowned.

"This is here for a reason," she said.

I looked at us reflected in the glass, thinking about us dying there, and how little we would've known about each other.

That's just how the metropolis had ordered us. Its scaffolding and thoroughfares were testaments to the might of its vertical ambition; but it took little interest in us, the flesh inside its mills.

I nodded. "I think she's right," I said.

My pile of papers was a profile. In it, there was a short biographical paragraph, followed by health records and what appeared to be a psychological report. I gleaned that the subject—a male whose name was redacted—was a substance abuser.

Methamphetamines and nyaope, it said. In the past month, he'd undergone electro-shock treatment. State-funded.

I looked up and asked the others about their files. Henry read from his, which contained the records of an ex-con who'd been arrested for armed robbery, before attempting to end his life in prison. Rose and Micaela's detailed the histories of an orphan and a homeless man with acute dissociative disorder. Lindani, frowning over his pages, revealed that his was about the widow of a miner.

"Maybe we should turn on the workstations," I suggested.

There was a request for log-in credentials. As we looked at each other through the glass partitions, I heard the door open and Phil came back, holding our clearance cards.

"Thank you for your patience. These are yours," he said. He passed the cards to us with log-in credentials. "Tomorrow, we'll meet again at G.R.O. Then we'll return here. In the meantime, take some time out to peruse the material."

He didn't mention the material we'd been given, and we were too disconcerted to ask about it. That, or too afraid.

007

The next morning, Phil was late. We dithered for half an hour in the G.R.O. basement parking lot, lined up like children on an excursion, blowing mist over the cold concrete and speaking about the Tower.

Since we knew nothing about the assignment, either on or off the record, we reasoned that we weren't in breach of contract when we shared our theories. The results were inconclusive, however—our combined knowledge too scant—and we weren't able to keep it up for longer than Lindani's cigarette. I followed the others upstairs and went to work.

Later that morning, Pius's widow walked in, followed by an assistant. He came to call me to our late boss's office, where she was waiting.

"Thanks Ronaldo. Please close the door behind you," she instructed. He left, and she turned to me. "Three women on the entire floor. There used to be laws against that."

"There used to be," I said.

She smiled. "Forgive me. It's been a while since I've been out of the house. Please take a seat. My name's Emilia."

"There's no need for forgiveness."

I took a seat at Pius's desk, and watched her fit herself into his large chair opposite me, running a manicured hand over his blotter. I took in her clothes, which were both elegant and modest, without the self-consciousness common in housewives from the northern suburbs.

"I get the feeling that a woman on her own would want certain assurances," she said.

"I don't follow."

"No? In a place like this, I mean. I'd assume she'd make sure her interests were protected."

"I don't have a nest egg, if that's what you mean. I belong to the building's worker bees. We do algorithms and data analysis. Programming. The cogs. We aren't important enough for that kind of money."

Emilia laughed. "Now I see what Pius meant. It's not just being a woman that sets you apart."

I watched as Emilia sighed. "Not like that. I'm not a scorned widow. My husband was a faithful man, perhaps to a fault, which is closer to the reason I've come." Smiling, she got up and started removing books from the shelves, dropping them into a small cardboard box. "Pius took on another man's burden. He let it kill him, in fact, when he could've stepped off the path."

"I don't know why I'm here."

Emilia nodded, but didn't face me. "Indeed, or is it the CEO that killed him? The shadow. The man who's never seen."

"I suppose I shouldn't be surprised."

"That I know about Ian Carpenter? No, you shouldn't be. Pius was my husband."

"Right. Then I take it this is where I learn what I'm doing here."

"It is, but understand before I go on, that I have two children on top of a dead husband. I need patience. That's the first thing. The second thing is that I was approached."

I met her gaze across the blotter. Emilia leaned forward. "I know about M/A/R/K," she said. "He's the one who sent me here."

The two of us stared at each other as the office computers hummed.

008

M/A/R/K recruited me a year and a half into my contract with G.R.O. I don't think it was too difficult. I met him on the darknet one afternoon. I'd been following a dead trail, trying to trace information about our CEO, Ian Carpenter, and his ventures outside Johannesburg. Naïve, I know, but it wasn't the only thing I was doing.

I was also looking for drugs.

I'd been on prescription medication—SSRIs—since the age of 12, but had had to taper off. I could handle dysthymia, but I was afraid of schizoaffective disorder.

I wasn't alone. In late 2022, not long after the second economic downgrade in a span of five years, our public health system had plummeted. National Health Insurance had been introduced—a calamitous trial, leading to almost immediate collapse. Rapidly reinstated, the private insurers had opted to cover less than a third of all common illnesses; which is how most of us had learned to live with our ailments. Then I'd discovered crypto and the darknet, which were both ancient.

I didn't believe M/A/R/K at first. He told me that he'd followed a trail that led to me.

At this point in the conversation, I moved from my desk to the inside of a toilet stall at work; we were using an encrypted phone messenger instead of email. I told him that I wasn't convinced. "Trails don't survive on the Tor network."

"For the most part, but that doesn't hold the same across the world."

I waited.

"This isn't extortion." Another pause. "I have what you need. Do you want it?"

"How do you know what I need?"

"The trail. The CEO and SSRIs. I can help with both. In fact, I have something better."

Still I hesitated. "Are you a criminal?" I asked him.

"The law doesn't arbitrate in this case. Do you accept?"

"I don't know."

"Let's meet."

I turned off my phone and sat motionless on the toilet seat. My throat felt parched as I listened to the hum of the ventilator, imagining it as an efficient vector of the plague. For the first time in over a decade, I thought of the hallucinations I'd suffered as a child.

I needed the medicine.

I met him at a Mexican restaurant off Fox Street, a block away from the apartment I used to rent when I first moved to Joburg. It was humid that afternoon, a Friday at the full onset of summer, but the place wasn't packed, which gave me a small amount of relief. I slotted myself in at a corner table at the back, planning to see him first as he walked through the door. Then I waited.

M/A/R/K was black—uncommon for a hacker, but not unheard of. As soon as he sat down, he explained his alias to me, which I took to be his way of telling me that I'd never know his real name.

"It means target," he said, and I wondered if I was paddling out of my depth.

I pushed the thought back down as a waiter delivered our drinks menus.

"I'm here for the medication," I said.

"I know." M/A/R/K reached down for a satchel beneath the table. "It's no secret that this is a troubled time for all of us."

"'Troubled time'? Does this mean we won't be speaking like normal people?"

He grinned, revealing four gold caps on his bottom incisors. "I'll be clearer," he said. "The nation's reaching a critical point. It's closing—our window of opportunity to do something about our totalitarians."

"That's better, but what am I supposed to do about it?"

"First, accept these gifts from me." M/A/R/K rested a hand on the satchel. "The contents come with verbal instructions. I hope that's not a problem."

"It isn't."

I was trying to impress him, I realized, irritated. I'd known that M/A/R/K was a hacker from how he'd found me. I'd expected him to be emaciated or obese, compromised in a visible manner, with an overbite or another species of debilitating defect. He wasn't. His skin was as clear as a child's and he was almost handsome, despite a veil of somberness.

Later, when I'd stop waiting on his approval, M/A/R/K and I would grow apart. It would take time, and we'd get close in the interim, but he couldn't lead without detachment.

"I'm listening," I said.

"Have you heard of The Tank?

I shook my head.

M/A/R/K had founded The Tank in 2020, he told me. It was a traditional hacker group: a multi-faceted organism with multiple heads and limbs that stretched from Romania to Kenya, specializing in leaks from multinational corporate accounts, telecommunications companies, intelligence agencies, and local law enforcement. In addition, M/A/R/K hacked the stock exchange, he hacked data start-ups, and he hacked eight out of ten of the companies that had signed on for the zone trials. The Tank's mission, he said, was to police those who controlled our information, from the data captured by our consumption to its distillation as intellectual property. To free information and return it to us, those who were being programmed by it and digitized into its commodities, our lives tracked and traded for market research.

Their name had never been scratched off the watchlists that flapped in the offices of cyber-security agencies the world over. They believed in the 99 percent, that it was the Hacker Class, and that the Hacker Class was the rightful heir to our means of production.

"We've been monitoring G.R.O. since it was founded," M/A/R/K said. "Enough to understand its architecture and the half-life of its data stream; but now I need extraction." He looked at the satchel again. "I know we share the same feelings about G.R.O. That's the reason we're both here. It's corrupt. It's a mistake to think that those of us who feel favored stand apart from those who don't—from those pressed hardest under the elites, the marked. I know this because I helped build their system. I left after I realized what it meant for Delta."

"Delta?"

"The titan. The zones aren't what the population thinks they are. This is a chance to make things right. There's more, but the task I have is urgent." He took something out of his pocket, holding it in his fist. "I left a backdoor in the network before I resigned. I've been unable to get back to it ever since, due to limited social access, with most of the hires afraid of the law and termination." M/A/R/K opened his palm, revealing a small 4.0 drive. "Insert this in a workstation and leave it in for one minute after booting. Then dispose of it."

I nodded. "Is that all?"

"That's all."

Even in the heat I felt cold. I wasn't really calm—it was a performance, and I wondered if he could tell. G.R.O. had seemed minor to me before then, but now its shadow had lengthened. To distract myself from my nerves, I reached over and patted the satchel on the table. "I'll do it," I said. "Now tell me how to use these."

Just then, a waitress arrived to take our order for coffee. M/A/R/K waited for us to be alone again before he leaned forward, knitting his hands. "Have you read Philip K. Dick's novel about androids?"

I nodded; in fact I had. "It took me time to forgive the awful title."

He laughed. "Fair enough, but do you remember the dialing? The Penfield mood organ. In the beginning, Rick uses it to take care of his electric sheep. Dialing different codes into the device makes the characters experience different moods. Panic, anger, contentment, hope. The effect is immediate." M/A/R/K pushed the satchel toward the center of the table. "The pills aren't that different."

"That sounds dangerous."

"It's efficient. Here." He took out a bottle and told me I could sample the pills there at the table if I wanted to. "They have an accelerated metabolic rate and the effect is immediate."

I took the bottle from him, holding it up against the light. I put it back down. "I'm on something else," I lied.

"That doesn't matter."

"How do they work?"

"Like I said. The Penfield mood organ."

"Let's see, then."

I opened the cap.

The pills worked, of course, which didn't surprise me, given the confidence M/A/R/K showed in his pitch. I slept more that week, and I thought less about the plague and the hallucinations I'd had as a child. I learned that I could space the pills out if I wanted to.

All this made M/A/R/K's request of me feel more than manageable—almost too easy. Even as one of only three female hires on the floor, I often passed unnoticed in our office—a woman seldom called upon for an opinion. That was the first point.

The second was that he was right. It was true that what I did at G.R.O. had grown to bother me. Not a small amount, either. I often wondered if my parents, having stood adjacent to the apartheid regime, were what drew me to my job. What repelled me too.

The flash drive contained a worm. The morning of the hack, I clocked in as usual and headed to the break room, where I boiled tea. I waited for one of the cleaners to vacuum in front of a particular workstation, one we kept in high rotation, and walked right into her. I dropped the cup, which shattered, and the two of us bent down to fuss over it, knocking heads—which is when I slotted in the drive, knowing her back would obscure me from the single camera in the lab. "Please wait here," I said. "I'll fetch something to clean with."

I turned the computer on, pretending to inspect it for damage, then headed to the break room for a mop and a broom. The computer had finished booting when I returned. The cleaner was still standing there and she bent down to help pick up the shards, concealing me again.

I pulled out the drive, carried it to the break room in a plastic bag with the broken porcelain, and crushed it over the basin. Then I left the workstation on and sat next to Henry, watching as my colleagues, a stream of them, clicked it off sleep mode and printed off documents.

The worm wasn't detected. I couldn't decide if I felt elated or relieved.

I thought about my parents.

I couldn't sleep that night. I rolled a joint and cued a podcast, then I walked out onto the balcony, watching the lights of the metropolis writhing over the grid like a net on fire. That's when

I received a text invite to celebrate with The Tank—as easy as that. M/A/R/K said he wanted me to have a look inside their operation. That I'd done a splendid job and so forth.

I met him downtown at an address close to the bridge. I parked on a street that dead-ended a block away from the CBD proper, and waited for him inside the car, watching the foot traffic.

The metropolis never stopped turning under our feet. Even though the sun had sunk, its cogs still churned out a familiar song for us, coughing men and women alike into underpaid labor.

M/A/R/K knocked on the passenger window, using his forearm to wipe the moisture off the pane. I rolled down the window and he smiled. "It isn't far from here."

He pushed himself away from the car, and I followed him. There was a light rain, powdering the world with a coating of static, making islands of orange streetlight shimmer against the worn tarmac. M/A/R/K led us a block down from the car and I waited with him outside a damp building with a brick façade and a caged door. The fire escape had collapsed, eons ago it seemed. Cars streamed past on the bigger roads down each end of the alley, but here we were alone.

"Is it secure?"

M/A/R/K nodded. "It is. Most of our operations take place in plain sight."

The door unlocked, and a tall figure stood in the frame. His width left no room in the gap, and he had to stand with his back to the wall to let us in. The sounds of the metropolis were drowned, now, under the fluorescent hum, behind thick walls. I followed M/A/R/K down a narrow staircase to the left, and waited for him to use an iris scanner on the narrow landing.

The room was located below ground. It felt like it, too, from the heat. It was divided into three sections and shaped like a gel capsule, with a curved ceiling. It was awash in an amber light that blended with the blue tint of computer screens. Those were present in numbers, each unit plugged into a workstation built against the wall.

M/A/R/K led me to a break room at the rear, where four of his people had gathered. He was curt with them. He introduced me as a covert agent, explaining that personal inquiries about me were not permitted. They nodded. It was not an unfamiliar ritual.

I decided to return the favor—I didn't ask for a name if none was offered, and I didn't initiate conversation. Instead, for the next half-hour, we drank and spoke around a steel table, as solemn as generals frowning over battle plans. I couldn't follow most of the conversation, but I retained what I could. For example, I learned that The Tank got its name from this bunker we were standing in, where it was founded. It was a cell of converts: two were former data brokers, one was a cyber security specialist, and the fourth, a man with a thick black moustache, introduced himself as a legal consultant. The rest, equal numbers male and female, were black-hat hackers, hunched anonymously over the workstations outside the break room. Each had defected from a different cell in order to follow M/A/R/K's cause.

As the night progressed, I suspected they'd retained older motives, too. I learned that the bunker doubled up as the base of a state-sponsored hacker cell, a new initiative from the Department of Defense—a grey site still in its beta phase—that was run by M/A/R/K. He'd offered each hacker in the team a chance to work in the open, to breathe and divest from the life of a fugitive, with expunged records and altered identities; and then he recruited them, along with their gratitude, from the government cell into The Tank. He kept the same address. He made use of the same resources.

I watched him command the table. "Here's the thing," he

said. "There's no salvation in regression. That's the pattern of evolution. It's unidirectional."

He was speaking to one of the former data brokers. The man had asked him about the possibility of working with a new eco-terrorist group in Cape Town—environmentalists with anti-tech leanings—if there might be strength in numbers.

M/A/R/K frowned, wanting to brush the question off. "Here's what I mean." He took a long breath. "Fine. Let's put an end to information. Humankind now has to find a new organizing principle, am I right? The dataset would remain the same. That's what would be at our disposal—the cumulative knowledge of humankind's past and projected future, which is what we have now. That would be the foundation of whatever new world we wanted to build. To advance, we have to build on more than the ruins required by a retreat from technology. To stamp on the heads of the powerful, we have to climb their cages and turn them into scaffolds."

There was a cheer around the table, but I couldn't help but cut in.

"I'm not too sure," I said. "For instance, what if one applies a novelist's perspective? Take drafting. There, a text gains refinement with each iteration, but the author must be willing, first and foremost, to destroy all that's before her for a do-over, if it's required. That willingness is paramount, and without it, there's a limit on how much a draft improves."

M/A/R/K nodded. "I like that." For a moment, he sounded like he might even mean it. "I do, but in the end, the trouble lies in our bodies, doesn't it? The human mind has advanced far ahead of its vessel, its source of energy. There's also been genetic wear." He raised his hands, indicating himself. "The point being, humankind couldn't survive a transition back to nature, even if it wanted one. Nor the time it would take to build new and egalitarian civilizations. Between our genetic weaknesses, autoimmune diseases, starch diets, immunodeficiencies, mental illnesses and limited resources, as well as the shifting climate of a scoured planet—the earth couldn't hold out for another go at us. The path backward is extinction."

I wanted to resist him, of course. To ask him if he was able to think outside the binaries he'd imposed on the thought experiment—Nature, Civilization, Past, Future—but we were disturbed by an uproar from the workstations.

A door had opened up in the left wall of the capsule. I hadn't noticed it on walking in. The hackers were cheering as they followed each other through the doorway.

M/A/R/K winced as I went over to him. "I apologize for the disturbance. I wanted to hear more."

I shrugged. "It's a party." Then I followed him through the door, up a ladder, through a trapdoor and onto an elevator landing. I squeezed into a crowded lift, pressing against M/A/R/K, noticing for the first time how young his hacker disciples looked. Their eyes, dilated or bloodshot under the lift's light, were agitated passengers in supple, fresh-laid faces. Fueled on caffeine or speed, I thought, as I watched two of them sharing a private anecdote.

The elevator came to a stop on the roof, where the rest of The Tank had gathered. From that vantage point, the metropolis was impressive—a vast machine of steel and concrete. In the distance, skyscrapers pushed up against the blurred horizon, piercing through the smog and giving the city a serrated edge. I heard laughter behind me.

"It's all a tool." M/A/R/K spread his arms out, framing the massive view.

Up there, he didn't sound irrational.

He pointed at a billboard in the distance—an announcement for a new construction initiative. "Even that." He gestured toward the sign. "From Delta, to the government, to the tallest building on the continent. It's all a tool, and tonight, it belongs to us."

009

There was a knock on the door, returning me to the chair in front of Emilia. She nodded to Ronaldo through the glass partition, sending him off again. Then turned to me.

"Does this have anything to do with Cape Town?" I asked. "The photos of me and Nathanial?" I asked her. "D., the artist I met?"

Emilia nodded. "M/A/R/K has interests in The Returners."

"Is she one of ours?"

"The artist is part of The Tank, but she's been living with The Returners for two years now. M/A/R/K wants to know if she's still an operative. He says it's important not to establish contact first. In other words, proceed as if nothing has happened. Let her get close."

"You couldn't have asked me?" I said. "I had to be used as bait, my friend threatened?"

"It's your first undercover assignment. Making sure you believed the narrative was important in establishing an organic bond with the subject. At least at first."

"How did M/A/R/K know we'd connect?"

"He says she's a great admirer of a book you wrote... I've never heard of it myself."

"I see."

"I think that covers it." Emilia picked up the cardboard box holding Pius's books.

I looked at them. "Pius wasn't a member?" I asked.

Emilia took a moment to answer. "No." Then she turned

back to packing up his effects—the summary of Pius's life at G.R.O.

I got up, too. I hadn't expected an assignment, but here it was.

010

The next morning we gathered in the basement parking lot, where once again we lined up like children and waited for Phil to steward us. None of us spoke—the humiliation of our shared obedience was too keen and recent.

I looked around, taking in the disrepair of our building. The paint had started to peel, the concrete had cracked, and small chunks had fallen off the pillars. A man, one of the grounds-men in blue overalls that were striped green at the wrists and shins like luminous shackles, was taking a bucket to the muck on a manager's car. In front of him, the security hut—a cramped room as narrow as a toll booth—squatted with a thick shadow draped over its mouth, while inside, the radio crackled as two guards whispered and rolled tobacco. These were the roots of the organization, I thought, which meant each man was famil-iar with dirt. All of us were denied access to the crown of the tree, even if that morning the five of us had been chosen to share a car with a superior.

Phil took a manager's space opposite us, the parking-lot lights slanting over his bonnet like melting ice.

"There's been a breakthrough in the work!" he beamed, roll-ing down his window. "The passing of an old bill! Let's not waste any more time. I'll explain the new directive in the Observation Room."

The hum increased as we approached the Tower. The machines creaked, the cranes dipping their heads at its feet like giants at worship. Lindani cleared us for entrance and we descended into the earth again, but this time, Phil didn't abandon us. He stood in front of a door we hadn't used yet and smiled, pressing his hands together.

"Now, to have a peek into the future," he said.

He led us into the Observation Room. It was a narrow space, short and rectangular. There was a counter with workstations and a row of chairs waiting for us; above it, a window hovered like a giant monitor on standby. Phil motioned for us to sit. The glass was opaque, giving us a chance to take in our faces. I looked like how I felt—Underslept.

Then a light went on behind the glass and revealed three technicians in blue scrubs and surgical caps standing on the other side. Before them were three hospital beds, occupied by two men and one woman, sitting up with their sleeves rolled to their elbows. Extending from their arms were IV drips, running alongside electronic cables that dug into the skin too. Nobody looked up at us; the window was one-way glass, I realized. I felt afraid of what I was looking at.

Phil cleared his throat. "The implants were legalized yesterday," he said. "The microchips will use wifi after their installation, but for now, we've had to make do."

The patients appeared docile. The technicians hovered over their stretchers with due diligence, prodding at them in soundless precision.

"Each patient was retrieved from a hospital," Phil continued. "They have no next-of-kin and are unaware of their presence here, or of our surveillance; this is necessary for accurate results."

I remembered the stacks of paper we'd found on our workstations. "Is this where those subject profiles came from?" I asked him.

He nodded. "Needless to say, the candidates have been reduced from five to three."

Henry furrowed his brow while the girls stared through the mirror. Lindani broke our silence. "I might be speaking out of turn, here," he said, "but I think we deserve to know what's going on."

Phil smiled. "It's not complicated at all. It's a deeper dive into our work at the office. Data extraction, collection, collation, algorithm building. The usual. This time, however, it's happening from down here—the cutting edge. The implants are encased in a bio-safe epoxy resin and biocompatible glass. No harm's done. The patients also have trackers on their scalps, which monitor neural activity."

We watched as the technicians placed blue caps over the patients' heads. Then Phil pressed a button, activating a speaker. "Hold it a moment," he ordered them.

Then he turned back to us. "This ground-breaking technology allows us to track and decode human desire," he grinned. "Those caps monitor electromagnetic pulses in the brain and create a data log. The implants monitor biochemical processes, endocrine secretions, and changes in DNA. The patients are also wearing contact lenses with imaging technology, capturing a frame with each blink. These are uploaded and motion-edited into video, allowing us to peruse the stimuli from the patient's point of view. In the near future, how and what we want will be mapped out—our desire centers located and even controlled. For now, however, we have a mountain of raw data to pile through, which is why we chose you, our best."

"What is it for?" I asked him.

"The future. Think of public health, for one. Left to their own devices, each of these patients will revert back to self-medication, or the other countless self destructive behaviors of the townships. Now, however, intervention will be possible for the first time. It will be within our power to influence them toward better choices. The true genius of this project, and what sets it apart in the field, is its focus on what we call 'neurological ravines,' formed during traumatic events. These ravines operate faster than the rest of the brain's impulse centers, we've learned, with more neurotransmitters at their disposal. The role of this team is to monitor how these ravines form and function through the data log. From there, a prototype algorithm will be built and tested against G.R.O.'s existing archive. In practice, of course, this means releasing the patients into the field for 12 weeks at a time, one after the other, and allowing them to reintegrate into their communities, before bringing them in again for data and surveillance downloads."

We were all silent, at that.

Back in Edenvale, I logged our time at the Tower as regular out-of-office hours.

I felt sick. I looked like I felt sick. I drove home and keyed into my apartment, went to the medicine cabinet, and dosed in front of the bathroom mirror. I stood under the shower until the water ran cold, then went into the living room to start up a podcast.

To keep from thinking about the Tower, I directed my thoughts to Emilia. I wasn't as surprised as I might've been by her visit. It was part of The Tank's mode of operation—to infiltrate the least suspicious members of the population.

I set the heat on the stove, emptied a can of diced tomatoes into a pan, doused them with olive oil and chopped some garlic.

The theme song came to an end and the dull, affable voices of the podcast hosts entered my apartment, their familiar timbre transporting me into the past. I remembered how, when I was still at the paper, I'd directed my enthusiasm toward stem-cell research; but my editor complained that most of it was mired in social discord, the reportage often indistinguishable from the breathless articles on Dolly the Sheep from two decades before. Hysteria saturated the field, but it's also what drew me to it. The arguments imbued science with an air of the supernatural, making its possibilities boundless. The same went for Dolly the Sheep. That mammals were being replicated inside labs had evoked thoughts of the divine in those who opposed it.

Humankind's technological advances, I often thought, were in service of a larger search, one that either led us inward, to our cells, or outward, into orbit. The rest, environmental science and artificial intelligence, was all meant to sustain us in the time it would take for humankind to achieve this goal, such that one day we could all claim comprehension of our origins and purpose. It was the reason I'd become a science writer.

I didn't tell him that, however. I listened to what he told me to do and did it. I took on the assignments I was given, which on more than one occasion might as well have been advertorials for fuel companies with inflated green ratings. That's what work became. I lost interest in journalism and learned a coding language. Now I wondered if that was a mistake.

I tipped the garlic into the pan. The podcast rolled into the next episode. I'd subscribed to it after stumbling across an episode on exogenesis late one night. This was a combination of humankind's two dominant searches, I remember thinking as the hosts spoke, in that it used molecular biology, biophysics, astronomy, and geology to postulate that microscopic life didn't exist on earth alone, but rather had been distributed across the universe on the countless asteroids created after the Big Bang. That this marked the beginning of biochemical processes which grew into cells, which grew into tissue, which grew into us, humankind.

I turned down the heat on the tomatoes, letting them simmer, and started boiling pasta. Then I pulled up an article on the truck accident on the N12. The driver had recovered, the reporter said, which gave me relief. As I turned to strain the pasta my phone went off, a message from an unidentified number, containing a URL linked to an encrypted messenger. M/A/R/K, I thought, assuming he'd found a fault with our old messenger. I consented to the download and it installed.

I sliced shallots and poured them into the pan, then rinsed my hands and uncorked a bottle of Moscato. I poured half a glass and took the phone to the living room, where I turned off the podcast and logged into the messenger. It wasn't M/A/R/K on the phone.

It was D.

"Hey."

The view was cloudless; a tide of sunlight poured across my lap. "Hey," I typed back. "How are you?"

"Excited."

"Excited?"

D. told me that she'd been impressed with the discretion I'd shown in Cape Town. Now she wanted to know if I'd made the connection to the exhibition.

I had. I mentioned Molope's paintings, the satellite images of the sabotaged mines. The messages we were sending disappeared after being read.

"No one was hurt," she texted. "That was the beginning. There's a lot more work to be done, but I've been given leave after our success at the mines. Do you know what that means?"

I got up and turned off the stove.

"It means I get to work on my art," she wrote.

"That's great."

"I'm moving up to Johannesburg to work and exhibit. I'm just not sure when. I still want us to work together. Is the offer still on?"

"Of course."

I said she could take her time; I'd fix the room up for her. I pushed down the part of me that wondered what she was after. That thought about Emilia's intel.

"I've told people I like you," she said.

"The Returners?"

"Not everything is about The Right Hand, but sure. Them."

"What did you tell them?"

"That I've met a great writer."

"I don't know about that," I said.

After our conversation, I was loaded with too much adrenaline to eat. I took out the notebook I'd bought after meeting Nathanial at O'Grady's, and read over the notes of a book I'd started thinking about writing, perhaps the one D. wanted from me. I imagined seeing her again.

TWO

011

For the next few weeks, our work at G.R.O. returned to normal. Despite our best efforts, however, Lindani, Rose, Micaela, Henry, and I couldn't hide the wide berth we'd started to give each other—our faces now each other's reminders of the Tower. Instead, we kept to our non-disclosure clauses.

Toward the middle of February, while test-running a new data collation app with the team, I received an email from Phil. It was a progress report, informing us that we'd be returning to the Tower in approximately 62 days.

We congregated outside the break room in silence, shuffling the albatross around our necks. Lindani showed us a photograph of his daughter. Then he smoked another cigarette and we followed him back inside.

I hadn't heard from M/A/R/K, not since Emilia visited our office, but I was making progress on the surveillance he wanted. D. and I had finalized a date for our flat-share. Earlier that week, I'd sent a message up the chain of command and received the green light from Emilia.

I hadn't reported on the Tower, however. I felt disconcerted that The Tank didn't know about it, and that sensation had coalesced into caution. I had the feeling that a hand was being hidden. Their operations were meticulous, I knew, but I was also a new agent. Expendable.

D.'s plane landed on a Friday three weeks later. Work had been uneventful that month, although we still hadn't acclimatized to the unease we felt about the Tower. It loomed and bred distrust between us. It would be the same again, the following week, I knew; D.'s arrival would be a break from the tedium and dread.

I'd offered to give her a ride from the airport, which wasn't far from the office. Outside Arrivals, I found a line of passengers standing with their luggage at their feet, their faces craned toward their phones as they waited for cabs.

D. looked as I remembered her; she was dressed in a green army jacket, a white t-shirt, and blue jeans. She didn't have a lot packed. Helping her put the luggage into the trunk, I counted two suitcases and a canvas bag of art supplies. I wondered if I'd noted this out of curiosity, or because of the assignment. I didn't like the feeling.

We were stiff with each other, which was to be expected, I supposed. I leaned forward to turn on the radio and D. started laughing. "That's an appropriate welcome for me," she said.

I followed her gaze out of the window. From nerves, I'd driven us into a traffic jam on the N3, and now we were stuck behind a fuel truck next to the Eastgate Shopping Centre—where the monument of a miner stood looming over the asphalt.

"The bronze plaques were stolen, but the figure's George Harrison," she explained. The miner was captured in a moment of triumph, holding up the first nugget from the world's largest gold field. "In some accounts, he was a prospector, in others, homeless. Some reports claim he discovered gold here, and others refute it. The fact remains, though, this is the epicenter of a disaster."

I'd never noticed the statue before, and I looked at it again now, thinking that we might not be as different as I'd first imagined, me and D. Not that I told her that.

Even before I'd realized I was doing it, I'd translated D.'s miner into a world that had, before that moment, belonged to me alone. I'd thought of him as a part of the plague. Its patient zero.

The traffic cleared and the rest of our trip didn't lag. D. wanted to show me around when we got to the flat. That's how she put it to me: that she'd been in the metropolis enough times and wouldn't play at tourist. I rolled her suitcases into the living room, unfolded an ironing board for her and poured myself a glass of water as I waited for her to change. Then I took her up on her suggestion of a bar in Melville.

The taxi dropped us off on 7th Street, in front of a low building with a corrugated zinc roof. It was split down the middle, both in color and function, with the blue façade on the right belonging to the bar we were headed to. I followed D. inside.

The room was a deep rectangle, with brick walls and wooden beams on the ceiling. A long bar counter took up most of the room, with a four-sided air vent hovering in the middle of the space, between a mirror on one wall and blackboards on the other. The patrons were scattered across their 20s and 30s; a machine close to the entrance cued their preferred anthems, ranging from ironic to nostalgic. I didn't mind the place.

D. found us a table near the rear, and ordered two drafts of light beer. Then she smiled: "I'm a normal person," she said, and lifted her glass as if to toast her statement. We clinked them together. "For example," D. said, "I never had sex in high school."

I couldn't tell if this was a provocation, but I answered like it was. "I slept with two people."

"Two?"

I nodded. "The three of us were friends."

Then she told me to hold on. The bar was filling up around us, awash in smoke and orange light: a din of laughter, bass. I watched D. wade around a drunk blond with black bangs, balancing two glasses of ice water to space out our drinks. I took the tumbler from her and asked her what she meant by "normal."

"I was afraid of people."

I nodded. "I had good grades."

D. smiled. "I can tell."

"I also knew about being afraid."

"I don't doubt that." She looked at me. "I was on heroin, before I joined The Returners," she said. "It started when I was 16. I drank a lot. That primed me for opioids in Cape Town. This isn't to shock, though. I just want us to be honest."

I nodded and took a sip of water.

"I went to art school," she went on. "That's when I started with heroin. In the 2010s, when opioids were picking up in Cape Town, I was a graduate student and had classmates with prescriptions. Diet pills and benzos. Codeine, tafil, Demerol oxy. There was also pethidine toward the end."

"Why did you need to use?"

D. leaned back. "I don't know. I grew up with a pit in the stomach. It's not uncommon. That was home for me, and it made me an anxious person. That's where the drinking came from. I didn't like being anxious, and in art school, opioids worked better than alcohol. The relief was instant, the euphoria full. The diet pills kept us awake to work after the downers wore off."

"So what happened?"

"There was a sting operation that compromised the doctor who wrote our prescriptions. There were more after that. Regulations tightened up, which is when we took the hunt to the streets. It was dirtier, but a bag of unga or white cost less than a sandwich on Kloof Street. It was less trouble, too. Even before the NHI bill." D. stretched. "I never got close to people when I was in high school, and I never got close to people when I was an addict."

"Then the Returners?"

D. nodded. "In the end, using depleted me. I developed the inevitable tolerance. I'd lost the chemicals I needed to keep alive,

I thought, as I walked into the Company Gardens, pretending each time that the bag I bought there would be the last. As I cut through the park, I'd think about the European settlers who'd built it. I wasn't being impressive: it was convenient for me to think like that. I had the right idea about the settlers, but not myself. I misplaced the blame."

"I see."

"That's good, because it took me longer to get it. It was gradual. Moments before a score, I'd experience a clear head; I'd feel relaxed and optimistic. It had to do with the anticipation of relief, I knew, but I took advantage of it. I'd stall on the purchase and walk a circuit of the park, thinking about the centuries between the 17th and the 21st. In our lecture halls, it meant a period that spanned from the Renaissance to postmodernism. Time had been neatened into aesthetic movements for us. The human cost of the passage was never tallied."

I waited for D. to go on, but she went quiet. The bar was still filling up. I told her I had to use the bathroom.

Inside the toilet stall, I thought about the cell. I took out my phone and looked at the messenger. It was empty. The same held for email. D.'s narrative didn't add up, I thought, but there was enough evidence to substantiate it. I'd seen the rails on her arms in the car when she'd taken off her jacket. Not that the scars were explicit: each was as small and faint as a freckle, a dark dot on her light-brown skin. D. also weighed less than was usual for a woman in her 30s. I'd bordered on an eating disorder when I was a teen, but she was even smaller than me, speaking to the stimulants in the diet pills. I couldn't reconcile her timeline, though. Emilia described D. as having left The Tank to join The Returners, but D. hadn't mentioned our cell. Instead, she implied she encountered The Returners straight after art school. The more I thought about it, the more the intelligence felt incomplete. Like it did with the Tower.

I pressed toilet paper between my legs and flushed. Outside the toilets, I used a bottle of sanitizer from my handbag, coating my hands in the clear fluid as I waited for the throng of shoulders to part enough for me to forge a path to the bar.

The bartender was a man in his 20s, tattooed, with a full beard and a shaven head. I ordered two mojitos in eight-ball glasses and started back to the table at the rear.

"I forgot it was Friday," she said.

"Me too." I shifted up the bench until I sat across from her.

"Now, where were we?"

"The park."

D. nodded. "It became a habit. I no longer got high, but I didn't want to increase the dose. I kept up the walks instead, savoring the moments of clear-headedness. Then I met the freegans. Dumpster divers. Living off waste, combing through garbage in the city."

"No, I know," I said.

She paused and looked at me. "What are you thinking?"

"Nothing."

"I can tell it's not nothing."

I shrugged. "I used to be a science writer, before I worked for the government."

"I know. I've read the articles."

"I once did a story on genetically modified food. There was an argument that advances in the field were stymied by capitalism's need for waste. Meaning that introducing GMOs would cast a stark light on our current surplus, which exists despite the hunger crisis on the continent. The article didn't run, but I managed to track down a freegan for an interview. Most food, he told me, was thrown out by the producers, if it couldn't be sold. The second biggest wasters were supermarkets, and consumers came in last, by a wide margin. That this was done to regulate market prices, and GMOs wouldn't change it. Instead, it would introduce foodstuffs with less nutritional value into an unwitting market. That was all."

D. smiled, looking impressed: she placed her hand briefly over mine. "There were four of them. Four freegans. It took me a while to notice them waving at me. Then I walked over and shared their blanket with them, spitting distance from the Rhodes statue. Those are the people who introduced me to The Returners."

We left the bar late. Neither of us was surprised that we had sex for the first time that night, in the early hours, on the pull-out couch in the living room. D.'s lightness fascinated me. I was drawn to it during the act, and to how the liquor had metabolized into a copper scent on her skin.

Lightheaded, I couldn't sleep afterward. I cued up the podcast episode on exogenesis again, dialing down the volume. I retrieved a duvet from my bed and joined her on the cushions, where we both touched each other for a second time, listening to the hosts debunk creationism for us, and in its place, laud the miracle union of cell and star.

Later, I'd often think back on these, our first weeks together. D. would often wake at noon, jot down some sketches on an A3 pad, then come to greet me at the G.R.O. reception with a shot of espresso. There were nights when we'd travel across time, roving through our 20s again, running a gamut that extended from the heart of the metropolis, from Braamfontein bars— where the music got turned up so loud that a single toke of cannabis, taken on the jagged stairwell overlooking a congested piazza, could make me feel 13 again—to Westdene, where, listening to Lee Scratch Perry with bearded men in berets and brown combat boots, we'd drink wine and talk until we heard the call for last rounds, waking up with our teeth furry and our lips crusted red.

D. often took me out to brunch, too, where we'd share a liter of passionfruit mojito on sunlit tables from Parkhurst to Illovo. We'd head indoors for beer at the Melville bar, before heading further up 7th Street to a dim Mozambican restaurant, where we'd laugh as we won and lost our change on the slot machines at the back. I'd think of all of that, in the future, and how each of us would stare at the other when she wasn't looking, leaning in and learning what we could about the new machine in front of us.

012

At the start of the fiscal year, March 1st, 2025, there was a bomb threat at the office. It took place in the middle of the week, during a heatwave that had rendered most of our building lethargic: a hive, I thought, with us orbiting each other like bees stunned by smoke.

Meanwhile, D. and I had fallen into a familiar routine—as fast and seamlessly as our flat-share, I thought—with lots of time spent staving off the heat on our balcony, overlooking the fading mural and the grid that writhed at Mandela's feet.

I'd clock in at the office, ignoring the loom of the Tower and the silence that presided over our floor. Then I'd come home, have dinner with D., sit at my desk and tinker on the computer while she sketched. D. and I also continued to have sex, and I looked forward to it as much as I did the angles of her limbs, the sound of her voice, the skin she'd dotted with damage for relief. I liked the exhaustion it bequeathed, too, collapsing us in a heap of oxytocin and communion. I was no longer alone, I thought, and the world had at last slid into place. I even began to think of the mission as an accident, some kind of mistake that Emilia would soon retract by text.

But I was wrong about all of it. I walked into work and there was a bomb.

It took me a while to register the alarm; it was because of Henry that I did. He'd turned to me and spoken, but no words had emerged from his mouth. Then I'd felt the air escape from my eardrums and the wail of the siren piercing through.

"It's not a drill," he told me. "There's a package on the ground floor."

I followed him to the break room, where the others were, and descended via the fire escape. Our colleagues were milling in the parking lot, looking up at the four stories in dread. Then the bomb squad arrived and confirmed it was a terrorist attack. From the entrance, we watched as two policemen carted a brown box out from the lobby.

It was later reported there was a pipe bomb in the box, along with a letter from a disgruntled grantee, addressed to the Department of Social Development, calling for our office to burn. The bomb was found to be defective.

I didn't expect to hear from the cell and I didn't. I drove home and told D. about it and she consoled me: "These things happen."

I agreed. It was the metropolis, I thought. Then we fell asleep on the couch, listening to the news, this time, instead of the cosmos.

013

Two weeks into March, a cold front rotated into Johannesburg, changing D.'s mood as much as it failed to affect mine. The office had stabilized and Pius had been replaced with new management—an inept, obsequious man named Leonard—while Phil had been assigned to the Tower.

Most nights, I watched D. bearing down on her sketch work and research. She was often hunched over from midnight through to morning, while I slept, tinkered on the computer, and clocked in at work. The layer of insulation between us didn't hurt. It was for a good cause, I thought, and I was also used to being alone.

One evening, D. went out without telling me. A Friday. She didn't come back that night.

I made breakfast the following morning. The flat was small enough for me to sense her absence. I prepared a batter for pancakes. I diced watermelon and paw-paw into a ceramic bowl. The sun rose over Kensington, streaking sunlight across the mural. I poured myself a glass of water and sat down on the couch, facing out to the balcony.

Then, all of a sudden, I felt the need to scan all the devices in our flat. I hooked my phone up to a scanning program on my computer; it took five minutes to discover a surveillance app. I opened D.'s laptop—she never locked it—and ran the same scan, with the same results. As I'd suspected. I did an internet search and opened the source code: it was a tracking program, using GPS to create a timeline of our movements over the past three months.

I didn't bother looking further.

I knew it was the reason the cell hadn't seen the need to contact me. I deleted the app and tried to put it out of my mind, but it lingered. I didn't know what I was a part of. I never had.

Then the door opened.

"I went out for coffee," D. said, handing me an Americano. "I also got champagne," she added, taking it out of a plastic bag with a liter of orange juice. We settled on the floor around the coffee table with our plates and mimosas.

Through a slat of sunlight, I took in the rails on D.'s forearms. Then I asked her if she'd ever been to Narcotics Anonymous, which seemed to surprise her.

"Is this about last night?"

"No. I'd like to know your thoughts on it, that's all."

D. sighed. "It's not an interesting a question."

"It is to me."

"I doubt that."

"It is."

"Then let's turn it into a game," she said. "Since this about me back then, interrogate me and I'll answer as the person I used to be."

"Okay." I said. "What do you think about rehab?"

"I don't know. Like most people, I often thought I was meant to be happier."

"But you don't now?"

"No. Now that sounds inane. I had to knock it off when I started painting."

"I don't think I understand that. So there's no point in working for happiness?"

D. shook her head. Her legs were crossed in her paint-spattered dungarees. "It won't last," she said. "How a person is is how a person is."

I took a sip of champagne, thinking about it. "Hold on," I said. "I still don't understand. I mean, what about your health? The fact that you could die."

"Then maybe that's what I want to be doing at the time. That's the choice I'm making."

I nodded, feeling like I might have understood her. We finished the rest of the meal in silence.

At last, D. said, "I'm different now, though. I can see I was being a casuist, delusional. I went to a center in Wynberg a few times, but it didn't take. I realized later that I wanted to get well, but I didn't want to re-integrate into society."

"You wanted things to be different."

"Exactly." D. smiled. "I wasn't using last night," she said. "I found a studio space."

The studio was close, in a walk-up a block and a half from our flat. Later, I'd bring her meals there after work, and sometimes I'd bring along a bottle of wine. We'd talk for hours, and I might convince her to talk me through a new painting.

That morning, though, the walls were bare. We christened the space with what was left of the orange juice and champagne, sitting on plastic crates and drinking out of paper cups that spilled whenever we toasted. As we took in the blank walls and high ceilings, D. detailed her intentions for the place, speaking her plans into ghostly presences against the pocked walls—indeterminate, inchoate, luminous. Her enthusiasm was infectious, her smile bright enough to turn the garret into an atrium.

Then she said there was something else she wanted to show me. We called a cab.

The sun still hung over the grid, burning down on us from a distance of 93 million miles. It was an indifferent source of power, I thought, as I pulled down the sunshade in the passenger seat, sustaining mammalian life without ever intending to. It bounced in a shimmer against the tons of steel and concrete that marked the architecture of the metropolis, drawing perspiration from the children who danced for change at its intersections.

The cab took us east to Braamfontein, parking below the Nelson Mandela Bridge. D. asked me to follow her and I did. Soon we were standing outside an art gallery: a six-story building with large glass panels built into a brick façade. There was a cigarette vendor on either side of us, and the street was beginning to fill up. Up ahead, the road had been cordoned off, making provision for a large green carpet that had been unrolled on the tarmac. It was a pop-up market—cluttered with the bivouacs and banners of corporations in competition. Through torrents of static, advertisements were projected over the heads of the metropolitan stream, coaxing them into products from data companies, international breweries and tobacco titans. Ever since regulations had been loosened to accommodate zoning, the nation's three largest multinationals had been untrammeled in their growth and influence, appealing to investors and end consumers alike, balancing the fiscus between carcinogens and communication.

I turned back to the gallery.

"For as long as I can remember," D. said, "I've wanted to be an artist. Even after I joined The Returners and the world grew larger, that didn't change. That's why I wanted to show you. There's being an artist, and then there's this side of it. This is what I'm choosing to be a part of."

I couldn't think of what to say. "Did you still paint, after you joined The Returners?"

"No." D. shook her head. "I read, instead. But last night, through into this morning, I filled two canvasses; they're the best paintings I've ever done."

"What's changed?"

"I don't know." We started toward another cab. "I think it's what's happening between us."

014

In the first week of April, the five of us were summoned by email back to the Tower. The first patient had been primed, we were told, and Lindani, Rose, Micaela, Henry and I were to collate the data that was extracted from them.

For the past two weeks, I'd become a regular at D.'s studio, watching her as she toiled or stood in repose over her canvasses. Toward the end of March, she'd been billed for a solo exhibition at the gallery she'd taken me to. I'd watched her laboring over her proposal, collecting files of older work into a portfolio. But as I read this email, I felt my anticipation for the opening, and the happiness I felt for D., shifting to make room for the Tower.

I looked up from my desk and took in the rest of the team, wondering what thoughts were taking shape inside each of them, and if those thoughts, like mine, had been set adrift and were shifting against each other with tectonic dread.

Lindani smoked three cigarettes as we stood in silence outside the break room. I almost joined him on the third.

D. wasn't in her studio when I got back. I found her in the apartment, sitting in the living room with a glass of wine she hadn't touched. I sat down with her on the couch and the two of us spent a moment in silence.

Then she sighed. "I don't know if I should be putting on this show."

"Are you worried about The Returners?"

"No. I haven't divested from civilization," she said. "That's a choice, not a demand for us. I understand the need to be conversant with the world we want to change—the times require that."

"I understand."

"That doesn't change the fact that I'm not sure if this is a good idea."

I couldn't find an adequate answer. I followed D.'s gaze. The sun was still setting over Kensington, washing an amber light into our living room. I walked to the window and observed the grid, the high-rises, the taxis and pedestrians—the worn, rutted thoroughfares and the men who heaved large carts of recycling along them, their muscles taut, working beneath layers of grime to feed us back to ourselves.

015

The following morning, Lindani, Rose, Micaela, Henry and I drove separately to the Tower, without Phil. Those were his orders. I'd left D. asleep, after packing her a thermos and a fruit salad—an attempt at a soft landing for her when she got back to her studio, carrying her doubts—and joined the traffic on Joe Slovo. The thoroughfare was clogged for six miles ahead, the morning bulletin informed us. As I took my place among the grid's countless commuters, I looked through the windshield and at my rear-view mirror, wondering what D. might've made of the clouds that extended across the horizon, pregnant with moisture and toxins and dust, and us beneath them: a groaning iron centipede, coughing more poison into the firmament.

I made it in an hour. The others were waiting for me outside the Observation Room.

Phil addressed us. "Now that we're all here, I want to talk about the two types of people who walk this world. The chosen and the unchosen. I was born in a village myself, you see, but much like you, I managed to find distinction in the metropolis."

We were silent. Then Phil opened the door and we followed him in.

This time, the workstations were on. We took our places in front of the blank mirror. Then the lights went on and we saw the technicians, all hovering over a single patient. It was the addict, Phil told us.

"Our first patient—I trust you've seen his report. Methamphetamines. Electro-shock therapy. The technicians have finished priming him for extraction."

The man was propped up on the gurney, his eyes closed.

"The electromagnetic pulses recorded by the scalp monitor, as well as the readings from his implant, have been collected into a data log," Phil continued. "There was significant illumination around an old ravine—the data corresponds. That helped us proceed. The team's job is to parse it and test it for patterns, in order to learn how ravines form and function.

"The first part of the process includes watching an edited video of three months spent in the patient's life, with a focus on those instances in which the pulses in and around the ravine were intensified." He motioned us toward our workstations and told us to put on the headsets. "During the screening, you'll be expected to categorize the stimuli and the responses. The latter will be divided into Constructive, Destructive, and Neutral. The first is when an illumination around the ravine—a reverberation of a trauma—compels the patient to take decisive action, either through consumption or labor. Destructive is when the patient-self-harms; and Neutral is when the patient does neither, leaning, instead, on their social bonds. The latter is rare, I should add, and often serves to undermine the strength of the dataset."

We put on our headsets, and the video began. It was from his perspective, from three months ago. He was strapped to the gurney, blinking at his reflection in the one-way mirror.

The five of us were seated on the other side of the glass.

Then he blinked again and we were no longer under the Tower: we were in Alexandra.

The video wasn't long. It was a 30-minute montage, in fact, with most of the footage cataloguing the patient's commute and labor schedule. The weekends were often a challenge for the technicians to retrieve, we were told, comprised of erratic, frantic movements, as well as spells of unconsciousness following intoxication.

Regardless, we catalogued what we could: the stimuli that affected the patient and the responses he gave to them, which ranged from violence to increased sexual activity to heightened concentration, social manipulation and substance abuse. We were supposed to isolate the gaps of time in between the stimulus and the reaction—the moment before the brain decided by which channel to seek comfort.

I looked at the patient. His life was a familiar one in the metropolis. I knew him, just as he would know me. He worked construction on the city's scaffolding, assembling Johannesburg, and then sought oblivion from the work. One of a multitude.

The video ended and we went to work. I was first to have a turn at heading the team. Lindani, Rose, Micaela, Henry and I called up the data log and integrated our entries on Constructive, Destructive and Neutral behaviors. Then we began to chisel him into coding we could test against G.R.O.'s archive. As we did so, I thought of D.'s miner again, George Harrison. I imagined us as prospectors too, seated in front of quieter machines, burrowing into what he'd left behind.

016

I found D. in her studio when I got back, but she wasn't working.

"I underestimated being here," she said.

The air conditioning was running, but the lights were off. I stood at the door and watched her on the floor, where she sat with her head hung between her knees.

"I used again," she said. "I relapsed."

I didn't know what to tell her. The traffic hummed outside, and the motorists hooted as trucks creaked under their contraband. D. sighed and I walked to her and helped her up.

"I don't know what to do in a situation like this, but I think we should go to a clinic," I said.

"I don't have insurance."

"We can discuss that later."

I helped her down the stairs, and as we reached the bottom landing, a bag of heroin the size of a ring finger fell out of her jacket.

I drove her to a clinic in Highlands North. The receptionist was a helpful woman who told us to download the clinic's application and create D. a folder, which I did. Then I sat down on the plastic chairs with her.

"I'm sorry," she said. "I'm a burden."

I told her it was fine.

"I'll sign up for an inpatient program."

"You don't have to do that."

"I'd prefer it." Then: "Again, I'm sorry."

I visited her all of that week, and the following. It would be three weeks in total.

I also continued to report to the Tower, where we helped to build an algorithm around our first patient.

In the meantime, D. told me she'd found a sponsor: a woman named Noni who'd been invaluable in her recovery. I expressed happiness at hearing that, and I meant it, too; I didn't mention the relief I also felt. It was important to display an unwavering confidence in D., I'd decided. To let her know I knew she'd be all right.

I couldn't sleep for most of the week. Our schedule had changed, Phil told us: the Tower's second patient had been brought forward. The code we'd built around the addict had been dispatched and that's all we were permitted to know. We took our places and waited for the next one.

It was the woman, this time. Her husband had died in a platinum mine, Phil told us. For work, she faced plastic tiles, scrubbing them, and her blood was thin from taking aspirin each night before bed. During the course of her surveillance, she was robbed twice, and toward the end, she acquired a King James Bible and began to make her devotions during her morning commute. Now most of her weeks were spent in the dark, with both eyes closed in prayer. The five of us set to work on her.

017

In the third and last week of D.'s stay at the clinic, after I'd tried and failed to reacclimatize to living alone in our apartment—thinking of the Tower most nights, and how the march of the metropolis had fallen under its shadow—I received a message from The Tank.

It was Emilia: she wanted to meet. I decided on the G.R.O. parking lot, where we could both muster up alibis if we needed them.

"I don't understand the sudden need for an intermediary," I said.

Emilia was sitting in the driver's seat, ignoring me. There was a man in an overcoat up ahead, fumbling with the keys to his car. I'd never seen him at G.R.O. before.

"I'm the intermediary, then?" she said.

"If M/A/R/K wants to tell me something, he should. No offence."

"This is a war." Emilia shifted in her seat and sighed. "The times call for precautions." We were both watching the man in the overcoat, now; he was no longer moving. Emilia went on: "M/A/R/K will establish contact soon. Even though he understands, he was inconvenienced by the deletion of your surveillance."

"I don't like being spied on."

Emilia laughed and watched the man, who was now on his phone. "That didn't stop you from working in this abomination."

I didn't answer. I could never defend G.R.O.

"Throughout our history," Emilia said, "oppressors have

always relied on our willingness to barter each other. From the Middle Passage to data."

I sank in my seat.

"I trust you haven't forgotten why you were chosen to be one of us."

"To make things right."

"That's correct. Now here's something you might not know. I was a member of The Tank before I married Pius, my late husband, and what separates me from you is how far I'm willing to go."

I told her I was the same.

"That's not how we found you."

"M/A/R/K found me. I'm sure you were fished out of your own well."

Emilia laughed again.

"What do The Returners have to do with us?" I asked.

"The assignment's still in progress. It wouldn't be prudent for me to disclose that. It's safer for all of us if we control the flow of information. That's our job, after all, or have you forgotten?"

I took a moment to think about it, before I pressed on. "The intelligence feels incomplete."

Emilia arched her brows. "It does?"

"I wasn't told how D. was recruited. If she ever was."

"I see. I'm not surprised you've developed sympathies for the subject. It's been almost a year. I had similar moments with Pius. I used to feel convinced that he could make me withdraw from the cause, but all it took was a thorough look at him. The man was a sleepwalker. Indifferent to his people, but beholden to his kin, like he was taught to be. I'm not saying I didn't mourn, I did, but his work will be put to better use now."

"I see. I'm not being an insubordinate. I probed her and found holes in the intelligence. Her life as an addict is what led her to The Returners. There's proof of it."

"Don't be naïve. Besides, those weren't your orders."

"I took the initiative."

"Please desist." Emilia started the car. The man had disappeared. "Everything you've been told about the subject is true. Perhaps you need reassurance on that point, for whatever reason, and if that's the case, then here it is. I'm offering it for free."

I nodded.

"Now, I have an important piece of intelligence. There's someone we're turning inside The Returners. The project started when our suspicions grew around the subject."

"Is that all?" I didn't bother asking for a name, knowing I wouldn't get one.

"That's all."

I reached for the door, but she stopped me with a hand on my arm. "I know this work can be demanding. The intelligence gathered on you described your personality as independent and thoughtful, but that's not what I'm getting, here."

I shrugged. "Maybe I've changed."

Emilia smiled and released me. "People don't do that."

018

D. was due for her release from the clinic that Friday. I drove up to Highlands North to fetch her after work, and we stopped at a dim coffee shop in Parkview to share a light dinner before heading home. In spite of our best efforts, the conversation was stilted.

D. suggested we go on a road trip together. "It's something that a couple in peril does."

I laughed, but I could sense more beneath the humor. I asked her what she wasn't telling me.

"I want to take you along on a mission," she said. "The Eastern Cape. The bus leaves in an hour. It'll be a chance to see our land."

"I'm from there."

"I know. It'll be a reminder—and a good start to our work together."

"I'm not packed."

"It doesn't matter."

I thought about it, and she was right. It didn't.

It was close to midnight when our bus pulled out of the metropolis. Exhausted, despite lingering traces of adrenaline, I drifted off an hour after we left, waking up the next morning to a different province.

D. was asleep and I didn't wake her. I looked out of the window, watching the view submit to an unending blanket of green, the one-room houses of rural settlements floating along its peaks like debris flung at sea. Up ahead, a woman wearing a pink doek carted her daughter down the aisle toward a narrow bathroom

MASANDE NTSHANGA | 275

stall. I could hear her voice behind the plastic door, scolding the child into urinating. Then D. woke up.

It was noon when our bus docked at the station in Stutterheim, in front of a Shoprite on a street called Hill. I followed D. out of the bus. "Let's sit somewhere quiet," she said.

We found a corner store with three plastic chairs arranged on the linoleum. A single cook was working the stove, her large legs brushing against each other as she approached.

"Today's breakfast special ends at one," she said.

D. and I settled on coffee.

"This isn't far from where I'm from," I said.

"I know. My cousin used to bring me here."

"In high school?"

D. nodded. "Tell me a story about growing up and I'll tell you mine."

"I've been writing one."

"I know."

I opened my notebook and pushed it across to her. She started reading it out loud:

This doesn't sound like a true story, but it is. For the length of one summer when I was a teenager, I worked as a recruiter for a new religion.

"Is this real?"

"Most of it."

At least, that's what the papers called it. I didn't know it at the time. I was 19, in my first year of university. At the end of that summer, the man we'd all known as The Professor was found dead in his penthouse, his face blue and a snapped noose around his neck.

D. looked up. I told her to go on.

That was also the summer I met Tiana, my second girlfriend—Part was my first—an exchange student from Jamaica Plain, Boston. We met in one of the libraries on campus. Her nose was covered in daisy pollen, I remember, and she told me that it shouldn't matter to me, but she was American and psychic.

I looked past D.'s shoulder as she read, watching a line that had grown outside a loan office. I thought about what we were doing there. D's mission was to brief three potential cell leaders in the rural Eastern Cape, based in Stutterheim, Cathcart, and Queenstown. It was part of the organic approach taken by The Returners: all their recruitments and briefings were in person. One face to give direction to another face; one hand to clasp another hand.

The overhead fluorescents in the aisle had fused, and the old books almost reached the ceiling. Tiana's hair was long and thick and it grew out in a bush that crested at the sides of her face. Standing in the narrow aisle, she balanced her outstretched arms against the shelves, each wrist adorned with a small leather bracelet. I watched her wipe the pollen from her nose, gather it in her hand, and blow it toward me. Then she said she could sense my unhappiness.

D. closed the notebook. "I still have to finish, but I can already tell it's about there being no trust between us."

I didn't answer her. D. packed the book into her handbag and we left.

The streets in the center of Stutterheim were wide, ashen and vacant. The residents kept to either side of them, as if avoiding a current, ambling along the pavements in search of shade under the worn awnings. D. and I followed suit. From one cover to another, we walked past a bank and then a social grants office. At one wide intersection, the path crumbled and sloped down toward a block of abandoned houses.

D.'s contact, who lived on the outskirts of town, had drawn a map to his location: a hovel built against the base of a low ridge. The directions were imprecise, but we managed. Half an hour later, we were standing in front of a one-room house built from misshapen concrete, peeling paint and sheets of rusting corrugated zinc.

There was a man weeding a mielie patch at the back. He shucked the heads he could save and tossed the rest. He sensed us and his back tensed over the plants.

D. drew closer and greeted him. "The Primary over us."

The man's shoulders dropped as he returned the greeting. "The Primary over us."

He sat us at a wooden table in a room that served as both his kitchen and bedroom. "I have little to offer," he said, "except a pail of water."

"That'll do."

He poured us both cups. "Thank you for taking the time."

D. smiled. "Thank the organization. It needs you."

The man had dark skin, muscular limbs, and a stern, narrow face. In the past, he'd been a citizen of the metropolis. A bank teller, D. had informed me.

"The numbers are growing, and it's almost time for our first meeting," he said, "but most of the flock still lives in the town."

"Don't call them that. The Returners aren't priests. In any case, it helps to be patient. It's a challenge for all of us to leave the grid."

The man nodded.

"I have two other meetings." D. pushed a folder toward him. "This is the material you'll need to establish your branch. There'll be someone along in a month to act as a guide."

"Thank you."

D. and I got up. "The Primary over us."

"The Primary over us."

I followed her out.

In town again, I walked up to the counter and asked for two tickets to Cathcart on the next bus.

"This is a late booking," the woman behind the glass said, and I apologized.

The Intercape pulled out of the station 15 minutes later, turning left onto Maclean Street, which turned into the N6 leading out of Stutterheim. The town began to recede. It was a dismal, but defiant, relic, which had witnessed the wars of the frontier and now stood to take on more centuries and governments. Little would change.

The landscape submitted to more green. I leaned back on the seat and tried for sleep, savoring the air conditioning and thinking of how long it would take for the planet to fold into itself and swallow all of these towns—if it would decide, in the end, that it wanted nothing more to do with us.

019

I was holding three hardcover books under each arm. They were on human anatomy. I couldn't feel their weight. My palms were sweating and I'd left my fingerprints in 10 different places. I looked down at the books and asked Tiana if she could help. I asked her: if someone wanted to kill her, would she have them shoot her in the head or in the back?

D. looked up from the notebook as our bus docked outside the Cathcart Police Station. It was a squat building that stood on the corner of Main and Carnavon. Following the map, we turned left onto Robinson Street and cut through Henry Elliot, heading north.

I started to feel faint. In front of us, the road stretched toward an endless horizon, dead-ending at the base of a barren hill. The tar looked worn, thinning back into the earth, in places breaking off into narrow dirt trails.

The house ahead was old, too. Its pillars held up a shingle roof, repaired with tin. Its plot, a thick apron of overgrown grass, was cordoned with a crosshatch of rusting wire, sagging open at parts. The air was moist, filled with the smell of old bark, and tranquil, undercut with the thick beating of insect wings. The road that led past the house bounded over a stream that led to a lake further north; from where we stood, I could make out mosquitoes shifting shape over the porch. When D. knocked, the woman who opened for us was stooped, with long white dreadlocks and an alert gaze, despite her apparent ease. She smiled at D. in recognition.

Inside, the house was crowded with firewood; the shelves

were filled with rows of tonics and herbal medicine. The corridor led out to a makeshift shade-cloth greenhouse at the back, and the other rooms gave off an air of being inhabited, despite their shut doors. It was a commune.

The woman said, "I know it isn't much, but it's enough for our needs at the moment."

Her demeanor and features were those of a woman my age, I thought, despite her white hair. She lit a stone pipe and drew in the cannabis fumes; we declined an offer to smoke. D. handed her a folder and we walked into the greenhouse, where she resumed watering her plants. There were eggplants, tomatoes and squash. There were robust sprouts of cannabis.

"Things have been going well for us," our host said. "I won't argue that our numbers are behind schedule, but we've had the best recruits in the nation."

"I don't doubt that, Khethiwe. How's the little one?"

"The same as she'll ever be: stubborn. I've told her it has to be her choice to join us. Not to trail after me. That it's a lifetime commitment."

D. smiled and embraced her. Later, I'd learn that she'd served as D.'s strongest pillar in The Returners. That afternoon, as we walked down her corridor, I turned to look at her again. The sunlight filtered through the shade cloth and lit up the kitchen, and for a moment, her figure appeared blinding inside the doorframe—as if she'd been lit on fire.

The next bus took us back onto the N6, heading toward Queenstown.

"There's supposed to be a river coming up." D. closed the notebook. "In high school, we had a geography teacher who told us there'd be no more natural water resources by 2020."

"I think I heard that, too."

"The teacher was an idiot, though. He'd make us leave class for making paper planes."

The sunlight intensified. I pulled a curtain across the bus window, narrowing the landscape to a crack. I remembered a teacher of mine, Mrs Osbourne, who'd told us that we lived in a semi-arid region, and as a result, drought was an inevitable feature of our habitat. I tried to forget about it as the air conditioning hummed inside the bus, descending over us like an invisible shawl.

020

It was for a paper, I explained. That's how I found out we had the same elective. The two of us had made it as far as the loans desk, queuing opposite the library's large casement windows. I still felt taken aback when she asked me out for coffee. I hadn't slept well, and I knew the caffeine wouldn't be good for me, but I also believed we could be friends. Downstairs at the student cafe, we found a free table next to the entrance. I asked her what living in Boston had been like. She shrugged, telling me that it was fine, like most cities, but beautiful in the winter.

In Queenstown, I could imagine the heat bubbling the tarmac. The bus dropped us off at a Sasol gas station on a road called Cathcart—the province looping into itself. We headed toward town, past a small park with a burbling stream. The water flowed black under weeping birch trees, their branches low enough to caress the plastic bags clotted on the grass. Even with the pollution, the green looked out of place. It was a small, verdant wound, I thought, on a torso of reinforced tar, steel and concrete; its edges scabbed with ancient refuse.

We arrived at a rutted intersection. Fast-food outlets with peeled and repainted signs led to bakeries and supermarkets with more of the same. Then an old building began to emerge from the horizon: a clock tower with a sharp, oxidized steeple. It overlooked the commuters who were clustered below. Later, I'd learn that it had been built in honor of Queen Victoria's diamond jubilee, and was now home to the town's municipal offices: an airless, purgatorial maze to most of the residents, whom it beckoned to spend lunchbreaks and weekends under its vaulted ceiling, lining up to pay for water or press bribes for social housing. Past it was the post office, which used to be City Hall, and then past that a line of hawker stands. Here women sat on beer crates, their ankles crossed under fading parasols, selling fruit, cell-phone covers, prayers—also the spells that could combat those prayers. But the building down the road was our target.

Inside the Cash and Carry, the fluorescent lights burned bright over the aisles; there were no windows on the floor. This was where D.'s contact worked. But when we got to the break room, we were told to meet her at the Hexagon. This was a public park, with monuments that reminded me of the ones I'd grown up under in King. There was a tiered water fountain that rose from the center.

I'd read about this park at school. It was built in 1853, intended to serve as a refuge for British citizens during invasion. The hexagonal shape would provide the battalion with a 360-degree view, allowing them to fire their cannons down all six of the incoming roads.

In front of us, the architecture stretched out under the sunlight, an unloaded weapon. Then D. found a note stuck to the base of the fountain. It was an address.

Tafelberg Road was long and shaded. Unlike the center of town, the green was abundant and didn't appear a laceration. Most of the houses were curtained behind dense shrubs, and canopied under tall oaks that obscured their façades.

D. and I walked five blocks to College Street, which is where we found her contact. It was a woman again. I watched her walk toward us in a maid's uniform.

"This is where I work," she said. "The misdirection is a new experiment of mine. Here in the suburbs, we're poised to cause more damage, but we're also closest to their defenses. The man whose house I clean? He snores with corpses at his feet. Do you know what that is, behind you?"

D. and I turned. It was a girls' high school.

"That's where I went. Now I clean up after them. I was six years old when they took down their Whites Only sign. In '92. Then, as a penalty for getting in, I was kept back two years. I grew up with them, and I know who they are. My mother cleaned for them, too.

"Now I'll tell you something else. I was here when that woman hired a man to strangle and knife her mother. The businesswoman. I remember her father, too, the serial killer, and how he shot 140 of us in three years. He was convicted in '92, the same year I started school here, and was given a hero's send-off from business owners."

I had only a vague recollection of the case.

D. gave her the material, leaving a hand on her shoulder. "I want you to organize your ideas and stand them in front of us," she said.

The woman nodded, her gaze lingering, as stiff as a soldier's.

"The Primary over us."

"The Primary over us."

We had one last stop to make, D. said.

It took me a while to notice she'd stopped walking.

"This is it. This is where I grew up."

I looked at the house in front of us. It was still in good shape: grey, with a tall white fence that tapered into sharpened edges; a narrow yard.

"My cousin took me everywhere," D. said. "That's how much I trusted him, which was a mistake; but I felt related to him, which was rare in this house. My mother thought I was too different from her. That's what she called being queer: I was being 'different', and it was pulling us apart. That was my mother, ever fragile... it was always my job to make sure she didn't slip and break. That meant I hid from her. But it was different with him. My cousin's parents lost their jobs, and he was attending a school near our house. He lived in a cottage at the back, and he didn't mind me being how I was. Later, though, I realized the reason he didn't mind was that he didn't care. Not about me or anyone. He was an alcoholic."

We stood looking at the house. I hadn't noticed that my hand was held over hers, but that's how we remained on the trip back to the metropolis.

The Professor was Tiana's father: a former biologist who'd lost his wife to a car crash. Tiana and I passed around flyers for his church, which combined the tenets of modern biology with those of The Nation of Gods and Earths.

The church was called XR03, after Clarence 13X, who founded The Five-Percent Nation in 1964, and the process of cellular respiration ('R'), which had been his field of research and the principles of which he had reconfigured into a theology. It was established in Cape Town at the end of 2003, to general indifference, until rumors of money laundering emerged. A special investigation ensued and the church backers were exposed as a node in a human trafficking syndicate. Tiana and her father hadn't known about all this, I believe, although I never asked.

Tiana told me that she'd had her first period in a bathtub—and that it saved her from using a razor on herself. This was after her mother's death. She'd looked down and seen the blood and changed her mind.

That's how it was, too, with the woman I'd met at the bistro in Cape Town. Living had reached over and pulled her back.

021

In Johannesburg two weeks later, D.'s exhibition surprised me. The canvasses she'd allowed me to see inside her studio had been blueprints: a foundation, I saw, established in pursuit of a larger pattern. Despite being constrained by white walls, a buffed wooden floor and the requisite LED lights, the space had been redone in her image, channeling us into her experience of existence.

In art journals, magazines and monographs, D.'s work would later be described in tones that ranged from deference to criticism to ambivalence. I would read every word.

The Johannesburg sun was beginning to descend below the smog line. We were given digital headgear that gave us access to an augmented-reality application—which made it appear as if the building was falling apart, the seams leaking a viscous red substance that looked like lava. The source of the fluid was a centerpiece that resembled both the Earth and an asteroid caught at the moment of explosion. Above it, computer monitors hung suspended from the ceiling on shredded fiber-optic cables; below them, in a circle around the spherical sculpture, were hominids in various states of evolution, each reaching for the paintings and photographs that were on the walls. These leaked a black fluid and depicted, in turn, complex star systems, binary code, and satellite images of disintegrating ecosystems. Many people would read a Molope influence into the latter, interpreting the images as a tribute to the missing artist, while situating D. within the local canon. By that evening, half of the work had been sold; the other half would be accounted for by the following morning.

I nursed a glass of wine, giving D. room to spend time with her gallerist. After my first circuit of the room, I realized the gravitas with which D. had embarked on her project. On subsequent circuits, I was almost moved to tears—both by the intimate experience of her turmoil, now on show in a room full of strangers, peppered as it was with her cautious optimism for our species—as well as from a feeling of genuine euphoria for the woman I now shared a life with.

Noni, who D. had also invited, hosted us for dinner afterward, and the three of us spoke well into the night: a rare moment of solace in the grid.

In the following month and a half, D. resigned herself to life as public property. That's how she put it. It meant submitting without complaint to interviews, profiles and exclusive vernissages, as well as dinner parties hosted at the tables of gallerists, colleagues, museum curators and prominent collectors. I went along whenever she'd ask me to, making an effort to remain inconspicuous, despite D.'s wish for me to anchor us both, which I was hopeless at. Not that I found the nights taxing. Expertise wasn't a requirement for the conversations we had at these tables. It was enough to mention who I'd arrived with— the requisite check of my network of influence, and whether I might provide gossip that could be used as leverage later—and which artists had caught my attention; followed by a predictable and shallow segue into Current Affairs. In most cases, it was acceptable to do even less. Nodding at the appropriate moment or commenting on the décor or the wine or the petit fours, all of which was manageable, I thought, until it wasn't.

It tired D., before it did me. One evening, returning late from a dinner in the northern suburbs and smelling of bourbon and lime juice, she told me she was done: that she would be going back to work, and even though her voice sounded hollow and unconvincing, I listened and believed her. I made room in bed.

The slide toward the end of 2025 marked 11 and a half months since D. and I had first met in Cape Town. The end of November arrived arid and vacant, with a third of the population leaking from the metropolis to vacation in the south and avoid the seasonal spike in crime. The protests had also decreased over recent months, indicating that Delta had, in the end, struck a balance in how it would handle the zones.

The two of us were cooling down, drinking light Mexican beer on the couch in the living room, when D. told me she wanted to introduce me to The Returners. There was a new mission in two weeks, and it would answer all the questions I still had about them.

She'd put the art world behind her, D. said. D. She'd been misguided in her approach from the beginning, and as a result, had failed to defend her work against co-option. It was a forgone conclusion, she now saw, that circulating art through markets was ineffectual. That the tables she'd sat at would've served better as kindling.

022

In the middle of December, I was called to the Tower for our third and last patient.

Phil was waiting for us in the Observation Room; the door was open and we took our seats. He seemed uneasy, clearing his throat before beginning. "This patient is different from the rest," he said. "He's undergone a new and riskier procedure—one that actually retrieves memories. This footage, for example, is from the recent past, before he was placed under our watch." Then he paused. "Ian Carpenter's a great man," he said, "but innovation has unique challenges and not all men are up to it. Keep that in mind as we watch the following video."

We put on our headsets.

The patient left the Tower and woke up in a hovel. He exercised and took Mandrax. There were sirens and a gang killing. The blood looked black on the tarmac. Then there was lost footage and a riot. Following that, three weeks of hunger and Mandrax. Exercise. Then there were phone calls.

Phil took a seat beside us. "Unlike the last two patients," he said, "this isn't surveillance, exactly. The technicians isolated what we need from the subject's memories."

The patient was in a parked car; it was night-time. He looked at his phone. Then he broke into a house.

There was a man asleep in the bedroom.

The man struggled, but succumbed to the chloroform in the cloth held over his face. The patient stripped him and laid him in a bathtub. He slit both his wrists.

He left the house with a laptop.

The video ended.

The five of us sat in silence. Nauseated.

The dead man was Pius.

Phil sighed. "Such things," he said. "This world needs to be delivered from itself."

We nodded.

"We believe he was hired by a competitor," he continued. "He was arrested a day later, and we had to work to make sure he received bail. We couldn't let him disappear into the system, you see. The information on Pius's computer was classified, and this also presented us with a unique opportunity to test the limits of our technology.

"This particular step has not been legalized, and the technicians believe the patient will remain in a vegetative state from now on. Mr Carpenter thought he would be of much more use here, instead of locked up. He can help realize the work of the man he butchered: a waste-not, want-not approach to justice. It goes without saying, of course, that this is all classified information. This will also be the last patient."

None of us spoke.

Phil told us that after we'd finished coding, we would resume our regular activities in Edenvale. Perhaps it was relief that gave us the strength to go on that morning, but Lindani, Rose, Micaela, Henry and I turned around and took our monitors off sleep.

I left G.R.O. two weeks later, after we were finished with the third patient. Resignation meant I was criminalized as a citizen, I knew, balanced on termination clauses that kept me on the edge of the law as long as I was alive and knew what I knew.

Rose and Micaela suggested we go bowling to clear the air between us, now that we were all done with the Tower, and

I agreed. It was how I wanted to remember us. Laughing and careless, invested in the unspoken comfort we'd cultivated between us in the office. The Tower would still loom, but that night, we held each other under its shadow.

023

The last week of 2025 arrived without ceremony. Not that it was unpleasant. Ever since I'd left G.R.O. and D. had terminated the lease on her studio, the two of us had settled into a peace that resembled our first weeks together. I continued to tinker on the computer and write in my notebook. My writing had intensified—accelerated—since our trip to the Eastern Cape.

I started driving D. to Narcotics Anonymous meetings, held in an old community hall in Brixton. She had no trouble remaining sober, even after Noni left for a post as a counselor at a clinic in Durban.

But one evening, D. seemed tuned-out and withdrawn on the way home. The meeting can't have gone well, I thought. When we got back to the flat, I let the car idle for a few moments; but D's silence persisted. I thought of Emilia and what she'd told me in the parking lot at G.R.O. That people never changed.

When we got upstairs, D. started packing.

"Are you all right?" I asked.

"I'm fine." Her movements were stiff.

I walked to the kitchen and poured myself a glass of water. "Do you want to talk about it?"

D. sighed, dropping her suitcase on the floor. Then she sat down on the pull-out couch, her head hung in her palms. "I have to leave," she said.

"I don't understand."

"For good. I have to move back to Cape Town."

It took me a moment to absorb. Then I asked her why, even though I could tell. I took down two wine glasses from a shelf above the stove and put them on the coffee table, took off my shoes and poured Baronne for us both.

"It makes sense." D. reached for her glass. "I failed."

I knew better than to talk her out of a mood. I nodded instead.

"I came up here to be an artist."

"I know."

"Now that that hasn't worked, I have to go back to The Returners, the life I know. I'd be a burden here, to myself as much as to you. I don't have to live through it to know there'd also be more danger of a relapse."

I listened, observing my apartment as she spoke. I'd moved up to the metropolis when I was 22, and had never grown familiar with it. I'd never established attachments, still responded to it with the compliance of a foreigner.

"I want to have a child." I said.

"Excuse me?"

I drank more wine, then repeated it. "I want to have a daughter," I said. "I always have." I turned to her and smiled. "It's how my life was meant to be. I want to make that known."

D. frowned. "Thank you for telling me, but I still don't understand the timing."

"It's because of how my life's going, right now. It means I'm coming with you. I'll pack up, too."

D. was quiet for a while; she asked me if I was sure, and I told her I was.

"I'm not talking you out of it."

"That's good."

I felt her head against mine.

I'm almost 40 years old, I thought, and my parents are gone.

The next day, D. and I took the last flight to Cape Town. I took her hand in mine and turned to look out of the window, watching the metropolis receding into a brown circuit board below us.

I couldn't tell if we were at an ending or a beginning, but I could no longer hear the machines in the metropolis. I looked down and watched the Tower shrink, as if it had been built on sand and was now sinking under the weight of its own ambition. D. was reclined in her seat, asleep. I watched the clouds, squinting at the beams lancing out from the sun. I looked through my notebook again, then leaned back and closed my eyes, feeling D.'s skin warm next to mine.

THREE

024

Two hours later, we walked into a veil of warm Cape Town rain. It was coming down as we gathered our luggage and walked out of the airport, an errant gust flinging the droplets into our faces. I squinted and held out my palm as a shield.

"There's a car for us," D. said.

In the parking lot, a tall man in a heavy coat and combat boots was waiting for us next to a black sedan.

"I have directions for a hotel in town."

We climbed in, and he told us his name was Peter. I ruled him out as a member of The Returners. As if reading my mind, D. turned to me from the passenger seat. "The meeting's tomorrow," she said.

I nodded, looking out of the window as the rain pummeled the glass, blurring the cars lined up in front of us. Peter took the highway, weaving through Mowbray up toward the CBD. The streets were sodden, with pedestrians on either side of the Main Road wearing coats under their umbrellas, each straining at an acute angle against the gale. We turned onto the highway overlooking the harbor and I began to write down what I saw in my notebook. Out on the ocean, the molten shapes of the lights burnt a line toward the shore.

This is where I would start our last chapter, I thought, before Peter enters the city center and heads toward Long Street. I packed the notebook back in my handbag, and Peter adjusted the heat and asked us if we were fine. D. and I nodded in the dark.

Peter parked in front of the large glass turnstile entrance of the same hotel I'd stayed at with Nathanial. D. and I stood aside while he waved the porter off, hefting our bags to the check-in counter himself. Then D. presented her ID and we all took the elevator to the fourth floor. Peter faced forward with our bags under his arms or balanced between his feet. He left us at the door to our room.

D. carded us in. The room felt warm, as if heated by an open oven, and D. suggested we leave the lights off. We left our bags by the door and sat in front of the window, watching the storm flashing over the city, both of us quiet as the air conditioning hummed.

"I saw you writing."

"I told you I'd start."

"I know."

"Do they know I'm coming?"

I turned and saw her nodding in the dark. "They trust me," she said, and paused. "What are you writing?"

"I'm writing down what I notice."

D. looked out of the window again. "This is an opportunity to change things. It might not look like it now, but it is, and soon enough people will see that."

I followed her gaze out into the thunderstorm, thinking of the flash floods that would inundate the homes in the townships that night.

D. turned to me. "Mali," she said.

"Mali?"

"That's how I thought my life would go. That I'd go there. I heard about it when I was young and I always thought I'd go when I was old enough."

Thunder shook the panes and I wondered if that was how it

was with me and the daughter I wanted, or if, as I often feared, it had more to do with the mother I'd lost.

025

The suite was booked for one night, and I couldn't sleep for most of it. I sat up against the headboard, listening to D. breathing in the dark. We got up at sunrise to more inclement weather, showered and went down for breakfast. I got us coffee and orange juice while D. used the wifi to make arrangements for the trip to Athlone. I had my notebook with me on the table, but I'd left it closed, watching her instead.

After breakfast, we stood outside the turnstile with our luggage in tow. D. told me we had to take a cab to town first, and then we'd be picked up outside the central library.

It wasn't far. Minutes later, we stood under the library's awning, with our luggage balanced between us. The streets were still vacant. This was normal: Cape Town had imposed curfews and enforced the regulation of commuter traffic into the CBD since 2022, providing room for tourists and affluent citizens. The townships hadn't been zoned in the province yet, but Delta had announced an impending project at the beginning of March.

D. looked up; a white minibus was pulling over. "They're here."

Two men in beanies and black jackets stepped out and took our luggage. They took turns to hug D., and she introduced me: "I can vouch for her."

"I've heard a lot about you." That came from one of the men as we pulled off. He had broad shoulders and a full beard, with dark skin. The accent was French, I thought. The other man, who was slight, with red hair and a pale complexion, sat in silence, facing ahead.

I asked him what he'd heard.

"That you're a genius."

D. laughed. He went on: "I'm a little harder to impress. I read your book and I liked it, I admit. I don't read a lot of make-believe—there's never enough time—but I liked the ideas. You seem to have knowledge of what's paining us, but I wonder what good that is, in the end." He grinned. "Most intellectuals are more than satisfied with talk. They have no real desire for change, as long as there's an audience and enough in their bellies. The Returners combine thinking with action. That's how we plan to return to the fork in the road."

D. glanced at me, her expression bemused.

"I'm not an intellectual," I said.

"Then what are you?"

"D. didn't tell you? I work for the government."

D. laughed again, and asked him about his manners.

"Right. Michel." He extended his hand and I took it. "That's Richard."

The driver glanced around and nodded. "Michel likes to act tough, but he knows we need all the help we can get."

"I'm not good with people," said Michel.

"Neither am I," I told him.

I spent the rest of our trip taking down what I saw in my notebook, observing the rising prominence of smokestacks as we neared our destination. The building was in a block of abandoned factories; an industrial graveyard.

The grass was overgrown around the warehouse, tufts peeking out from between rocks and concrete, together with discarded paint cans and rusting motor parts. More Returners were waiting for us at the entrance; I was introduced to them, too.

There was a girl whose expression didn't shift when she shook my hand. Her name was Ling. Next to her stood an older woman, Mari, with white hair and strong shoulders, who studied my face, smiled and shook my hand, too.

Inside the factory, the concrete floor was powdered with dust. Rusting pipes hung on walls speckled with graffiti. Under the exposed rafters, there was a mezzanine, with an office missing a door. On the ground floor, two more men were sitting in front of a large steel desk rigged as a workstation with multiple computers.

Mari stood at the threshold. "There's still no access." Her voice was low and hoarse with exhaustion.

D. nodded. "How did it go with Michel's contact?"

"He pulled out."

"What was the problem?" D. asked, sighing.

"I'll tell you in a moment."

I waited for her as she walked ahead and spoke with Michel and the other two men. Then she asked me to follow her. She led me to a room at the other end of the floor, where we found two crates to sit on. "How are you feeling about all this?"

"I'm fine. Is there a problem with the mission?"

"There's a place we need access to. It's tiered. First, we need to infiltrate the building, and then we can execute."

"That's vague."

D. laughed, palming her forehead. "It's an old habit."

"Let's start with the building."

"It's a paper plant. We need someone to infiltrate the headquarters, first, and plant a device which will allow us to disable the security system when the time comes."

"So what's stopping you?"

"The problem is gaining access to the headquarters without raising suspicion. We haven't been able to locate a candidate. The security's strong. I suggested Molope, but he's been admitted to hospital with renal failure. He's critical."

I thought about it for a moment. "I think I can help," I said.

"How?"

"I need to make a call."

. . .

It took me three tries before I reached Nathanial. He was in New Zealand already, but he'd set up his phone to divert calls from his local number. He was on a fishing trip, he told me. I could hear the ocean roaring behind his voice.

"How long will it take to return to shore?"

"Ten minutes. Is something the matter?"

"I need a favor."

Nathanial told me he'd call me back. I waited, watching The Returners across the floor as they discussed their mission. I couldn't make out what was said, but I nodded at D. when she looked my way.

"First of all," Nathanial said when he called me back, "tell me this has nothing to do with the people who sent those pictures."

"No. None of it will come back to you, but I need help. I need my old press credentials," I said. "I need you to unlock them at the paper's database."

"I don't know how to do that."

I told him I'd mail him the instructions, including my password, as soon as we got off the phone.

He paused. "It's better if I don't know what this is about, isn't it?"

"It is. How are you?"

"New Zealand's good. Doreen and I are better." He paused. "I'm worried about you."

"Don't be."

I emailed him the instructions, and 10 minutes later, he replied with my bar code and ID from the paper. I went over to The Returners. "I can get access. I'll plant the device inside the building," I said.

They all looked at me in shock.

"How?" asked Michel.

"I'm a science writer."

Fifteen minutes later, D. and I were in a different, smaller vehicle with Michel, headed to the plant. As we drove, he explained how the device worked. It would jam and hack the security system for 10 minutes, he said, after remote activation. He asked me twice if I understood and I nodded.

As we entered Belville, D. asked if I needed to change clothes.

"Not really. I need the barcode and the ID on my phone, that's all. There's no uniform for science writers, that I know of."

The landscape gave way to dirt, gravel and sparse grass. Table Mountain and Devil's Peak were distant now. He parked outside the headquarters, and I walked toward the boom gate, drawing my coat against the wind. I waved at the guard inside the booth.

The building was modern, with white, curved walls and large plate-glass windows. Behind it, hidden from view, were the less alluring paper mills.

"I'm a reporter," I said. "I'm here for an article about the company's new green policy."

The guard let me in and I walked up the driveway to the entrance of the five-story building. Inside, I waited for the woman behind the desk to get off the phone.

"I'm here to interview Mr Richelin," I told her. "He's in Sustainability."

"Right, please sign in, ma'am, and I'll get through to him. Can I see your pass?"

I gave her what Nathanial had sent me and she scanned it. It cleared. Then I waited for her to look up again, and asked her if I could use the restroom.

I sat on a toilet lid and counted silently to 100 to calm myself. I wondered if the jamming device could withstand the moisture inside the tank. I took it out of my handbag. It was small, but with a strong signal. The mission was planned for tomorrow, meaning it would have to escape detection for two complete cleaning shifts. I decided to plant it behind the bowl. Then I flushed and walked back to the front desk.

The receptionist winced. "Mr Richelin has two other meetings scheduled—I don't understand! Did you set up an appointment?"

I shook my head. "No, for this article, we're catching our subjects off guard. It helps to make the stories seem less like advertorials—seeing as the write-ups are usually very positive."

"That makes it all the more unfortunate! Is it possible for you to wait? I would love to be the one that introduces you to Mr Richelin."

I pretended to think about it. Then I told her she shouldn't fret, and asked for her name. "I'll try to return in two hours, and if you're off shift, I'll mention you to him."

"Thank you."

I walked out, wondering if I was now a member of D.'s cell.

That night, The Returners prepared dinner for me. It wasn't much, leek soup and rye bread, but I appreciated the gesture. Michel and the two men we'd found in the warehouse, Liam and Lelethu, got out beer and bourbon. I tried not to ask questions, observing and listening to them instead. There was a fire going outside, and minutes after midnight, all of us walked out into the field behind the warehouse to look at the constellations.

Gathered around the fire, The Returners began to talk about the fork in the road and The Right Hand. I was surprised that it was Ling who spoke first, in a low voice, staring into the fire like a woman caught in a trance.

"History isn't written before it's lived. For as long as there's life, there's time. The human animal is poisoned, but not dead. In undermining the rulers of our age, we chart the course back to the fork and reveal The Right Hand to people."

Ling threw a twig into the fire, and Richard took over, sharing her tone.

"The planet doesn't end where we begin, but The Path of the Machine has severed us from a communication that predated sentient life. From the beginning of what we know as time, all living creatures have been part of a universe in conversation with itself. The impact in Vredefort, the asteroid, was a communication and warning for which our landmass, the birthplace of humankind, was chosen in particular."

I drew closer to the amber light of the fire. Lelethu took over: "In The Right Hand, there is no separation between matter in the universe: from energy, to chemicals, to us multi-cellular organisms. The sustenance of the human animal is as much a giving as it is a taking from the planet, a conversation in loop, adding knowledge to an ever-accumulating core, the location of the universe's conversation with itself. In death we return, before we are redistributed once more into other, different iterations across the universe, from where we add, again, to its core."

Then D. joined them. "Now the conversation is fragile. Having created consciousness, or evolved into having consciousness as one of its limbs, the core worked on its potential and not on a prediction of its course. The human animal, in particular, a new being, was privileged to be the first carrier of consciousness, to appraise itself and look at the universe's conversation from the outside. The forces it was then beholden to couldn't have been predicted, not least loneliness, and the feeling of being a lone god in a sea of objects, including its fellow creatures. The fork in the road and The Right Hand are all attempts to heal our confusion."

Later, D. and I got our luggage from the car and walked up the stairs to the second floor to unfurl our sleeping bags. I asked her if The Returners had been reciting from a book.

She nodded. "There's a manifesto and a tract authored by the first Returner, whose identity and whereabouts aren't known to any of us."

"For safety?"

D. nodded again. My muscles felt relaxed from the alcohol, but my mind was adrift, floating on a mercurial sea of wonder and disbelief. I was still thinking about it when D. and I brought our sleeping bags together and went to sleep, the universe communing with itself.

026

Protopa Paper, the target of the Milnerton mission, was a subsidiary of Protopa Incorporated, a manufacturing company established at the end of the 20th century, and which over the last two decades had diversified from fossil-fuel extraction and the distribution of petrochemicals to energy production and electronics, growing to be one of the largest conglomerates of the third millennium. Its subsidiary, a paper plant, possessed the longest track record of illegal dumping in the region, and in addition to that, was one of the main stakeholders in the Delta Urban Renewal Project: a sizeable target.

In recent months, Protopa Paper had branded itself a major proponent of recycling, concealing the fact that the sludge created by the de-inking at their plant was a major component of their illegal dumps, second alone to the enormous amounts of pulp they discarded in local landfills. This was on top of the fact that the plant's processes themselves, D. told me, resulted in millions of gallons of effluence. Using chlorine to bleach the wood pulp, the plant emitted large amounts of dioxins, a persistent organic pollutant and one of the most toxic substances released by human endeavor. D. likened the plant's degradation of the region to the BP oil spill in 2010, except Protopa's effect on the environment was gradual and still undetected.

That morning, we used the basins at the back of the warehouse to wash. We spent the morning going over the plans for the mission. Then I received a phone call from Henry.

"I thought you'd want to know," he said, after a curt greeting.

"Know what?"

"The Tower. I know what it's for. I dug around. The new

manager, Leonard, was careless with protocol." Henry cleared his throat. "G.R.O.'s helping Delta source labor for the zones," he said. "That's what the experiments were for. To draw from a pool with limited rights and no relations. Then to program their compulsions toward products supplied by the companies signed on for the trials."

I didn't know what to say.

Henry sighed. "I'm risking a lot, but I thought you should know."

I thanked him. Then I put the phone down, wondering if I'd ever stop shaking, if the Tower would ever stop looming.

When I walked back in, D. told me she wanted to take me out for a drive. As she started the engine, I began to feel light again, remembering I'd stepped outside the Tower's shadow.

D. drove us into the Cape Town CBD proper, the skies clearing and the sun beaming down in a brilliant shimmer against the tar. She stopped outside the bistro where we'd once shared apéritifs, and led us to the same table we'd sat at, that evening in January.

"Do you know why we used artificial cobalt at the Molope exhibition?" she said. "Think about it. In 2016, a report was released that children in the DRC were mining the mineral to answer a demand for lithium batteries in the West and the East. "They were orphans as young as four, breathing in toxic fumes." D. paused. "Now I want to be honest with you."

"I'm listening."

"We're burning down the paper plant," she said. "There's the potential for long sentences if we get caught, and it's a dangerous mission to begin with; which means you'll be staying behind in the warehouse, even though I know being in the field isn't new to you."

I felt the insides of my ears contract. "What do you mean?"

For a long moment, D. watched me. "I know that you're a member of The Tank," she said.

It was back. The feeling of being dropped in the ocean. I looked up from my coffee. "How?"

"I found the surveillance in my computer, months ago. It didn't take much for me to connect it to M/A/R/K, since you worked at G.R.O. and he has history with them."

I watched her, not knowing how to respond.

"I tried to think what to tell you, but then you deleted the software on my computer, which made me pause. I didn't know which side you were playing for, so I waited."

"I thought The Tank was wrong about you."

"I'm not surprised. They work on withholding information."

"Then you know M/A/R/K?" It sounded inane, but I didn't know what else to ask.

D. sighed. "The freegans didn't help me with my addiction, like I said, but one of them, Lindanathi, knew about The Returners. I was growing curious about them when M/A/R/K found me trying to score and offered me a substitute for methadone."

"That's what he offered me, too."

"The methadone substitute?"

"No, but drugs. It was a substitute for SSRIs." I reached into my handbag and took out the pills. "I have schizoaffective disorder and persistent depressive disorder. I was diagnosed at 17."

"I never saw those in the apartment."

"I hid them."

D. leaned back and asked me what M/A/R/K wanted from her.

"I didn't get orders from him. He sent a woman from The Tank. Emilia. It was surveillance, and I had to get close. I wasn't told more than that."

"Is that all?"

"They needed to know if you were still a Tank operative, and still following orders to infiltrate The Returners."

D. laughed. "His suspicions were right. The Tank wanted to keep our world as it is, and that's why I left. M/A/R/K had misgivings about The Returners targeting Delta and disrupting his plans. That was my mission. To spy on them."

"Did they? Target it, I mean."

"No. Except for now, through Protopa, but that's because of me. I designed this action, but I wasn't thinking about M/Λ/R/K when I did. The Returners don't know that I started off as an operative and I don't intend telling them."

I nodded. "That leaves Emilia."

"First, when you mentioned her, I thought she was a plant from Carpenter, but now I see that in her world, only The Tank and the Renewal project matter. That she believes in M/A/R/K as much as I believe in The Right Hand." D. paused and looked at her hands. "In the end, I agreed to meet with him."

"Excuse me?"

"He's here."

I looked up and she was right. M/A/R/K had entered the bistro and was headed to our table.

027

For a moment, without expecting to, I thought about the life I'd had and how it had led me here. I thought about the Accelerated Christian Education program I'd attended as a child—an operating system, I now saw, unsuited to the continent's hardware—along with the various other iterations of formal education I'd encountered; all harmful, but necessitated by our dispossession and status as immigrants in industrialized South Africa. I thought of how I'd lost my mother along the way, of her losing her own mother, of my work at G.R.O., of my father, and of the Tower. Then my vision settled back on D, an immigrant who fell sick whenever she tried to integrate, and M/A/R/K, who'd taken a seat in front of us.

"Now that it's all over, do you want to know why I started The Tank?" he said.

It was obvious he'd heard our conversation. I didn't bother asking him if he'd hacked us.

"I know that you helped build G.R.O.," I said. "You told me that the day we met."

M/A/R/K nodded. "I did, but I also downplayed my role," he said. "Ian Carpenter and I were partners. We approached Delta together, after we'd bought and restructured G.R.O., but then we fell out on whose model to use."

"I don't understand. Did you come up with the zones?"

"No. Zones weren't our idea. The first ones were in Asia. Ian and I knew that expansion into the developing world was inevitable, and that it wouldn't be as egalitarian. The development of the townships and slums through zoning was always set to come at a great cost. In the end, both models were a form of slavery.

There was the idea that, despite the human cost, slavery expedited development, and when enough time had passed, it would be abolished again, on the other side of progress. The difference was, I didn't believe that we should consolidate the structures we already had. My model worked on a rotating system, with both haves and have-nots trading places after an allocated time. "

I winced.

"I know. I was an idealist. Ian, on the other hand, wasn't. He believed that luck and merit determined people's destinies and there was no need to tamper with that, and Delta, of course, was amenable to his thinking. The idea was to introduce basic services, education and employment, while decreasing civilian movement to and from the zones, locking the residents in sites of indentured labor and consumption."

My coffee had gone cold.

"I started The Tank to steal data and sabotage the renewal project. I wanted to submit my proposal again, but now it's too late and that's all over. That's why I'm telling you this. The government's approved a plan to zone the North West Province and use G.R.O.'s data and Carpenter's model to source residents and labor."

M/A/R/K caught D.'s eye. "I knew you'd decamped to The Returners." He turned to me again. "I wasn't sure she was wrong, either. When you joined us, I saw how much potential you had for our cell, but I wanted you to make an informed decision about both sides. The Returners and The Tank. I wanted you to decide after going to the Tower and seeing what they were doing there. If it was something you could work with to achieve our goals." M/A/R/K sighed. "It's true, in the beginning I wanted to sabotage G.R.O. and approach Delta with an alternative vision for the zones, but now I see it was all headed here."

Then M/A/R/K got up from the table. "I'm disbanding the cell," he said. "I have to reconsider strategies."

Then, as abruptly as he'd arrived, he was gone.

I asked the waitress for a double bourbon, while D. got more coffee. It was the last time we'd ever see M/A/R/K, I thought. "That leaves me with one last thing," I said. "Why did you live with me?"

"I wanted to," D. said. "And after all, I was from The Tank too. I also read *Obelisk*, and I meant what I said about it. It reminded me of our teachings, and I knew then that you could be one of us." She sipped her coffee. "What about you? Why did you let me live with you?"

I finished the bourbon. "The answer to that is simple. I wanted you. And I still do."

028

Hours before the mission, I unfolded D.'s sleeping bag on the second floor of the warehouse in Athlone and unrolled mine over it, planning to keep it warm while I read over the notes I'd written about us. I could hear The Returners who'd remained behind—Mari, Richard and Ling—pacing on the floor below me, speaking in hushed, urgent tones. This went on for hours. Eventually I decided to dose again, in an effort to calm myself down.

I went back to reading; and then—for the first time in over two decades; and exactly when the device disabled the security at Protopa Paper, it turned out—I saw the machine again, floating above me between the high warehouse rafters. I'd never seen it with so much precision, and I felt immobilized as it extended to cover my field of vision, filling my ears with a drone and my eyes with the paper plant.

I saw The Returners installing explosives and following the escape route I'd heard them plan. But then D. stopped in a corridor, hearing voices from behind one of the doors. They hadn't foreseen that there'd be a team working overtime to integrate a new method of bleaching pulp. It didn't take her more than a moment to decide to remove the devices and try for another date. Lelethu, Liam, and Michel followed her, but by the time they finally made it out, the police were there and opening fire.

I saw nothing after that, until the triangle returned.

It was superimposed over a map of our landmass, now, its center placed between the Vredefort Crater, the Cradle of

Humankind, and the Greater St. Lucia Wetland Park. Which is where I saw her, too. My mother, Nobomi.

In the week that followed, the news would report on how Oscar Molope, the dying painter, had aided the police in preventing a terrorist organization from bombing the Protopa Paper plant—an act of arson that would've killed the 15 researchers who were still working inside the labs.

Having suffered from amnesia upon his admission into hospital for renal failure, following his escape from kidnappers who'd held him captive since January, Molope was put under deep surveillance. A message from one of the terrorist leaders, D.—identified as local artist, Dudu Gumedze—was intercepted, tipping off authorities to the planned attack in Milnerton. There was resistance from the group, it was said, and multiple fatalities were incurred, but none of them police.

That night, Mari, Ling and Richard were standing over me when I came to, their faces blanched from shock. They described how I'd been in a trance, and then told me we had to go. The mission had failed, they said, and The Returners were dead.

PART B: 2035

Journal LOG 01

Maybe I was born to be told what I am. I have a rule where I don't kill mammals, but it's three in the morning when a spring-bok lopes onto the highway overlooking the harbor in Cape Town and dies, paralyzed by my headlights as we collide. The moisture from the rain draws a sheet of mist across my windshield and I can't decide if I should drive further. I sit back and wring the steering wheel, watching as the blood slides down the cracked glass and past the license disk. The rubber feels like meat beneath my palms. I squeeze it and let it go.

I wake up with the alarm clock spilling red light over D.'s brow. I close and open my eyes again, turn over and feel for her pulse next to mine; but she isn't there.

It's been a decade now.

It's difficult to comprehend the propagation of human life, given the odds against us, but here I am, a mother now. I met my daughter when she was nine and gave her the nickname Mali, after the nation D. adored when she was the same age. Earlier this year, Mali left for university in Tokyo, and I am retired, left alone again in the metropolis, wading through the recollections of an aging woman. G.R.O. closed down in 2026, and for a while I survived as a consultant, planning on retirement as soon as Mali had finished high school. The zones are still not in full operation, although Delta is. There was a five-year hiatus in the urban renewal projects, but news of their revival has been gaining ground. I suspect M/A/R/K and Emilia were responsible for the blockage, months before The Tank was dismantled. I never spoke to either of them after the Milnerton mission; both rendered ghosts now, receding into memory.

Journal LOG 2

I have resolved to write again, after I leave the metropolis. Things that were once opaque to me are now clear. Last week, for example, I looked up Jean Piaget's guiding principle, and understood it for the first time—what Marianne had meant with her distinction between assimilation and accommodation all those years ago. I was too young, then, of course. First, I had to learn what a schema was, and how it worked as a shortcut that organized the world's overabundance of information in the human mind.

When I was a child and saw that skin tone for the first time, the one like Marianne's, I'd called it skin. I'd assimilated it into the schema I had for skin, she would've said. Then, as I grew older, absorbing more of the world, I noted the difference between that skin and all the skin I'd known before, designating it as skin, still, but with different defining properties, now: brightness and power. It became bright and powerful skin, until, when at last I learned the word *European*, it became distinct: information I then had to accommodate anew. I had to set it aside as different. It wasn't skin, teachers tried to point out to us, it was European: of a land that had set out a table and divvied up our landmass for itself.

The Returners were right in their war. For generations afterward, men traveled in congested trains, passing water between cars and falling asleep on their feet, before descending into the earth through shuddering mine shafts, weakening in the dark; later seeing the light again with their lungs eaten into strings, while on the surface the air grew more noxious. This is who we'd become. The Left Hand.

Journal LOG 3

In March of this year, 2035 CE, as our government officials convened in a Delta-owned conference center in Durban to discuss melting ice caps, population growth, urbanization, food shortages, and preparations for the drought that was expected to arrive this December, I received a call. The voice belonged to an older woman, and sounded familiar, but she declined to reveal who she was over the line. I'd been expecting to hear from my daughter, I realized, which made me feel embarrassed, having spoken to her only the night before; but still I allowed myself to stew in disappointment as I listened to the woman. She told me that she knew me and suggested a meeting, and I agreed—both from curiosity, and from not having much else to do. I was a pensioner now.

Journal LOG 4

I met her in a drought-relief center, as per her suggestion. The space, an abandoned basement parking lot in the CBD, was crowded with volunteers and those who'd be most in need in December. I saw her waving at me from a table with purified water. She asked me to join her in a coffee shop on the same block.

Her face was beginning to return to me, I thought, but recognition was slow. In the coffee shop, I continued to stare, until she smiled.

"I'm amazed," she said. "There's still no recognition."

I began to apologize, but then there was no longer a need. "Mari, I'm embarrassed," I said, as it all started to come back: the warehouse in Athlone, 10 years ago. She'd been one of The Returners who'd remained behind as the others were being killed.

"I'm much older now."

Her coffee arrived and I poured out my tea. "It's been a long time."

"The Milnerton mission."

I nodded. "I was inconsolable. I left Cape Town in a daze. It was a year before I could look at the world again."

"I remember. Molope died, too, not long after that, and we scattered."

I stared into my tea and thought of The Returners. Looking up again, I saw the color had dropped from Mari's face. Her gaze was fixed on her hands now, and I heard her take a long breath. "It's not the first time you haven't recognized me," she said.

I thought back to that night in the warehouse again, when I'd seen the machine and stared through the saboteurs' eyes.

It was as if she'd read my mind. "It wasn't that night," she said.

"I don't understand."

"It won't be easy to." Mari reached for my hand, but I left it on the table under hers; I looked at her, filling up with fear. "I'm Marianne," she said.

It took me a while to register what she meant. I made her talk me through it. "When I was 17," I said, "I answered an ad in *The Daily Dispatch* for gifted children. Was that you?"

Marianne nodded. "2002, I remember. Yes, that was me. We knew we would find you, but not so quickly. The ad was just the first attempt, while we were settling into town and conducting our secondary research. None of us predicted our luck."

I enquired about her colleagues: most of them had continued to work with her, she said.

"Even in 2025?"

Marianne nodded. "I never stopped being a scientist," she said. "Even in The Returners."

Journal LOG 5

Over the course of that week, I continued to have tea with her. Two old biddies, I imagined us, frequenting a student coffee shop close to the relief center and speaking with lowered voices. To clear my head, on some afternoons I followed her back to the parking lot and helped her distribute water purifiers.

That Friday, I invited her over for dinner. She expressed both gratitude and relief, before settling on consternation; she told me it would be fitting to hear the rest in familiar surroundings. Thus far, her revelations had varied from the expected to the implausible, but all had proven true under observation. That evening, I made us tea while I left an eggplant stew to simmer on the stove. I placed a cup in front of her and pulled up a chair.

Marianne sat in silence, creasing her brow. "I feel like you've been kind to me," she said, "and now I have to break your heart."

I got up to turn off the stove. When I heard her weeping, I went back to her and took her hands in mine, leading her to the couch. "What's the matter?"

"Please forgive me," she said, "and understand, all of us would've done whatever that woman wanted us to do: Devon, Paul, Maanika, all of us."

Holding her, I wondered if it was natural for her hands to feel that cold.

"Which woman do you mean?" I said.

Marianne looked up at me with tears seeping into the folds in her skin. Then she told me: it was the woman who'd given birth to me. Nobomi.

Journal LOG 6

This time, the shock left me feeling weightless and parched. Over the following hour, the words came out of her in a downpour. I sensed relief behind her confession, which filled me with both aggravation and nausea.

Marianne spent the night. I stayed awake.

The next morning, the two of us sat down to a barren breakfast table, drinking our tea in silence. I didn't know what do to with this woman. I no longer dosed, but I remembered a bottle of cognac sitting on the shelf above the refrigerator. I helped myself to a glass, ignoring her, before pouring her one along with my second. Then I asked her to repeat herself.

Marianne accepted the drink and nodded. She began speaking in a low voice. "Nobomi believed that the machine was an alien communication, one that had grown fragile from being filtered through human consciousness. That's what we were testing for in 2002, and it's also the reason she was never in that room with us, even though she wanted nothing more than to see her girl. Nobomi believed that she'd been the first to receive the signal, but that it was compromised in her; that she hadn't been strong enough to hold it. Now her purpose was to decipher and protect it in her daughter. The shock of seeing her, after that long, might have disrupted the signal in you, she thought."

"I don't understand," I said, thinking about my mother and the sacrifice Marianne was implying she'd made. "Who gets the signal?" I asked. "How does it happen?"

"None of us know for sure. It might be evolutionary—was Nobomi's deduction. Or a rare mutation."

"I can't believe scientists believed this."

Marianne smiled. "None of us did, at first. We were trained scientists, and Nobomi was self-taught. But when we observed her, we discovered anomalies in her cognitive functions. Nobomi could also see things, we soon found."

I glared at her. "Why come to me now?" I asked. "I no longer see the machine."

"The communication you had in Cape Town was the last, we believe. The research leads us to believe that the source of the signal has gathered enough information on our planet, and concluded that we are the ones responsible for its degradation, and by extension, for causing discord that has had a ripple effect on how the universe balances itself."

"That sounds like what The Returners taught," I said.

Marianne nodded. "It would. Nobomi wrote their manifesto and created them: she was The Primary. Their text is based on the last communication she received. It was a way to influence the culture, she thought, when our approaches to the scientific community and the authorities had failed. I wasn't sure about it, I'm still not, but she'd grown frustrated, and the frustration had made her erratic. The signal was starting to wear on her mental health. I'll be honest. I was surprised when I heard of your involvement. That's when I joined."

I poured another drink.

"There are others now, but they follow a different cause. They call themselves The Returned. They believe humankind doesn't deserve to survive. They work in a direction opposite to that of The Returners. They attack natural monuments with the intention of making humankind's destruction inevitable. The last I heard, they were planting timed explosives on the cliff-face of Table Mountain. They even have a symbol." Marianne dug a notebook and a pen from her handbag, and drew four circles. Then she turned it around so I could have a closer look. "Have you seen it before?"

I studied it and shook my head.

"It doesn't matter." She packed the notebook away. "Right now, we have more pressing issues at hand," she said, "and I want be honest with you."

I watched her place her teaspoon across her saucer. Then she faced me. "Nobomi did what she did in order to spare all of us. Nothing less. Even if it meant losing her child. I know I sound like a mad woman, and I might be, but all I'm asking for is a chance. The team and I need to know what you saw in Cape Town."

I finished my drink and looked at her, thinking of my daughter. Then I told her I would come along. That I would pretend to believe.

Journal LOG 7

I fell in with them. It took another week for Marianne and her team to feel satisfied with the tests they ran on me. I was driven to a facility behind a large residential home in the north of Johannesburg. It was a scientific estate: four white, rectangular buildings housed laboratories and conference rooms. I didn't recognize Marianne's colleagues, except for Paul, who had greyed over the years but managed to retain the same haircut, which made him easier to recognize than her. When he saw me, he embraced me, perhaps too hard, and thanked me for coming. I would be sleeping on the premises for the duration of the tests, Marianne said. When I asked her who the property belonged to, she shrugged and said all of them. "That's something we picked up from The Returners."

Journal LOG 8

That Saturday, I was invited into one of the labs on the grounds. The tests on me had all been processed by then, and I'd endured numerous interviews. I hoped to be spared another, and I was, but the experience still unsettled me.

I saw an image of the triangle—in the presence of other people, for the first time—superimposed over a map, with red marks for the Vredefort Crater, the Cradle of Humankind, and the Greater St. Lucia Wetland Park. The image was projected by a small device at the back of the room.

"In the end, the message was simple," Marianne said, "like most true messages are."

"I don't understand."

She walked to the image and pointed to the center of the triangle. "It means we have to go there."

Journal LOG 9

Two days later, I was on the road with the scientists, headed toward the Vredefort Crater in the Free State. I thought of D. as we drove—the five of us in a minibus, not unlike the one I'd ridden in with The Returners. In my years at G.R.O., before I'd met her, I'd always walked the world as a collection of veiled vulnerabilities, a closed and cautious system, all the more defenseless for being so. D. was different: she wasn't afraid to push her face out of the window of a speeding van, even in traffic; all it took for her to take a risk was liking how it felt—not the need to prove herself, like it had so often been for me. As I drove with Marianne and the scientists, I thought of her, and how once, in a one-room city apartment, we'd given each other five weeks of peace.

An hour and a half later, we stopped in the middle of a barren field, with dust, rock and dead grass stretching out to all the compass points.

"This is as far as we can go," Marianne said, handing me a map. "Head in this direction."

I turned and walked away from them.

The car receded from sight and it started getting dark, the sun dimming from view. I couldn't tell how far I'd walked, but I grew tired. My thoughts were mercurial and my arms hung heavy at my sides. I needed to rest.

I laid myself down in the dust. And this is when the hum arrived, and the machine appeared before me, breaking the arid horizon and standing larger than I'd ever seen it. There was a narrow rectangle of light at its base, and I understood that it was a door. The hum became a murmur, and it vibrated through me with a motion that tugged at all that surrounded me, until I felt nauseated and emptied of thoughts. I got up and approached the rectangle; I walked through the light and into the dark.

Inside, it felt narrow, its blackness disturbed by motes that resembled distant, cascading stars. I could feel the hum inside my body. And then I heard it speak in what sounded like 10 different overlapping voices, mixing accent and inflection.

"This our voice, and it has traveled across the stars."

I asked it why it had come to me.

"This our voice, but you have to want to listen to hear it."

There was a whine and I covered my ears. I made out the sound of my own breathing, and realized that it was emerging from the walls.

Then the voice flattened into coherence. "Thus far, only two humans have been able to hear us. The woman who was your mother, and you, her daughter."

I asked it why.

"It is unclear to us. Humankind is host to an organism it has termed Evolution. It is benign and acts to preserve sentient life on Earth. That is what we know. It is our understanding that it has intervened, but it is unclear, as our kind does not evolve. It is our understanding that the mother was the first to hear us, and she passed this on to the daughter. In those who are receptive, our voice provides them with both gifts and illness, but never comprehension. That is, until you and your mother. You both bear gifts and illness—the daughter has less illness than the mother—but also comprehension." .

"I used to see a triangle."

"The triangle is a mistranslation."

"I don't understand."

"The human mind comprehends existence through three dimensions: the past, the present and the future. This is not the case with our kind, as our comprehension is not fixed to a shape. This discrepancy causes a disruption in our signal. That is the triangle you see."

"But what does it mean? The message."

"The communication is a warning."

"Of what?"

"Of the destruction of humankind."

I didn't know long I'd been shaking.

"There is a celestial body on its course to Earth. It is twice the size of the celestial body known as 3122 Florence. It will emerge from a declination of 32.03 degrees, from the galaxy M33, inside the Triangulum constellation, making it the second interstellar object to enter this solar system since the one humankind called Oumuamua. In 15 years, the impact will obliterate Earth. The goal of our signal is to communicate that saving this planet is conditional. The celestial body will be intercepted if humankind changes its trajectory."

"How?"

"The tip of this continent, from which humankind emerged, has taught us vital lessons about your species. Human history has availed itself for our perusal: even from this field, we can observe your oldest remains and trace your passage through Evolution. Your idea of time and how it splits existence gives rise to what you call Will: a human trait capable of affecting radical changes in behavior. It is our understanding, too, that our intervention would be in conflict with humankind's principle of Evolution. However, it is also our hope that you will be inspired into greater empathy and your trajectory will change."

"What is the condition?"

I was thinking: this has burdened me my entire life. This question.

"The existence of the universe is predicated on balance, but humankind has not heeded this. This planet's conscious life has grown to deter the universe's transference of the energy required for it to regenerate and sustain itself: a chain that passes through all sentient life on this plane."

As it spoke, everything went dark, so dark I couldn't see—and then I found myself back with D., in the living room of our old apartment. I could see myself there; D. had walked in late from her studio. She asked me what my parents did when I was growing up. I didn't want to answer. It wasn't the first time she'd asked me. I looked at the time on my phone, and asked to talk about something else. D. sighed. She walked to the window and faced out into the metropolis, and I knew that I'd never forget her in that moment.

Then I could see again, but the room began to fade, and the machine was speaking again. This time, I felt it resonate through me from end to end.

"If the corporatization of Earth does not end, then humankind will advance, but it will destroy this planet. It will seek other worlds and its imbalance will infect and spread, disturbing the universe and its calibration. The wars it will ignite, and the sickness it will spread, will result in the destruction of numerous worlds before the universe rectifies itself and regains its balance. This has been the goal of our signal, of gifting humankind with our voice, and now it is accomplished."

I wanted to ask it more, but there was only silence.

I couldn't hear the world or myself in it.

Neither machine nor voice.

I blinked, and I saw the barren skies again. For a while before the scientists came searching for me in the field, I felt found, even cured, with an insurmountable feeling of peace and purpose. It spanned a lifetime, and was accompanied by the knowledge that not only were we not alone, but it was also not too late. There was still time to find our balance and survive.

To clear the plague.

Journal LOG 10

Later, I'd think of home, King William's Town, and how as a child I'd visited the Cattle Killing mass grave on Edward Street. The plot was divided into two sections, and in the first half, holding pride of place at the end of a narrow strip of gravel, and rising up in a color and shape that reminded me of the machine, stood a war memorial for British settlers who'd died in the Frontier Wars, from 1835 to 1878, when King William's Town was still part of the Cape Province.

Then behind it, obscured from Edward Street and hemmed into a narrow rectangle of unconsecrated ground, was the mass grave. Its memorial stone was molded into a headless woman and there were ears of maize and thin figures etched into its base. It was meant to commemorate the amaXhosa men, women, and children who'd died between 1856 and 1857 as a consequence of having followed the vision of Nongqawuse, a 14-year-old prophetess, who'd claimed that killing their cattle and burning their lands would resurrect their dead and push the British back into the ocean. That a new grain would be dug up and cultivated. New kraals and homesteads would be erected. New herds of cattle would be reared, uncontaminated with the lung sickness of the Europeans. A reset: to begin again from the beginning.

But the cattle were sustenance, representing food, wealth, and social cohesion to the amaXhosa, and their decimation rendered the people vulnerable to both starvation and British invasion. The resultant deaths numbered in the tens of thousands, with casualties occurring each week in King William's Town. The colonial government of the Cape Province disposed of the corpses in a mass grave hidden behind their military cemetery—at the foot of their testament to conquest.

I wondered if the prophetess and I were alike. If she would've tolerated being put on pills. If she'd seen the machine—the obelisk I'd written about—that had led me to the metropolis, where I'd worked and loved, to D., and at last to that dark field in Vredefort, to the threshold of death. I wondered if her message had been scrambled, too, like it had been with me and my mother, Nobomi.

I thought of how many others could be out there now, those like us, suspended and lost, touched by the signal and teetering between comprehension and madness. I didn't have an answer, not then; but I resolved to find one, since I knew now what I was meant to know my entire life.

That Nobomi had been the penultimate link.

That I was The Primary.

III

TRIANGULUM

Litha calls me while I'm watching TV. The three of us haven't spoken, except by text, since last week, when we slept over at his place.

"My fosters know," he says. I've never heard him stammer before. I ask him to slow down. "They found the condoms and talked to the neighbors."

I get up from the living room, where my aunt's blowing on a bowl of minestrone soup, and walk out to the backyard, making sure the kitchen door doesn't bang.

"Jesus."

"I know."

"Is there no other way to look at it?"

"I don't think so," Part tells me when I call her afterward.

We meet up at the park after my aunt's gone to sleep.

Part beats me to the question. "What did they say?" she asks Litha.

"That I'm a Satanist and everyone should know. They're sending me back to the children's home, where I'll probably get shipped off to another foster family. They're that religious. Tonight's the last time we'll see each other." He pulls a water bottle from his backpack and takes a sip. "But I have a plan. I figure we should make the most of the time we still have. It's about the three of us finding your mom."

"I don't get it," I tell him.

"I didn't see this before, but if we form another triangle from Triangulum, and then superimpose it over town, we can project another direct route from the constellation to King. Look—" He takes out a new hand-drawn map and shines a flashlight onto it. "It isn't much, but here's the idea. Stand over there, across from Part, and I'll stand over here."

He makes us step back, Part and I taking up two points of Triangulum.

"This is what I thought. The triangle cuts through the nature reserve, Grey Hospital and the graveyard. Each is a monument, and simple enough to locate from space."

"Those also stand for birth, illness and death," Part adds.

I kneel down next to Litha's map. "What does it mean?"

"It's a starting point. We should investigate each angle of the triangle."

"Looking for what?" Part shuffles back toward us from Andromeda.

"Clues."

"In the dark?"

"In the dark."

I take another look at his map. "Let's start with the nature reserve," I decide. "Here. The star at the top of the diagram."

Litha agrees, suggesting we take Maitland, the second biggest thoroughfare in our town.

"It's the safer route," he explains.

Part and I don't argue with him, or with the light beaming in from the incoming traffic. The two of us don't have variant chromosomes, which means we have to listen to what he tells us when it comes to being safe.

When we get to Daleview, we cross over to the other side of Joubert Road and head up Maitland. It feels like I've walked out of a tomb and into an air vent.

"I've never been out here at night," I tell them.

"Not even for New Year's?" Part asks me.

"I'd never been to a party before Friday."

"Really?" She laughs, and tells me she's the same.

We walk past the Dale fields toward the reserve. There's no

one there when we get to the fence, but it's solid, and bolted shut with an iron lock. Litha drops his bag and Part pushes her fingers through the links. "Do we have to go inside?"

I nod. "To find the landing traces."

"That's true," Litha adds, pulling out his drawing again. "It's dark, but I have a plan."

"Triangulum?"

"It's the same principle... imagine a smaller triangle fitted inside the triangle that took us here. For example, take a look at this."

Part and I draw closer and look over his shoulder.

Litha traces a finger inside the triangle, marking a smaller one. "It should be on that hill," he says, turning to look. "Next to the obstacle course."

I make out the silhouette of the hill, beyond a grove of trees. There's enough moonlight to forge a path.

"Let's go, then," says Part, and starts hauling Litha's backpack over the fence. "These wires aren't electric."

We reach the foot of the hill and climb up to the top in silence. Litha pulls out a towel from his backpack and tells us we can sit if we want to.

I lie on my back as he searches his bag for the flashlight again. In between the trees, the stars burn bright against the planet's lid, blinking like white mites in oil. I turn on my side to look at Part, who turns on her side to look at me, too. I can hear her breathing. Her hand reaches toward mine and our fingers knit, her lips soft against my own. As she brushes her thumbs behind my earlobes, Litha heads back down the hill, beating a path through the bushes below.

Part pulls back from me and sits up on the towel. Pointing toward town, she asks me if I can name the constellation above the Missionary Museum.

I sit up too, and follow her finger. "It's Orion."

She nods. "Do you still think a lot about her?"

"More than I can say."

Then we both lie back.

"There's nothing here," Litha says, coming up the slope again. He turns off his flashlight. "I checked around the base of the hill and a little further down. It looks like we'll have to go deeper."

I nod. Part and I get up and pack his towel back in the bag.

We thread into the forest, following Litha's flashlight, coming out into a small meadow pooled with blue moonlight. There are remains of a campfire in the center, still smoldering in a ring of stones. Litha walks to the woodpile and crouches, hovering a palm over the glow. Then he takes a page from his exercise book and feeds it into the coals. "Let's take a break."

We sit on the stones, listening to the hum of the forest. I wonder who was here before us, and if they'll be returning.

Part touches my knee. "Do you still have the acid? Let's take it."

"It's just one a tab. I don't know if it's enough."

"I don't care."

We split the paper and start chewing. I stare into the amber light of the flame.

The earliest known sighting of a UFO took place in Ireland, in 1490, I remember reading, when an object shaped like a silver disc flew over a church during morning mass. In its wake, a path was burnt on the ground, a bell was dislodged from its tower, and cows were found with their hides singed in a field. The craft was never recovered.

"I was thinking," Part says. She looks through Litha's exercise book and runs her finger over his notes. "I've been to Queenstown before. To a farm near there. It was for a birthday party and the whole class was invited. I remember I went, even though I had chicken pox. I didn't even scar. Look." She raises her arms and we look. "Anyway, this thing happened."

"Thing?"

"It was fine at first. Everyone was having an okay time. The girl's name was Haley, and one of her lungs had collapsed earlier that year, and she'd had to spend a week at the hospital. Her parents still felt like they had to make it up to her. They had all these activities planned. Haley's dad took us on a tour of the farm, showing us the pig pens and the milking machines. He had us taste a mug of buttermilk, and promised us a tractor ride to the mielie fields. Most of us weren't used to farms. The feeling of being around livestock and seeing how milk is pasteurized. That things could have a smell."

Part pauses. "Then things got interesting," she says. "The class caught onto a rumor from one of the workers that there was a crocodile in the farm lake. The class lost its shit... but here's what happened, afterward. Haley's dad still felt guilty about his daughter having spent a week in a hospital ward, and was surprised at how much satisfaction he found in pleasing us, other people's kids. It restored his confidence in himself as a dad. So he decided to go along with it. He told us the crocodile was real, hooked up a flatbed trailer to his bakkie and told us to climb on." Part closes the exercise book and hands it back to Litha. "I'll wrap it up, now," she says. "In the rush down to the lake, her dad didn't notice that Haley, who knew there was no crocodile, hadn't climbed onto the trailer with us. Instead, she was back in her room with Joss Philips, our class monitor, who we all wanted to impress at one point or another. Though I think Haley's thing was deeper that. I mean, Joss was beautiful, even back then, and she looked older than us.

"No one missed them until the group came back, having given up on the crocodile that wasn't there. Haley's dad was chuffed. Or at least until the van came to a stop in front of the farmhouse and the class jumped off, and he couldn't find her.

He wasn't alarmed, since Haley was home, but it soon came out that Joss was also missing. The group broke up and we all went back to our snacks, not too worried. No one thought to look in her room. That's the first place I would've searched, if I cared, but I wasn't really bothered."

Litha and I nod, agreeing.

"In the end, I think a group of us wanted some board game Haley had in her room. It sat on top of her bookshelf, and her dad offered to take it down for us. Later, the entire class claimed to have been there when he opened the door and found them. Haley had Joss straddled on the floor next to her bed, and both of them had their tops off.

"For a moment, Haley's dad must've thought the girls were wrestling. I don't know." Part laughs, and then goes quiet again. "I just remember him standing there, quite still, before turning and closing the door and leading us back to the living room, at which point we all knew we had to be quiet. Then he went upstairs to get his wife. It wasn't funny at this point. Joss and Haley came out of her room and just sat watching TV in the lounge. Then Haley's mom came down and took them upstairs. Not long after that, Joss got picked up by her mom, and when she came back to school on Monday, Haley had been moved to another class."

I think about it. "Do you think Haley planted the crocodile rumor?" I ask.

"I've never doubted that, but I can't tell if it was about Joss Philips or getting her dad off her back. Or both. I never got to talk to her, after that. Haley was moved to another school in the next quarter. I don't know where, but we never saw her again."

Part stops speaking, and I turn to the fire again.

In the year 1842, in the Russian Empire, small metallic hexagons were found dropping out of the sky after a strange cloud had hovered over Orenburg. Reports also exist of a craft seen in

1663 over Robozero, emitting fire and noise, before searing the clothes off a group of fishermen.

"I didn't tell the entire truth," Part says. "About Haley, just now. The truth is, I used to be good friends with her, and I did see her again. This was before you worked at Mr Movie, Litha. My dad had been drinking after his shift and he'd come home with a jar of coffee and margarine, instead of what we needed for dinner. I went with him when he drove back to town for pies." Part sits up, but doesn't turn her head. "Then he wanted to make it up to us by renting a movie," she says. "That's when I saw her. I didn't recognize her at first, but when I did, we had this moment I couldn't make sense of. Haley looked at me with a frown at first, confused, and then she smiled; but when she did, it showed her teeth, which were small and brown, almost like a child's, and her expression was childlike, too. I noticed she was still holding her mother's hand, and that scared me. That and the fact that I felt embarrassed about Dad, hefting a bag of pies. He hadn't changed and was drunk in the middle of the week. That was the last time I saw her."

Part breaks a twig and throws its parts into the flame.

In 1972, a farmer in Fort Beaufort reported to authorities that he'd witnessed an object floating 40 meters above his farmhouse. He'd opened fire on it, he said, but the bullets slid through the casing without damage. The sergeant and the police station commander who reported to the scene opened fire on it, too, to similar effect. The object resembled a 40-gallon drum, with three legs protruding from its base. Each one switched to a different color as it flew. Later, dents were found in the ground where the legs had rested; the sighting remains a local legend.

"Do you guys remember Mongezi?" Litha asks, and I nod.

Mongezi used to be Litha's bunkmate at the children's home. I remember Litha telling us he'd wanted to burn down the building.

"Mongezi once started hoarding all his food," he says. "He'd find bags to pour his meals into, keeping them in his locker and in a corner under his bed. He started wearing his clothes in layers, too, and said he was preparing for escape. But of course the food started going off, and the staff noticed him sweating under his clothes at breakfast. He was taken to counseling and we all waited for the worst—but then the unexpected happened. His biological parents came for him. I understood how he thought; I'd almost hoarded, too, but I got too hungry. He had this pocket knife, which we used to carve our initials on most of the trees at the home. Those are faded, now, and I don't know where Mongezi is." Litha uses a twig to scratch the soil between his feet.

I'm not sure if I feel the acid.

The fire starts to die down. "It looks like we'll have to go to the graveyard," Litha says.

Part and I get up and follow him for a long time through the forest. Or at least that's how it feels. Following the map, he leads us back toward town, where we jump another fence. At Headlands, we turn left and walk down the hill toward the graves. We're only two blocks from Part's house. I point across the road at their roof, flanked by a pair of gum trees.

"You could walk home from here, if you wanted to," I tell her.

"I know I could," she says, "but I won't."

December 18, 1999

That week, more relatives and friends, old diplomats and people I'd never met, began to show up at our house to see Tata. My aunt and I had to meet them in our driveway—after we'd tidied and aired his room—and then lead them down our narrow corridor. Doris was familiar with most of them, I could tell, even Tata's old colleagues from the Homeland Office, and introduced me. I'd smile in response to their pitying expressions. They never seemed to hear us when we asked if they wanted more tea, instead looking 'round and taking in what little we had left after Tata's doctors' bills.

His hacking, wet coughs and chest pain.

I also made tea. I toasted white bread and slathered it with peanut butter or margarine. Then I carried it to his room on a cloth-covered plastic tray, where his would go cold while his visitors drank theirs up. I often had to make another cup for him after the people left, and he'd appear calmer to me when he sat down for it at our kitchen table.

"The two of us are the same," he'd sometimes tell me. "I no longer like making a fuss over food."

Then he'd smile and repeat that: "The two of us are the same."

RTR: 031 / Date of Recollection: 07.17.2002 / 4 min

The graves don't offer us the evidence we're after. First, we circle the plot. Then we climb the gate and cut a diagonal path across it, from one end to the other, and then we add another length and another width, completing the triangle. Nothing.

"It has to be the hospital," Litha says.

"Then let's leave," Part says. "I can't stand it here."

We climb the gate again, and take the hill back to Maitland. As we head past the De Vos Malan fields in the direction of Alexandra, the lights split our shadows behind us.

"I like that we did all this," I tell them, as we get to the hospital turn-off. "No matter what happens afterward."

"This is the last hurrah—I still can't believe it." Litha pauses. "I'm glad we got to do it, too."

"Me too," Part adds.

And then in silence we follow Cambridge down the hill to the hospital.

We can't get inside. The building has spikes on the gate and barbed wire on the fence. We search around it, finding nothing again. Then we hear a call from a security guard, who motions us to his wooden booth next to a locked pedestrian entrance. There's a bottle in his right pocket.

"Do you know what time it is?" he asks. "Turn around and go home. No one gets into the hospital at this hour."

"What about a visitor who has to see her mother?" I ask.

"Mother? Come back in the morning." He pulls the bottle from his pocket and takes a sip, then pinches his lips. He's teetering on his feet.

"How long have you worked here?"

"I can't hear from there." He gestures me closer. He opens his wooden booth and pulls up a crate to sit on. "For what?" he says.

"I'm doing a school project."

"Then it's been a long time," he sighs, rocking the crate.

"Night shift?"

The guard laughs. He takes another sip and points the bottle at me, nodding. "Night shift. That's the reason I don't have a wife anymore."

I ignore that. "Have you had any strange experiences here?"

He laughs again, and his face settles into a grin, his brown teeth pale against the darkness of the booth. "This right here is something strange."

"No. Maybe in '95," I say.

"I don't know. Lots of strange things happen at a hospital. Tell those two to go around to the exit and the two of us can figure it out."

I take a step back from the booth.

"Lights," Litha cuts in from behind me, drawing closer and placing a hand on my shoulder. Have you ever seen a bright light hovering over the hospital? It would've been a flattened circle with a dark center. With other lights around it, too."

It's the most common description of sightings in the southern hemisphere. I remember it from *UFO Diaries*.

Part and I watch as the guard's face goes still. He pulls out an A4 exercise book from his drawer and sits on it, cushioning himself against the hard plastic. Then he frowns, and slaps his face lightly. "I apologize," he says. "You're only a child. I should know better." Taking another drink, his face settles into a pained smile. "How did you know about that light? I can't lose this job."

We don't answer. I hear his labored breathing. "I remember it," he says. "The following day I met my ex-wife. I was told by a sangoma that I would have good fortune from that night, but I've never known it in all my life."

"What did it look like?" I ask him.

"It was a ball. It was too bright to look at. Like an angel." He gets up and licks his lips. "Those were better times. Hard, but at least we got a little of what we worked for."

I wait, but he doesn't speak again. "What direction did it go?"

"There—where else? To Johannesburg. That's where my wife wanted us to go."

He gets up and teeters again as he steps into the light, raising his arm and pointing toward Joburg. His skin is light and his face is hairless, pocked with blackheads. Our eyes follow his finger. His walkie-talkie goes off and he fumbles for it. The voice on the other end sounds muffled but amused. Without another word, he stumbles out of the booth and starts down the road, disappearing around the corner.

Left standing there in front of his wooden booth, I turn to look at Litha and Part, who look back at me, confused.

"I'll take it," I tell them.

"Are you sure?" Part asks. "He didn't seem right in the head."

"I think he's sad, that's all. I've lost someone, too."

Litha packs the map back into his backpack.

"I'll take it," I tell them again, and for the first time since Mom was taken from us, I feel I have the measure of how little there is to hold on to in our universe.

December 20, 1999

When I think of Mama now, I often feel that her absence, and what followed it that summer of '99, actually began some time before her abduction, when my parents settled on the couch in our living room in Bhisho to watch the release of Nelson Mandela from prison. I was seven years old.

It was to be broadcast on our old Panasonic TV, a color set Tata had bought second-hand from a Cantonese dealer in '88. In that instant, Mama told us, our town, the capital of the Ciskei, would become an anachronism: a place that belonged less to what was in front of us than to what had passed. She was right, but it took longer than an afternoon to sink in.

One August morning two years later, Mama woke up and complained about needing more rest to recover from a recent flu. Tata offered to take me to school himself, which wasn't unusual. He sometimes dropped me off on his way to Parliament Hill, since our school wasn't that far from his office.

I forced down a bowl of oats, left the TV and got into his car. He squinted under his sunshade, saying the rubber of the steering wheel was burning his fingers, which made me laugh. I copied him, pulling my shade down too, and felt the same helplessness against the tide of light washing in from the horizon. Although it was still morning, the sun hung in the middle of the windshield, pressing down its might against the console and our thighs. It was a heat that reminded him of the mines in the Transvaal, he said, and of labor that had almost left him blind one summer, before his parents died and he went back home to sell their homestead for his varsity tuition. I nodded, not making sense of it, but feeling it was important.

Tata drove straight past the school turn-off. He shifted gears and asked me if I wanted to see where he worked, and I said I did. He continued up to Parliament Hill and drove us through a boom-gate flanked by soldiers in fatigues carrying automatic weapons. We stopped at the back of a large parking lot, next to a squat brown building with narrow, blue windows that bounced back squares of sunlight.

I waited for him in his office. It was cold, but felt foreign enough to keep me occupied with its modern fittings—filing cabinets, artificial plants and blinds—while Tata received men from the Transkei legislature in a boardroom down the hall.

In later years, I'd often think back to this morning and won-der about Tata's diligence. Unlike most second-class citizens in the republic, his service to the apartheid government was direct.

The feedback from the meeting was agreeable, he said; he appeared calmer than usual. He went over what he called the minutes with his assistant, nodding and smiling at her. I took in her perfume, which smelt nothing like Mama's.

Later, after he'd bought me a cream bun and a boxed toffee milkshake for lunch, a call came through to his line.

It was Mama. I heard her voice say, "catatonia," before it went quiet again.

Later, Mama's explanation was that her head had felt burdened.

Tata took his time replacing the receiver, even though the line was dead. His response to Mama's behavior, her moods he couldn't understand, was often to drive us to Zeleni, where the matron, Mama's mother, owned a homestead in Gubevu. a small rural district above the Sikobeni River.

It was a half-hour drive. That Saturday, I sat strapped in the backseat, holding a thesaurus Mama had pushed on me to solve a recent crossword puzzle; but I ignored it. Instead, I waited to pass Bhisho Hospital, when I could look up and see the shacks and mud huts beginning to sprout from the mottled hills on either side of Komga Road, hills pocked with animals that were absent from our suburban neighborhood back home.

The matron's kitchen was a small square of uneven, red-polished cement. A counter of rough plank, surfaced with vinyl, stood opposite a meat freezer connected to a generator that coughed outside, its legs speckled with rust.

Inside, I was drawn to the smell of Madubula: the disinfectant was so strong it seemed like it was seeping out of the walls. A flytrap hung down in a straight line from the ceiling, clustered black with a million gleaming insects.

Over a lunch of tripe, butternut squash, spinach and samp in the lounge, Mama's mood improved, like Tata thought it would. Her conversation took a familiar turn: a plea for her mother to move in with us to be looked after, which the matron declined, stating that her own house needed keeping. She got up and retrieved a calabash of amasi that sat fermenting in the cupboard under the kitchen window—a batch drawn from the cows milling in her kraal—and poured mine into a tin cup, offering Mama and Tata theirs in dimpled glasses.

"Mandela's out of prison," she said.

Tata sighed, and stretched back on the couch. "He's out of prison, yes," he said, "but who's he negotiating for?"

No one answered him. I could make out the tick of the matron's clock.

Later, I looked out of the window as Tata drove us home. It had turned dark, and I watched as thin lines of lightning plastered themselves against the horizon, as if to demonstrate that the world was an ornament that could be cracked. Back in Bhisho, we ate in more silence, marking another dinner in front of our TV, and then I went to bed.

Seven years later, after Tata had begun to receive his final visits in '99, I woke up one morning to the same silence: a feeling of heaviness, of wading underwater. I spent that summer watching the clock, fearing the return of the migraines I'd suffered at the Diocesan College, where I'd begun to see the machine across the stone benches, its hum loud and hostile as it replaced the teachers' faces. I woke up in front of the TV each night, with a spread of completed homework slipping down to the floor; I'd go to bed and wake up in class. This happened over and over.

Then there were the mornings Tata couldn't get up from his bed.

I often watched people's mouths moving without hearing them. Once, when I was dozing off in the science fiction aisle of the library, fending off torpor from a new prescription that gave me tremors in the morning, I looked up and saw a torn book with the title *Eden* written on the spine. It looked old, but I took it out and went home. Maybe it was the cover—an illustration of a landscape that reminded me of the machine—that made me choose it. I read long passages from it at night, keeping myself occupied through Tata's coughing. Later, I felt that I wanted to write something, too, a story that made me feel the same way but had us in it, but I didn't know how to start.

In *Eden*, a spacecraft carrying a crew of six—a Captain, a Doctor, a Cyberneticist, an Engineer, a Chemist, and a Physicist—crash-lands on a distant, alien planet. Left stranded, and with no recourse but to explore the surrounding terrain, the crew comes across a large-bodied alien species. These aliens, called doublers due to their ability to pull and push their torsos until they split into two separate bodies, exist under an advanced system of governance based stratified and manipulated information, a framework designed to mold them and their civilization in accordance with the wishes of a hidden ruling class. The aliens regulate themselves in a cageless prison, rendered their own jailors, their rulers watching.

In '92, two weeks after we visited the homestead, the foundation Tata had leaned on for all his adult life began to crumble. The town he knew fell silent. On the streets, white armored trucks cruised through the grids of our suburbs, while soldiers sauntered in and out of the corner shops we frequented in town. Once, driving us back from school, our contract driver came across a vacant bus parked in the middle of the road. Fearing explosives, he reversed his van and told us we had to walk the rest of the way home. When I told Mama about it, she wouldn't stop looking out of the window.

There was no school for us on the Monday the gunshots arrived; we could hear them from our yards. Most of us had been warned. Later, we'd learn that the Secretary General of the African National Congress, along with its armed wing's chief of intelligence, had led a crowd of 80,000 to the stadium on Komga Road, a plot nestled on the green outskirts of the capital, in protest against the government Tata worked for. They were calling for the resignation of his immediate superior, Brigadier Oupa Gqozo, and for FW de Klerk to approve the instatement of a new government: one that could oversee the absorption of the Ciskei into the larger democratic state—in effect, its dismantling. The stadium was guarded with razor wire, but the protestors sought and found a gap in the fence, unintentionally rousing a phalanx of hidden soldiers who opened fire on them without warning. The marchers scattered; 28 were reported dead and more than 200 were injured.

I finished the novel and read it over again while Tata worsened.

In the last pages of *Eden*, once the crew manages to repair the spacecraft, two of the doublers stand up against the ship's exhaust funnels as it takes off, allowing their bodies to be incinerated instead of being returned to the regime.

That's what I'd taken from it, I realized.

That the doublers were us.

Two nights before Tata died, he got Doris to buy him a handle of Old Buck gin and a carton of cigarettes, before calling us to the kitchen to share them with him. I was surprised when my aunt didn't put up a fight. She rinsed three glasses and set them on the kitchen table, poured herself a drink and took it down without looking at either one of us. I felt light-headed after the first sip.

I listened to them talk, like the young siblings they once were, as if each drink served to knock off a decade. I leaned back in my chair, warm from the gin, as Tata lit a cigarette, drew on it and then handed it to me.

"This can't do me much more harm," he said. "Me and those men had to breathe the air in those holes. We climbed back up with pocket change and polluted lungs."

I didn't know what to say.

Tata often mentioned the mines in the Transvaal, as well as his old office on Parliament Hill, but he never elaborated. Instead, he'd change the subject and redirect talk to his pension, which, he often repeated, by chance hadn't sunk along with the homeland.

I inhaled and coughed, and he laughed and took the cigarette from me. "Now don't ever do that again," he said.

Doris got up and began to draw the curtains. Tata and I remained seated at the kitchen table, both grinning from the gin. He poured himself another shot and then the two of us went quiet again, careful not to bring on more of his coughing, listening to the tick of his watch. I could hear us breathing.

Then Tata sighed, as if coming back to life and shrugging off his sickness. His hand found mine on the table.

"You're my greatest accomplishment," he said.

RTR: 032 / Date of Recollection: 07.18.2002 / 6 min

I think of him, now, as I prepare for school.

The morning he died, Doris and I were woken up by the loudest coughing we'd heard since he'd fallen ill. Without discussing it, we both knew we had to break down the door. He was on his side, a stream of blood flowing from his mouth, through the sheets and down onto the floor. He was announced dead an hour after the nurses found him a bed on the second floor of the hospital.

They let me sit through assembly. Then, 10 minutes later, at the start of math class, I get called to the headmaster's office.

"This is beyond belief," Mr de Silva tells me. He turns back to his window in his swivel chair, reminding me of the time he'd pulled the monitor pin off my school uniform. But somehow I manage to face him, this time.

He takes a deep breath. "I'm left with no words," he says, raising his hands. "I had to keep the news from my wife, do you know that?"

I don't answer him.

"To do such things. I mean, this is a schedule 3 offence, without question, written in clear print in our regulations... the chaplain agrees we don't need a hearing." He looks at me. "Make me understand this."

For some reason, I think of the guard at the hospital and his ex-wife, and Litha and Part standing behind me.

"I don't know," I tell him. "They're my friends."

"That's your explanation? That you don't know and they're your friends?" His neck turns red above his tie. "You'll have to leave the school grounds at once," he says. "There'll be a let-ter sent to your aunt, declaring your expulsion; but for now, go home and have a hard think." He shakes his head. "After all we do for you people."

I say goodbye to Ms Isaacs, who embraces me for a long time in her office. She hands me the *Far Side* cartoon, her eyes averted as we pull apart. Then I leave the premises.

I wait for my aunt to come back from work. I help her with the groceries, and then I tell her I've been expelled. Doris pauses for a moment, then carries on unpacking. Afterward, she sits down at the kitchen table and watches me as I join her.

"Tell me what happened."

I do. I tell her about what we did, and about Litha's fosters.

"I see," she sighs. "And the two of them have the same punishment?"

I nod. "Part and Litha go to different schools, but I can't see it being different."

"Right." Doris stretches and gets up. "Pass me the pots on the rack and let's get started with dinner."

I watch her turn to the stove to boil a pot of water. Then she stops. "This is it, then," she says. "The morning I got here, Lumkile told me this would happen. That there'd be challenges."

I listen without facing her, opening and closing the knife drawer.

"That's who he was," she says. "He couldn't be told a single thing about you and your mother. I never knew where his head was, but I was certain of that."

I take two plates from the cupboard and set out the spoons. "He never talked about Mom," I say. "Did you know her?"

"I did."

"You never talk about her either."

Doris sighs. "Hand me the mixed veg."

She tears the packet open, spreading the frozen carrots and

broccoli across the skillet. "Lumkile didn't want me talk about her; but of course, I knew Nobomi. I was there when all of us went to see her in Fort Beaufort."

I stop and look at her. "I don't remember that."

"I know. The nurses were in panic when you passed out in Tower. Nobomi told Lumkile to spare you after that."

"Tower? Mom was in a mental clinic? You didn't tell me that."

"Tell you what? You were there yourself. And your father told me not to discuss her. He said he would give me the house if I took care of you. That's all."

I take a seat at the kitchen table, feeling light-headed and nauseated.

"And I don't know what happened to you, that day," she says. "The two of you were sitting in the common room one moment, and the next you'd fainted and she was screaming at ghosts."

"The common room?"

"I don't know. It was a long time ago, but they had books there. I'm sure she had you reading something."

My throat tightens. "Do you remember the book?"

"I think it was about ships. That's all you kept talking about on the drive back."

"UFOs?" I ask, laying my head on the table, feeling the heat growing behind my forehead.

"I can't hear," Doris says. "Stop talking through your teeth."

"The book." I look up at her. "That's what we read. It was *UFO Diaries*."

"*UFO Diaries*," Doris repeats. She raises her eyebrows. "I don't know about that."

"He lied to me, then," I say. "He said she went missing and he didn't know what happened."

Doris turns down the heat. "Not in the end. Lumkile never believed Nobomi had lost her mind. He thought she was stubborn, and that she'd grown tired of him. That it was just a thing that happened with her. He wouldn't listen. Nobomi was committed in '95, and he went to see her each month, right up until the accident in '96."

"The accident?"

"There was a fire at the hospital. It broke out at night, and lots of patients were found dead, but others had gone missing. Nobomi was one of those. There were searches that followed, but all of them were reported dead in the end, even without their bodies. Lumkile never entertained the idea. He took it as proof her abandonment, although he still chose to wait for her. That's the reason he told you he didn't know. He left out Tower, because he was frightened. You showed no memory of the afternoon, and that's what he came up with."

"No one else asked after her?"

"Nobomi had no relatives after her mother passed. There was a memorial service at the clinic, but Lumkile didn't attend. He waited for her."

"Do you think she died?"

"I do. Nobomi's condition was bad. There's no chance that she could've survived. Let alone learn to make it on her own."

I nod, thinking about *UFO Diaries*. Doris squeezes my shoulder. "If you don't get up and help me with these potatoes, you'll have to look for your own school," she says.

My smile comes out weak, but it's there. She's allowed me that. I get up, wipe my tears, peel the potatoes, and julienne the onions over a side plate. Then I thank her.

"For what?"

"For today," I say, "and for everything else."

"Nonsense." Doris dials the heat down on the pot. Her hands feel damp against mine. "The two of them made a good child," she says. "That's all most of us could ever hope for."

January 1, 2000 + **[RTR 033 00:15 min]**

Later, I would learn to project myself into the future: an attempt to walk the last lap of the maze Litha had presented to us with Triangulum. It didn't matter that we hadn't found the path that led to my mother at the end of his map; we had found a start.

This is how it went. When Litha and Part walked me home that night, I looked up and found that we were charting a deviation from his triangle of stars.

It made me wonder about my mother and father: if I was moving closer or further away from them. Triangulum, I could tell, now, had been a form of traveling through time and not space. My parents and I formed an incomplete triangle, made of only two sides, the past and the present, and I could see now that I hadn't needed the future because I'd thought one replaced the other—that the past was erased by the present, and that the present would be erased by the future.

I was wrong. Marianne and I hadn't connected Block Time to travel, but this felt close.

We deviated further, heading down into Fort Hill to the house I shared with my aunt. Traveling the map had given me the sensation of tracing someone's footsteps: even if the prints were cosmic, they had belonged to my mother, a movement into the past from the present, I thought; but that wasn't true either. It had been a movement through the past as much as a movement through the present. Triangulum was not a system of tracing, but of combining. The triangle, I now realized, meant that I'd been joined with my parents all along: that each of us held a position reserved for us on its slopes, which met at the center, where memory converged with the imagination.

Using memory, I took a taxi to Bhisho and touched the walls of my old house, imposing the present I owned over my parent's past, revealing them to be one. We had been there together, and in memory, we still were.

Using imagination, I could project myself into the future, and bring it back into the present and the past, converging time.

Maybe that's what I would write about, I thought; or maybe I'd move to Johannesburg, following the light, and become an astronomer. I didn't know.

When we got to the road that led to my cul-de-sac, I told Part and Litha to stop. The air was cool and the night was lit with constellations. The street felt deserted, devoid of human life, as if somehow we'd escaped unscathed from a scourge that had claimed it.

Part asked, "Are you sure you'll be okay?"

I nodded. "I'm sure. Now look up."

They did.

"The three of us have gone as far as we can," I said, "and I feel closer to her, now."

Litha and Part nodded, and I decided to take it as fact—at least for now, while each of us stood alone in the bright dark.

That we had escaped.

That we were the sole survivors.

Now what to do with the future?

RTR: 034 / Date of Recollection: 09.19.2002 / 1 min

I tell Litha and Part what happened with my aunt when I see them next, around a month and a half later. The three of us have been banned from each other's presence and scattered into different low-fee schools for the rest of the term; none of us escape the whispers.

Doris surprises me in her resolve to stand in my defense against our neighbors. The two of us grow closer, although we still fight. Half a year from now, Litha will get returned to the children's home by his new fosters, before being taken in at a boarding school in Bloemfontein on a scholarship. Part will go to Graaff Reinet, and then on to Kingsridge in Grahamstown. I'll go to Pietermaritzburg. The three of us will never speak again after that.

The night before Litha goes back to the foster home, though, we meet at the corner of Alexandra and Queens Streets and walk to the Shoprite. We use the scaffolding in the next alley to get onto the roof, and we walk from one rooftop to the other, covering half the town. We end up sitting on the edge of the Kwik Spar roof, next to the hospital, as the sun begins to rise, dimming the town's streetlights.

"Maybe heaven isn't dead because there is no heaven," Litha tells us. Part and I are silent.

I look in the direction of the hospital, where a man once saw a ball of strange lights hovering over the sick.

Did you hear that, Mother? I think to myself.

Did you hear that, Father?

Hovering over us.

NOBOMI

1950 – 1996

LUMKILE

1948 – 1999

. . . .

ACKNOWLEDGEMENTS

Thank you to my friends and family.

Thank you to Imraan Coovadia, Henrietta-Rose Innes, Fourie Botha, Eric Obenauf, Eliza Wood-Obenauf, Brett Gregory and also the good people at Jacaranda Books.

I'm also grateful to the following writers, whose output was invaluable: Victor D. LaValle, Stanislaw Lem, Thembinkosi Lehloesa, Ted Phillips, Jon Scaramanga, Colson Whitehead, Percival Everett, Samuel R. Delaney and Wallace G. Mills.

Thank you to Mbali Khanyisile Sikakana.

Two Dollar Radio
Books too loud to Ignore

ALSO AVAILABLE Here are some other titles you might want to dig into.

THE REACTIVE NOVEL BY MASANDE NTSHANGA

→ **A Best Book of 2016** —*Men's Journal, Flavorwire, City Press, The Sunday Times, The Star, This is Africa, Africa's a Country, Sunday World*

← "Often teems with a beauty that seems to carry on in front of its glue-huffing wasters despite themselves." —*Slate*

A CLEAR-EYED, COMPASSIONATE ACCOUNT of a young HIV+ man grappling with the sudden death of his brother in South Africa.

THE WORD FOR WOMAN IS WILDERNESS
NOVEL BY ABI ANDREWS

← "Unlike any published work I have read, in ways that are beguiling, audacious…" —Sarah Moss, *The Guardian*

THIS IS A NEW KIND OF NATURE WRITING — one that crosses fiction with science writing and puts gender politics at the center of the landscape.

AWAY! AWAY! NOVEL BY JANA BEŇOVÁ
TRANSLATED BY JANET LIVINGSTONE

→ **Winner of the European Union Prize for Literature**

← "Beňová's short, fast novels are a revolution against normality."
—Austrian Broadcasting Corporation, ORF

WITH MAGNETIC, SPARKLING PROSE, Beňová delivers a lively mosaic that ruminates on human relationships, our greatest fears and desires.

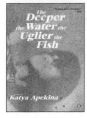

THE DEEPER THE WATER THE UGLIER
THE FISH NOVEL BY KATYA APEKINA

→ **A 2019** *Los Angeles Times* **Book Prize Finalist**
← "Brilliantly structured… refreshingly original, and the writing is nothing short of gorgeous. It's a stunningly accomplished book." —NPR

POWERFULLY CAPTURES THE QUIET TORMENT of two sisters craving the attention of a parent they can't, and shouldn't, have to themselves.

Thank you for supporting independent culture!
Feel good about yourself.

Books to read!

Now available at **TWODOLLARRADIO.com** or your favorite bookseller.

FOUND AUDIO NOVEL BY **N.J. CAMPBELL**

← "[A] mysterious work of metafiction… dizzying, arresting and defiantly bold." —*Chicago Tribune*

← "This strange little book, full of momentum, intrigue, and weighty ideas to mull over, is a bona fide literary page-turner." —*Publishers Weekly*, "Best Summer Books, 2017"

SEEING PEOPLE OFF NOVEL BY **JANA BEŇOVÁ**
TRANSLATED BY **JANET LIVINGSTONE**

→ **Winner of the European Union Prize for Literature**

← "A fascinating novel. Fans of inward-looking post-modernists like Clarice Lispector will find much to admire." —NPR

A KALEIDOSCOPIC, POETIC, AND DARKLY FUNNY portrait of a young couple navigating post-socialist Slovakia.

THE DROP EDGE OF YONDER
NOVEL BY **RUDOLPH WURLITZER**

← "One of the most interesting voices in American fiction." —*Rolling Stone*

AN EPIC ADVENTURE that explores the truth and temptations of the American myth, revealing one of America's most transcendant writers at the top of his form.

THE VINE THAT ATE THE SOUTH
NOVEL BY **J.D. WILKES**

← "Undeniably one of the smartest, most original Southern Gothic novels to come along in years." —NPR

WITH THE ENERGY AND UNIQUE VISION that established him as a celebrated musician, Wilkes here is an accomplished storyteller on a Homeric voyage that strikes at the heart of American mythology.

SIRENS MEMOIR BY **JOSHUA MOHR**

→ **A Best of 2017** —*San Francisco Chronicle*

← "Raw-edged and whippet-thin, *Sirens* swings from tales of bawdy addiction to charged moments of a father struggling to stay clean." —*Los Angeles Times*

WITH VULNERABILITY, GRIT, AND HARD-WON HUMOR, Mohr returns with his first book-length work of non-fiction, a raw and big-hearted chronicle of substance abuse, relapse, and family compassion.